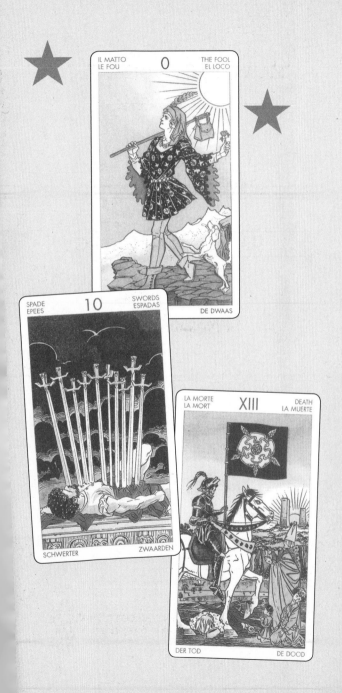

D0251633

CAVALLO DI BASTONI — KNIGHT OF WANDS
CHEVALIER DE BATONS — CABALLO DE BASTOS

RITTER DER STÄBE — STAVEN RIDDER

L'EREMITA — IX — THE HERMIT
L'ERMITE — EL ERMITAÑO

DER EREMIT — DE KLUIZENAAR

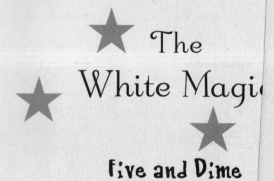

The
White Magic

Five and Dime

SPADE — 5 — SWORDS
EPEES — ESPADAS

SCHWERTER — ZWAARDEN

New York Times bestselling author

Steve Hockensmith
with Lisa Falco

The White Magic

Five and Dime

A Tarot Mystery

MIDNIGHT INK
WOODBURY, MINNESOTA

The White Magic Five & Dime: A Tarot Mystery © 2014 by Steve Hockensmith with Lisa Falco. All rights reserved. No part of this book may be used or reproduced in any manner whatsoever, including Internet usage, without written permission from Midnight Ink, except in the case of brief quotations embodied in critical articles and reviews.

FIRST EDITION
First Printing, 2014

Book design and edit by Rebecca Zins
Cover design by Lisa Novak
Cover illustration by Miles Hyman/Lindgren & Smith, Inc.
Steve Hockensmith photo by Cecily Hunt
Lisa Falco photo by Picture People, Topanga Mall
Tarot images from Roberto de Angelis's Universal Tarot;
used by permission of Lo Scarabeo; further reproduction is prohibited

Midnight Ink, an imprint of Llewellyn Worldwide Ltd.

This is a work of fiction. Names, characters, places, and incidents are either the product of the authors' imagination or are used fictitiously, and any resemblance to actual persons living or dead, business establishments, events, or locales is entirely coincidental.

Library of Congress Cataloging-in-Publication Data
Hockensmith, Steve.
  The White Magic Five & Dime / New York Times bestselling author Steve Hockensmith, with Lisa Falco.—First Edition.
      pages   cm.—(A Tarot Mystery)
  ISBN 978-0-7387-4022-5
1. Psychics—Fiction. 2. Psychic ability—Fiction. 3. Death—Psychological aspects—Fiction. 4. Mothers and daughters—Fiction. I. Falco, Lisa, 1970–
II. Title. III. Title: White Magic Five and Dime.
  PS3608.O29W458 2014
  813'.6—dc23

                                                           2014003332

Midnight Ink
Llewellyn Worldwide Ltd.
2143 Wooddale Drive
Woodbury, MN 55125-2989

www.midnightinkbooks.com

Printed in the United States of America

With his pack over his shoulder and his head held high, the
Fool boldly begins his spiritual journey. But watch out for
that first step, Fool. It's a doozy!

Miss Chance, *Infinite Roads to Knowing*

THE PHONE rang, and I answered it.

I know—pigeon move, right?

You look at the caller ID and it says something like VALUTECH LLC or LUXURY LIVING or (in this case) WHEELER AND ASSOC and you know what that means. Or I do, anyway. Because usually I'm the one on the other end of the line, and I only need a few minutes of your time to discuss an exciting opportunity that could radically alter your financial outlook, but it's a limited-time offer and you'll have to act now.

Maybe it was curiosity. Maybe it was professional courtesy, one call-center phone monkey to another. Maybe I was just in a "what the hell?" mood—that wasn't uncommon.

Anyway, I picked up.

"Hello?"

"Alanis McLachlan?" a man said.

I pulled a Coke from the fridge and briefly considered leaving the phone in its place. Let the guy try to sell his time shares or hot-hot stocks to my leftover pizza and moldy tofu dogs.

"Yes."

I popped open the can and took a drink.

"Also known as Sophie Harper?"

The old training paid off.

Never let them see you sweat, Biddle used to say.

And never let them hear you spit-take Coke all over your kitchen.

I managed to swallow.

"Yes. That's me, too."

"I'm calling about Athena Passalis, also known as Barbra Harper."

The first name I'd never heard before. The second made me grit my teeth.

"Does she want money," I asked, "or is she dead?"

I knew it had to be one or the other. Either she needed something from me or she'd never need anything again.

"Oh, um, actually…" the man stammered.

And that answered my question.

Athena Passalis, aka Barbra Harper, aka Mom had finally done the one and only thing she ever could or would do to make the world a better place. She'd left it.

Or "passed on," as the man put it.

I let that sink in a moment. Then I asked the first question that came to mind.

"Who killed her?"

What else were you going to say when you found out someone like my mother was dead? "Was it the hepatitis she picked up in the Peace Corps"? No. "I told her donating a kidney to a stranger was crazy"? No. "I can't believe she went back into that burning building for a cat"? No.

The man on the phone gave me another "oh, um, actually…" Then: "The police don't know."

"Of course they don't," I could have said. "Whoever finally got Mom was going to be smart."

"What happened?" I said instead.

So the guy told me the details. There weren't many to tell, apparently. A simple case of *burglarus interruptus*. You know the old story: innocent citizen finds herself in the wrong place at the wrong time. Just a tragic stroke of bad luck.

Yeah, right.

"I'm very sorry," the man said. "I'm sure all this comes as a great shock."

"Eh," I said.

THE GUY's name was Eugene Wheeler and he was an attorney and he did manage to give me a great shock eventually. He told me Barbra had a will, and I was in it.

When we were done talking, I hung up and walked to the kitchen table and took a seat.

My mother was dead.

My mother was dead.

My mother was dead.

I even said it out loud. "My mother is dead."

I waited for the tears to come. All I could manage was a sigh.

I didn't owe the woman more tears anyway. She'd had plenty from me already.

There was a debt, though. One I hadn't been sure I'd ever repay, but now perhaps I could.

I owed my mother justice.

I CALLED my boss.

"I'll be out the rest of the week. My mom died."

"You have a mom?"

"Biologically, yeah."

"But…wait. Didn't your mother die two years ago?"

"That was my I'm-going-to-Hawaii mother. This is my real mother."

"You lied about that?"

"Wanna fire me?"

My boss thought it over.

"You have till the twelfth. That's it. And no horseshit about a dead father."

"I don't have a father," I said. "My mother carved me out of wood."

I WENT to Berdache, which is easier said than done. When you find out you're going there, certain questions arise.

"What the hell is Berdache?" (Answer: A town you've never heard of.)

"Where the hell is Berdache?" (Answer: Yavapai County, Arizona—if that helps.)

"How the hell do I get to Berdache?" (Answer: Fly to Phoenix, drive up to Sedona, keep driving into the craggy, scrub-crusted desert until you're thinking, "Really? People actually live out here?" Stop when you see buildings.)

And last but not least, "Why the hell am I going to Berdache?" (Answer: It's complicated.)

A LONGER answer:

In the rocky hills around Sedona there are "vortexes" of powerful psychic energy, they say. Of course, "they" want to take you on tours and sell you maps and books and crystals and guide you through ancient Indian ceremonies that will purge you of bad juju and excess cash.

Apparently there are vortexes around Berdache, too, but they aren't as powerful. You can tell because the signs for them are smaller and their psychic energy is only strong enough to support half a dozen occult bookstores and New Age trinket shops. One of these stores is the White Magic Five & Dime.

According to Eugene Wheeler, it belonged to me.

My mother had died inside it.

EUGENE LOOKED like a Eugene. He had small-town anchorman helmet hair and a gray mustache and a layer of belly blubber that bubbled up out of his chinos like lava. He was wearing a corduroy jacket and a powder-blue oxford shirt and a red-and-yellow striped tie with a knot as big as my fist. I got the feeling he'd looked and dressed like this since he was eight, mustache included. Maybe if his parents had called him Rocco he would've turned out differently. But they'd made him a Eugene, and that's destiny.

There's a reason people don't name their kids Eugene anymore.

This particular Eugene had a small storefront office on Berdache's main drag. WHEELER & ASSOCIATES read the sign out front, but the associates were either on vacation or imaginary.

Eugene couldn't work up much enthusiasm when I walked in and introduced myself. On the phone, he'd played up the advantages of "monetizing" my new assets. Selling them, in other words—

with a percentage of the revenue going to the executor, of course. Him.

But no. Instead I'd come to look everything over before deciding what to do.

Some people hate it when you do that. Con men, for instance. And your average, everyday, ordinary businessman, which is what Eugene Wheeler looked like.

Sign here, he said.

And here.

And here and here and here annnnnnd…here.

Now sign this and initial this and don't forget to date that and would you mind giving a blood sample?

It took two hours, mostly because I always read everything I sign. Always. Everything. I don't put my name on a Christmas card until I've double-checked the fine print on the back.

"Sorry this is taking so long," I said.

Eugene tried to smile. "No problem. You're doing exactly what I tell all my clients to do."

The difference being *they* never actually do it.

I went back to reading.

WHEN EVERY here, here, *here,* and *there* had been signed and dated and sprinkled with holy water, I was the proud owner of not just the White Magic Five & Dime but the apartment above it and the black Cadillac behind it and the $45,246.79 in the bank up the road. I could go back to my crappy Chicagoland one-bedroom richer than I'd ever been in my life.

But I wasn't done in Berdache just yet. There was one more bit of business to attend to—one I couldn't clear up by simply signing on the dotted line.

"Anything new on my mother's murder?" I asked.

Eugene winced. He'd still been trying to slide by with references to her "passing." So much less murdery.

"No, not that I've heard," he said. "I'm sure it's our police department's number-one priority, though. A nice, respectable lady attacked in her place of business—that's thrown quite a fright into people, as I'm sure you can imagine."

A nice, respectable lady?

I studied Eugene's face for any trace of sarcasm. I didn't find any.

"How well did you know my mother?" I asked.

"Not very. I mean, I knew her, of course. There are only five thousand people in Berdache. I know everybody. But..." He shrugged. "Some better than others."

"So you never did business with her?"

"No. Not until about three weeks ago. That's when she came to see me about a will."

"Did she say why she suddenly wanted one?"

"Oh, she gave the usual reasons—reaching a certain age, wanting to be sure her affairs were in order. But you know you're never too young to have a will drawn up. That's something everyone should do, especially if they've got property or a lot of money in the bank to think about."

"I think you're probably right."

Eugene smiled.

"That's why I've had a will since I was nineteen," I went on. "Everything goes to my cats."

Eugene kept smiling, but his eyes weren't in it anymore.

It was a lie, though. I don't have a will. I operate on the assumption that I'm going to live forever. I haven't been proved wrong yet.

I don't have any cats, either. They remind me too much of my mother. Beautiful, finicky, aloof, and you're the one who always has to clean up their crap.

"Did my mom give you my phone number or did you have to track it down yourself?" I asked.

"She gave it to me, of course. I wouldn't let a client designate an heir without current contact information."

"Did she say how she got it?"

"Got...your phone number?"

Eugene furrowed his brow, but the hair patty just above it didn't move an inch. It looked like a gray beret taped to the top of his head.

"I haven't spoken to my mother in twenty years," I said, "and the last time I saw her, I had a different name."

"I see. I'm sorry. No. She didn't say how she found you."

"It doesn't matter. She was always good at getting information... when she wanted it."

I stood up and thanked Eugene for his time.

"Guess I'll go take a look at my new place."

"I'm afraid we're not quite done yet. There's something else we need to discuss."

"Yeah?"

"Your mother."

"What about her?"

"You need to decide what's to be done."

"What's to be...? Oh. You mean with *her*."

Eugene nodded. "The body's at the county morgue. Once the medical examiner's finalized his report, they'll release the body to you. You should know what your plans are."

"It was right there in the will. She wants to be cremated."

"Yes, but where? What kind of service would you like? What kind of urn? What kind of marker? I know it's overwhelming, especially at an emotional time like this, but you have a lot of decisions to make, Alanis. I'd be happy to make all the arrangements, if you'd like."

Who says chivalry is dead? And I'm sure he'd only charge me ninety-five bucks an hour instead of his usual hundred.

"That's awful sweet of you, Eugene, but it doesn't have to be that complicated," I told him. "Where would you go around here to pick up some charcoal briquettes?"

I WAS standing across the street from the place where my mother had died—a place I now owned—and I had two thoughts in my head.

#1: What happened here?

#2: Wow, Mom…tacky.

I was looking at a dingy white two-story building between a mom-and-pop hardware store and a mom-and-pop "psychic massage studio." (Everything in Berdache looked mom and pop—or maybe mom and mom or pop and pop. You can never tell with the New Agey types.) A neon OPEN sign hung in the big picture window facing the street. Off, of course. Around it, painted on the glass, were tarot cards and a crystal ball and assorted signs of the zodiac—Leo the Lion and Cancer the Crab and Alvin the Chipmunk or whoever.

And there were these words:

THE WHITE MAGIC
Five & Dime

Divination * Revelation * Bargains

For obvious reasons, Mom had left off her true stock in trade: lies.

I'D COME a long way for this—to see for myself who my mother had become and what had become of her. All I had to do was step off the curb and walk across the street and use the keys Eugene had given me. Yet now, with only fifty feet to go, I found myself frozen, unable to move forward.

Why was I really here? Did I truly think I could bring my mother justice? Did someone like her even deserve it?

Anyone? Anyone…?

I turned my back to the road.

Directly across the street from the White Magic Five & Dime was its mirror image. House of Arcana, it was called. Inside I could see books, candles, incense, cards, crystals, bullshit, horseshit, and crap. And a woman looking back at me from behind the counter. She had frizzy gray hair and a macramé shawl wrapped around her shoulders and a welcoming smile on her placid face. Her baggy yellow frock looked like something Obi-Wan Kenobi would wear, and I got the feeling it was either woven from hemp or meant to look like it was.

Hello, Earth Mother. The only things missing were flowers in her hair and the smell of patchouli.

I waited for her to start belting out "Aquarius."

She just kept smiling.

Fine.

Maybe my mother wasn't around to explain her last scam, but she wasn't the only one running it.

I went inside.

THE WOMAN'S name was Josette, and she was good. She projected all the right vibes—warmth, curiosity, a touch of disarming ditziness—while stifling the sound of gears turning, turning, turning in her head. She kept smiling as she sized me up, no doubt thinking, "Stranger in her mid-thirties, alone, casual clothes, no jewelry, no makeup, no manicure, short Supercuts hair, radiating bemusement and amusement but, underneath, confused."

I knew that's how she saw me because that's how I would've seen myself. Every con artist of every kind knows how to cold-read a mark. I'd been doing it since before I could read books, and I was good at it. Mom and Biddle had made sure of that.

Of course, every con artist knows how to hide vulnerability, too. But I wanted mine to show. It's good bait.

I poked around for a few minutes, answering the woman's carefully bland questions ("In from out of town? Been out this way before?") while pretending to take an interest in her rune stones and anointing oils and plastic-wrapped spell kits. It took her five minutes to get to the pitch.

"I have a feeling," she said, "that you've come here with questions."

"Wow! How did you know?"

I expected to hear that her spirit guides had told her. Or maybe it was my troubled aura.

12

"You were staring at the store across the street for a long time," she said instead. "It looked like you were trying to work up the nerve to go in."

The lady wasn't just good, she was very good.

Short con or long, it has to start with trust. And what better way to begin building that than with a little dribble of truth? Just enough to clear the way for the snake oil.

"I was," I said.

"Thought so. I'm afraid the White Magic Five & Dime isn't open anymore." Josette's smile grew a little wider. "But I do readings, too."

"So the Five & Dime went out of business?" I said as I shuffled the cards Josette had handed me.

We were at a table in a curtained-off nook at the back of the store. Before sitting down, Josette had locked the front door and hung up a sign saying BACK IN 15 MINUTES. So we wouldn't be disturbed, she'd said, but I figured it had more to do with sticky-fingered tourists who might wander in and help themselves to handfuls of healing crystals and pentagram pendants.

"Focus on your question," Josette said. "What is it you'd like to ask the cards?"

What the hell was my mother up to around here? I thought.

"How do I become a happier, healthier person?" I said.

Josette held out a hand.

"Good. Now give me the deck."

I handed it over. I'd paid in advance (naturally) for a seven-card reading. I didn't feel like shelling out thirty bucks for the "standard ten-card spread" when with three cards and five dollars less I could get the same old crock.

Josette laid the cards out like this:

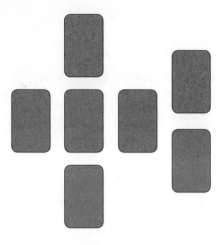

"Looks like an airplane."

Josette seemed pleased with herself. "It's a spread of my own. I call it the Weather Vane. It's good for showing which way the wind's blowing."

"You can just make up a 'spread' yourself?"

"You can do anything with the tarot." Josette reached out and touched the card at the center of the crisscrossing rows of three—the middle of the airplane. "Ready?"

I nodded.

"All right, then. Let's begin."

"Ahhh," Josette said as she turned over the first card. "This is your present—your current situation—and we've got the Two of Swords. A sword is an instrument of war—of conflict—but it can also bring liberation. It cuts through the things that bind us. The woman here has two swords, but look: She's not using them. She's just holding them over her chest, blocking her heart. She thinks she doesn't need her emotions and her instincts, but that's blinded her. She can't truly see herself or her situation, so she's paralyzed. Stuck.

"Moving up to the next card, we see what's in the conscious mind.

15

"More swords! Only the swords on the Six here aren't being used as weapons. They're going with someone on a voyage. Does that boat remind you of anything? The boatman? The dead being ferried across the River Styx, maybe? Perhaps someone close to you has died—though it doesn't have to be that. It could refer to any important life passage. A painful time is being put behind you. You're continuing on to someplace new, but the pain goes with you.

"Moving down now, we see what's going on in your subconscious.

"Swords again! The Eight. In this card, the swords form a wall. A pen. A prison. But see that gap? The wall's incomplete. She could walk away anytime, yet she doesn't because she can't see the way out. Swords is the suit of intellect, of the mind. Here that's a trap, though. This woman—she's imprisoned by the things she *thinks* she knows.

"Going back now, we look at the past.

"Interesting. The Queen of Wands. Wands is the suit of energy, will, ambition, action. But the Queen's reversed, so what we have is a strong, intelligent, creative woman who's turned herself to unproductive pursuits. She's a powerful influence, but not a good one. Whoever this is, she's a bit of a…well.

"Moving forward, we step into the future. And what do we have?

"Oh! Lovely! The Two of Cups! (Some people call them Chalices, but I like Cups. More down to earth, don't you think?) Anywho, Cups is the suit of love. That can be all kinds of love, of course, but would you just look at that couple there? Aren't they adorable? I think you might have something special to look forward to. Someone special.

"Now, in the last row, hopefully we'll find a little guidance for you. Going up, we've got the energies you should be trying to harness. And what we find is…well, well.

"The Fool. Now don't get the wrong idea about him! The Fool's actually someone we should respect. He's brave. He trusts his impulses enough to take what looks like a dangerous step. He could be going right off that cliff, but at least he's taking the first step toward something. Don't give in to fear is the message here. Do something.

"Finally, moving down, we'll see what energies you should avoid.

"The Four of Pentacles. Hmm. I see two possible meanings here. First, the obvious. Here's someone who's clinging to something— a big coin. That could be money or it could be material things or it could be a belief in material things and material things only. A rejection of the spiritual side of life. Do you see the other pentacle over his head, though? It's almost like a halo or a crown. That's some achievement of his—some gift; a special ability, maybe. But he's hording it; keeping it to himself. He should share it, use it, not hide it away. He needs to be more like the Fool. He needs to just go for it! And I think that's what you need to do, too.

"Now…how would you like to start going for it like a Fool by buying a nice big expensive bag of healing crystals I scooped out of my fish tank this morning?"

JOSETTE DIDN'T actually say the thing about the healing crystals from the fish tank, but I wouldn't have been surprised if she had.

Her advice boiled down to this: Turn off your brain. Let your emotions take over. Don't worry about what you know or don't know. Just focus on what you *want.*

It's the starting point of every con.

Clearly she thought I'd turned my brain off a long, long time ago.

I respected the woman's technique, though. Forget good or very good; she was masterful. Cold reading will only get you so far. Then you have to start asking leading questions and throwing out vague comments the mark can interpret however they want. You have to fish. But not Josette. Somehow she'd pegged me as the product of a Mommy Dearest without a single word about it from me.

I wondered if she knew who I was.

I faked my way through some follow-up questions, but Josette was admirably patient. She didn't try to tap me for more cash. She was working Biddle-style.

A fool and his money are soon parted, he liked to say. *So why rush it unless someone else is trying to part the fool from it first?*

Eventually Josette went to the front of the store and opened the door again.

"So," I said, "your main competitor's gone, huh?"

I pointed at the White Magic Five & Dime.

"There are still plenty of other readers around Berdache and Sedona," Josette said.

"So I've seen. But the person running that place across the street must not have been one of the better ones. If they could really tell the future, they'd still be in business. I mean, you *all* oughta be millionaires, right? Just gaze into your crystal ball until you see tomorrow's *Wall Street Journal*, then call your stock broker and wait for the dividends to roll in."

Josette smiled at a joke I'm sure she'd only heard a million times too many.

"I don't believe readers see the future," she said. "I believe they see the possible."

I nodded as if this made sense.

"So what happened to the Five & Dime's owner, anyway?"

Josette's smile wavered. "I'm not really sure."

Nice dodge. The Berdache Tourism Bureau would be pleased.

I thanked Josette for the reading—it had been so insightful, really it had—and left.

THE READING had provided some insights—into my mother.

No wonder she'd opened the White Magic Five & Dime. Twenty-five tax-free bucks for a sprinkling of Fairyland pixie-dust bullshit? It was too easy.

Only she wouldn't have stopped there. Not Mom. All that trust being placed in her—all that pain and confusion being shared—it would add up to one thing for her: leverage. And she would have used it—to push. Until someone finally pushed back.

Mom hadn't just met her death over in that store. She'd invited it inside, done business with it in there, tried to cheat it in there. And if I gave a rat's ass about that, I'd go in there, too.

But did I? Should I?

I found myself standing on the sidewalk again, staring at the White Magic Five & Dime across the street. Wondering why I would avenge a woman I'd never even forgiven.

I was still wondering even as I stepped off the curb and started toward the store.

"He's called the Magician," you say, "but what the heck is he doing? Where's the rabbit coming out of the hat? Where's the MAGIC?" Hey, just because you can't see it doesn't mean it's not there. Are powers surrounding you right now, influencing and perhaps even controlling you, that YOU can't see? Well, duh.

Miss Chance, *Infinite Roads to Knowing*

JOSETTE HAD better inventory, but Mom's place had all the atmosphere. Walking into the White Magic Five & Dime was like stepping into Indiana Jones's trophy room. African masks hung on the wall beside Japanese tapestries and Indian dreamcatchers and a crucifix with a Jesus so battered and bloody he looked like he'd gone ten rounds with Freddy Krueger. There were statues of the Buddha and Shiva and the Virgin Mary and that tubby, armor-wearing warrior-guy you sometimes see near the cash register at Chinese restaurants.

My mother had always been a stone-cold atheist, of course. Churches were just competition working a different kind of con. So either she'd done a one-eighty and had gone from believing in nothing to believing in *everything* or (more likely) she'd simply overdone it with the pseudo-mystical set dressings. Christian, Buddhist, Hindu, Satanist—it was all the same to her.

The chintzy merchandise—crystals, candles, charms, etc.—was limited to a few tables and shelves along the walls, and the one display case was stocked exclusively with tarot cards and a cheap-looking book about them. Near the picture window at the front of the store was a waiting area: a couch and chairs that would have been at home in a stereopticon slide of President Taft and Family, a coffee table covered with *Reader's Digests* and yellowing newspapers, a fountain (off), a lava lamp (off), and a fern (dead). Here the sheep would sit, patiently perusing year-old headlines and "Life in These

United States," until it was their turn to step through the beaded curtain at the back of the room and begin their latest fleecing.

Now *there* was a heaven my mother would believe in.

I pushed through the beads and found myself in a narrow hallway lined with oversized tarot cards. The nice ones, of course. Strength. Temperance. The Lovers. The Star. The Sun. There was no Fool here (unless you counted me). And no Death—at least on the wall.

At the end of the hall were stairs leading up to the second floor. Beside them was a door that opened into what looked like a storage room or office. There was another doorway—this one doorless— about halfway down the hall.

That was the one I went through. As I expected, it took me to a small, nookish room with a table and two chairs.

This was where my mother had done her readings.

It was also where she had been murdered.

It should have been creepy, standing on the spot where my mother had died. But there was no sign any crime had been committed there, other than rampant fraud. The local cops had been very tidy.

Their IQs I wasn't so impressed with. What would a burglar have been after back here? Hardened criminals aren't going to bother with a B&E just so they can score zodiac charts and incense. And if the killer was an amateur—a tweaker on the prowl for loose cash, say—the crime scene would have been a lot messier.

Meth heads and amateurs freak out. They stab you with ball-point pens and beat you with lamps and rip out chunks of skin and hair. They don't strangle you unless they've done all that other stuff first. And Eugene Wheeler had said my mother had been strangled.

I pictured it in my mind. Mom on the floor, a man's hands around her throat. After a moment, I had to blot out the image. My mother might have been dead to me, but I hadn't wanted her dead to *everyone*. Thinking of her murder still sickened and saddened me.

I couldn't let that stop me, though. I brought the image back, only with stick figures this time. I had to run through the scenario and see if it could make sense in this little closet of a space.

The room was like a confessional without a screen between penitent and priest. There was barely space for a game of Scrabble, let alone a life-and-death struggle. Two people could squeeze past the table, sure, but it wasn't like Mom to be cornered in any way, shape, or form. It was easier to imagine her thinking she was the one in charge, looking her killer straight in the eye.

The way she'd always look at people when she was back here. Over the table.

Over the cards.

It wasn't hard to figure out where my mother would have been sitting. From one of the chairs, you could look down the hallway and see the waiting room beyond the beads. That would be Mom's spot. She'd want her soft murmurs drifting out to the next patsies in line, keeping them in their seats with the promise of wisdom or solace or good news or whatever it was they wanted to hear.

I took a seat in the pigeon's chair and stretched my arms out in front of me.

Lean forward. Grab hold. *Squeeze.*

Sure. It could work. If you were strong. And if you were pissed enough—pissed in that special way Mom could make you—you'd find the strength.

So all I had to do was figure out who in town my mother had screwed over. The population here couldn't have been more than two or three thousand people. Once I had my list of suspects, I'd…

Something.

I SAT. I thought.

Who goes to see a fortuneteller?

Suckers.

What kind of suckers?

Superstitious suckers. Supersuckers.

How do you find supersuckers?

You give them what they want.

What do they want?

You just said it, Sherlock. Fortunetellers.

Where do you get a fortuneteller?

You don't get one. You make one. You become one.

Ah.

And there it was.

The killer would come to me.

I was congratulating myself on my genius when the back door opened.

THERE WERE footsteps. Then the door closed. Then more footsteps.

The footsteps stopped.

Someone was in the room at the other end of the hall—the office or whatever.

That someone stayed still for a very, very long time.

I stayed still, too.

Eventually a thought occurred to me. *Wait—I'm not the one breaking and entering. I own this damn place.*

"Who are you?" I said. "What are you doing here?"

I made my voice firm, assertive, self-assured. Yet I also got up as quietly as I could and started moving slowly down the hall toward the front door, just in case I didn't like the answers I got.

"Who are *you*?" a woman said. "What are *you* doing here?"

"I'm calling 911, that's what I'm doing."

My phone was in my jacket. My jacket was in my car.

"*I'm* calling 911," the woman said. "That's what *I'm* doing."

"Hello? Yes? Operator? I'd like to report a break-in."

"Hello? Yes? Operator? I'd like to report a break-in."

I'd made it all the way down the hall to the beads. I could turn and run for it, if I wanted.

I stopped.

It was very, very quiet.

"You didn't call 911," I said.

"*You* didn't call 911."

"Would you please stop repeating everything I say?"

"Would *you* please tell me who I'm talking to?"

"My name is Alanis McLachlan. As of this afternoon, I own this building."

"Oh. Shit."

"And who are *you*?"

The woman stepped out into the hall and started toward me. She was skinny and tall and pretty, in a gawky way, with frizzy hair and big brown eyes. Her skin was the color of chocolate milk—the good kind with lots of syrup.

As she got closer, I realized she wasn't a woman. She was a girl—seventeen at the most.

"My name's Clarice Stewart," she said. "I guess I'm your tenant."

"Excuse me?"

"I live upstairs."

"I thought Barbra lived upstairs."

"Who?"

"Sorry. Athena."

"Oh. Yeah. She did. Her real name was Barbra?"

"I doubt it, but that's not the point. Are you saying you *and* Athena lived upstairs?"

"Yeah. We were, like, roommates."

"Really?"

"Really."

My mother. "Roommates" with a high-school junior.

Riiiiight.

"Look," I said, "we can work all this out later. Right now, I don't see how you can even be in this place. I mean—don't you know what happened in here?"

The girl gave me a look so toxic I'm surprised I survived it without a hazmat suit.

"Of course I do," she said. "Don't *you* know who found the body?"

CLARICE LED me up the stairs. The second floor was an apartment. Communal living room, kitchen, bathroom. And, yes—two bedrooms.

It wasn't hard to guess which one belonged to Clarice. The dirty clothes covering the floor had spilled out through the door, as if the room had vomited wadded-up jeans and wrinkled T-shirts.

The rest of the place was a mess, too. Dirty plates and bowls were everywhere. From what I saw on them, it looked like Clarice had been living on Hot Pockets and Cap'n Crunch.

Clarice started scooping up the dishes and carrying them into the kitchen.

"Sorry about the mess. I haven't been in the best mood since… you know. But I'll do better."

I walked to the other bedroom and looked inside. Names, identities, accents, ethnicities, hair styles, hair colors, glasses, contacts, whole wardrobes—these things came and went with my mother. But one thing had stayed the same all the way to the end.

The woman was a neat freak. A place for everything and everything in its place—so you can grab what you need quickly when the inevitable time comes for a quick, quiet exit out the back. Clutter could slow you down.

People, as well. Mom always kept that streamlined, too.

There were no pictures in her room. No mementos. No hint of a past, a family, a daughter. It was as if I'd never been born—which was what I assumed my mother would have preferred.

So why was I here now?

"How did you end up living with Athena?" I said.

Clarice was jamming glasses into an already overloaded dishwasher.

"My family's kind of messed up. Athena took me in."

"Out of the goodness of her heart?"

As if there was any.

Clarice glanced back at me, and there was the slightest pause—a second's reassessment and recalculation—before she answered.

"In the beginning, yeah. But before long I had to 'earn my keep.' I was her little slave, basically. I cooked, cleaned, ran errands, helped out downstairs."

"You worked in the White Magic Five & Dime?"

"When I could."

"What did you do?"

"Took messages, made appointments, made sure no one walked off with anything, got hit on by creepy guys, dusted, vacuumed. That kind of thing."

"How about the behind-the-scenes stuff?"

"What behind-the-scenes stuff?"

"The readings. What Athena told her clients. Her advice, guidance, services. How much of that did you know about?"

"None of it. That's all private. Like doctor-patient stuff."

"No one ever mentioned any special—?"

"Although you know," Clarice cut in, "I would overhear things sometimes. Just a phrase, a few words. There was this one time I had to go to the bathroom, so I was walking down the hall during a reading, and I thought I heard Athena say to this lady, 'What you need are llamas.' I was like, '*Chuh?* Did I hear that right?' I *so* wanted to stop and listen. But of course I couldn't or Athena would be all up in my grill later. That lady never came back in or I would've asked her, 'How's it going with the llamas? They look like they'd smell.'"

I smiled and nodded and thought *llamas, my ass.*

"There was this other time…"

And Clarice told me about this other time. And this other time. And this other.

30

You want to know about the business? Sure! Let me tell you about the llama lady. And the Transformers guy. And the woman who thought Bruce Willis was following her.

It was verbal sleight of hand. A minute into it and you'll have forgotten what your original question was. Five minutes and you wouldn't remember that you'd asked a question at all.

I'd learned it from my mother, of course.

So had Clarice.

Mom was dead. Long live Mom!

"There was this other time all I heard was 'never, *ever* with asparagus,' and the guy was like, 'How about a carrot?'" Clarice went on.

And on and on.

I let her prattle. I could've given her some pointers—"It's called obfuscation, dearie, and it requires a lighter touch"—but she was trying so hard, it was endearing.

I wondered if I'd been a better liar at her age. I would've had more practice, certainly, but there's a lot to be said for natural talent.

"Wacky," I said when I'd had enough.

"Totally. The people around here…man. I could tell you stories all day."

"I bet."

Clarice started the dishwasher, dusted off her hands, then gave me a well-I-guess-you'll-be-going-now look.

"There's something else you can do for me, though," I said.

"Yeah?"

"Tell me about the night Athena died."

SHE WAS reluctant, but I was the new landlord and she obviously wanted to stay. So it only took a little wheedling to get the girl to talk.

"I'd been out with friends," she said. "Just hanging, goofing around. I got in really late and came in the back way, like always. And I noticed that the light was on in the reading room. That was weird. Athena never had anyone in after nine. She might stay up messing around on the computer, but she wasn't in the office when I came in, and it wasn't like her to leave lights on after she went upstairs for the night. She was always so particular—so anal. So I went down the hall to check it out. She'd been kind of extra-moody lately, and I thought maybe…well…I don't know what I thought."

"And you found her."

Clarice nodded.

"I freaked out. Screamed, ran outside, called the police. It was obvious someone had killed her. Her eyes were…"

The girl's words trailed off, and her jaw clenched tight.

Then she shivered and swallowed and started again.

"Her eyes were all bugged out, and I could see bruises around her neck. So far as I knew, the guy might still be inside. When the cops came, they checked the place out, but he was gone."

"How'd he get in?"

"Through the window in the office, they think. The front and back doors were both locked—I had to let myself in with a key. And the window was cracked open, so there you go. The guy didn't take much. Just some money and whatever electronic stuff he could grab from downstairs. The police think I probably missed him by, like, thirty minutes."

"And they let you stay here after that?"

"Oh, god no. They kicked me out. Can't have some kid messing up a crime scene. So I stayed with friends and then snuck back in a couple days later. I figured they'd already done their *CSI* thing in the Five & Dime, so what would it matter if I'm up here? It's not like they were going to come back and find some new clue that would crack the case open. Naw. It's gonna be some druggie saying, 'Hey, man—wanna buy a camcorder? I killed a lady for it' to a scumbag friend. And then the friend gets arrested for possession and tells his lawyer, like, 'Hey, I know something the cops'll want to hear.' I think that's how these things usually work out. Or maybe that's just the way it looks on *Law & Order*."

"Were there cards on the table?" I asked.

"What?"

"On the table. In the reading room. Were there any tarot cards?"

"I guess. There's always a deck on that table."

"But were they spread out? Like for a reading?"

"I didn't stop to check. I was a little distracted—you know, *by the body*."

"Try to remember. It could be important."

The girl's bearing—her aura, Josette might have said—suddenly changed. Her face turned hard; her eyes darted.

She was going fight-or-flight on me.

"I don't even know why I'm talking to you. Who are you, anyway? You claim you just bought this place, but then you call Athena 'Barbra' and start asking questions like a cop."

"I didn't say I bought the building. I said I own it."

"What difference does that make?"

"Eugene Wheeler never spoke to you? You don't know anything about the will?"

33

"What will?"

"My mother's will."

"Your—?"

Clarice's eyes widened.

"Oh my god," she said. "Athena was your mother?"

"Yes."

"And she left everything to you?"

"Yes."

Clarice looked away. She shook her head. She started to laugh though she looked like she wanted to cry.

"That bitch," she muttered. "That goddamn bitch."

Not the most tactful thing to say to a grieving daughter, but I couldn't argue.

"Look," I began.

I was going to tell her she wasn't getting kicked out. I didn't know what I'd be doing with the place, but until I decided, she was welcome to stay.

I didn't have to bother, though.

"Bitch!" Clarice shrieked, and the tears finally broke through as she ran to her room.

She had to kick dirty clothes out of the way, but after a few seconds she was able to give the door a nice loud slam.

WHAT A very special woman my mother was. Dead and gone, she could still make people cry.

I've never had any desire to be a mom myself and have always acted accordingly. There are many, many reasons for this, and here's one: I don't like the idea of a teenager screaming "bitch!" at me as she runs to her room in tears. And here it was happening anyway.

Old news: life's not fair.

I STOOD there a minute feeling stupid. Should I knock on Clarice's door and ask if she was all right? It would be a dumb question. I could hear her sobbing. What could I do about it?

No one ever taught me how to console someone. No one ever taught me to care. I'd spent the last two decades trying to teach myself, but it was still a work in progress. *I* was a work in progress.

Eventually I just went back downstairs without saying anything.

I headed to the front of the store and turned on the big neon sign in the window. Then I walked to the display case and pulled out a copy of the tarot-reading book—*Infinite Roads to Knowing* by someone called Miss Chance.

I started reading.

Open yourself to new ideas and new people, and you could
be like the High Priestess—a reader of minds and diviner
of dark secrets. Just look into those eyes. They're already
looking into YOU.

Miss Chance, *Infinite Roads to Knowing*

It didn't take me long to decide that Miss Chance was full of crap. Her introduction I skipped. Ditto the history of tarot cards and "divinatory" readings. I wanted to get straight to the how-to: You see this card, you say that. You see that card, you say this. That's all a "guide to the tarot" needs to be, right?

Yeah, maybe. But apparently Miss Chance didn't feel that way. Each and every card got its own chapter: as many as eight pages devoted to one little drawing that looked like it came from some weird-ass medieval comic book.

And what was on those eight pages? Stuff like this:

> *If in the four suits we see the four elements that the ancients believed make up all things—earth (Pentacles), air (Swords), fire (Wands), water (Cups)—then in the twenty-two cards of the Major Arcana (the Fool, the Magician, the High Priestess, and so on) we see something separate from and beyond the trumps and, consequently, separate from and beyond the material realm. Looked at like this, the cards of the Minor Arcana (the Queen of Pentacles, the Ace of Swords, the Eight of Wands, the Two of Cups, etc.) are depictions of the physical realities that surround us—our world and the things we do in it—while in the Major Arcana*

(Latin for "big secrets," remember) we find reflections and refractions of the archetypes that can define human identity and act as signposts on the road to knowing.

Miss Chance didn't just lay it on a little thick. She backed up the BS truck and poured it out by the ton.

Eventually, however, with much perseverance, I was able to find passages that seemed to be written in English. A few I even understood. Kind of.

I found a pen and started underlining.

I was putting a star next to a particularly sane sentence when the front door opened.

"That isn't going to fill customers with confidence," someone said.

I looked up.

A man stood in the doorway. He was tall, dark, and handsome. (His hair and clothes were dark, anyway. He was a white guy, so he could only get so dark without being sunburned.)

He was smirking at the tarot book.

"I'm just looking for typos," I said. "I wrote it, and there's a new edition coming out next year. Are you here for a reading? I'm the new proprietor. Returning clients get half off their first session."

The man's smirk grew smirkier.

"No. I never got my fortune told here, although I did always come with a lot of questions."

He pulled his black leather jacket aside to reveal a badge clipped to his belt.

"Now it looks like I've got questions for you," he said.

I stifled a sigh and walked to the window and turned the sign off again. It had been on for all of twenty minutes.

"Come on," I said. "Let's go for a walk."

His name was Josh Logan, and he was the head of the Berdache Police Department's detective division.

He was also the entire staff. The Berdache Police Department had seven employees, and he was the only investigator in the bunch.

His smirk disappeared fast when he found out who I was.

"I'm sorry," he said. "I didn't know Athena had any children. When I saw the sign was on, I just assumed some crony of hers was trying to pick up where she left off."

"I look like a crony to you?"

Logan winced.

"An associate. A colleague," he said. "You know what I mean."

"I do, actually. And where exactly is it that you think my mother might have left off with one?"

Logan took a few strides in silence. We were walking up Berdache's main street, Furnier Avenue, which doubles as a short stretch of Highway 179. Every quarter block or so, someone would say "hey, Josh" or "afternoon, Officer." From their smiles, I took it Detective Logan was a popular man. Given his looks, I wasn't surprised. He was like a taller, younger George Clooney, only not so homely.

"So you're a fortuneteller, too," he finally said to me.

"Not really."

"But you said you wrote a book about—"

Logan cut himself off with a snort and a shake of the head. I knew what he was thinking.

Like mother, like daughter.

"Look," I said, "I hadn't spoken to my mom in a long, long time. I can't imagine she changed much, though. That's part of the reason I came to Berdache. If she hurt anyone here, I want to find out who. To do that, I need to connect with her clients—particularly the most vulnerable ones. The most gullible. Do you think that's something you could help me with?"

"You want me to round up your mother's dumbest customers for you?"

"I didn't say dumb. I said vulnerable and gullible."

"You've got to be kidding."

"Why? Because I say I want to track down the people my mom swindled and make amends? You find that so hard to believe?"

Logan said nothing.

"It's because I look like a crony, isn't it?" I said.

Logan gave me a long look.

I batted my eyes at him.

I do not look like a crony. I look like a 4-H beauty pageant runner-up. Not tall or thin or blond enough to win, but the big brown eyes and sweet smile would knock the judges dead in the Q&A.

That's why I used to make such a good crony.

"There must have been some complaints," I said. "I assume all those questions you wanted to ask my mom weren't about your love life."

Logan gave me another sideways look. He held it for seven or eight steps, glancing away just in time to glide around a lamppost. It was as if he had every inch of Berdache memorized.

"Maybe I can help you, maybe not," he said. "Why don't we see if you can help *me* first?"

I couldn't.

He asked about my mother's methods, her tricks, her partners. And though I could have told him stories all afternoon—not that I *ever* told those stories—none of it would have done any good.

"I'm not denying it: my mom was a con artist back when I knew her," I said. "But I have no idea when or how she got into the fortunetelling thing. We didn't even have a Magic 8 Ball when I was a kid, let alone tarot cards."

"'Back when I knew her'? That's a weird way to talk about your mom."

"Not when you haven't spoken to her in twenty years."

I got yet another of Logan's long looks as we continued up the sidewalk. It was a miracle he hadn't steamrolled a tourist.

"You go all that time without contact of any kind, then you just waltz into your mother's place and take over after she dies?"

I shrugged. "There was a will. I was in it."

"I doubt if it's that simple."

"Then you're smart. Don't make it too complicated, though."

"What do you mean?"

"I mean *there was a will. I was in it.* I assume I'm your number-one suspect now. And I shouldn't be."

"Hold on. I didn't say anything like—"

"I can put you in touch with my boss. He'll tell you I was at work in beautiful Lombard, Illinois, the day my mother was murdered and the day after, too."

"Whoa, whoa!"

Logan finally stopped walking. We were at the edge of town by now. The rocky red bluffs in the distance darkened as twilight approached, and the clouds over the desert turned purple. The Lone

Ranger wasn't riding off into the sunset over Logan's shoulder, but he should have been.

"I'm sorry if I gave you the wrong impression," Logan said. "You are not a suspect."

"Why not? I ought to be."

"You just said you shouldn't be."

"I meant I didn't do it, not that you shouldn't wonder if I'd done it."

"Um, okay. I take it back. You *are* a suspect."

"Good. I'd hate to think you weren't being thorough."

"I am being thorough."

"Then you can tell me who your other suspects are."

"No, I can't."

"Because you don't have any?"

"*Because I can't.*"

"All right. 'Can't comment on an ongoing investigation.' I get it. I mean, I'm next of kin, not *60 Minutes*, but okay. You've got rules to follow. If they say to keep a brokenhearted daughter in the dark, keep a brokenhearted daughter in the dark. Why should you talk to me about any progress you might have made? I'm all alone here in town—in the world, really—but you don't know who I might go blabbing to. You can't violate confidentiality just to offer a little comfort to *me*."

When I was done, Logan was wincing.

I'd been hoping for a grimace.

"Look, I'm sorry, but—"

"I mean it, Detective. No need to apologize. Really. I'm just trying to make some sense of my mother's murder, but hey—protocols are protocols. They're more important than people, right?"

I got my grimace.

"I tell you what," I said. "Forget the suspects. Just tell me who I should avoid here. I'll be sticking around a while, and I'm guessing my mom had enemies."

"Well...*enemies* is a strong word."

"Rivals, then. Competitors. People who didn't care for my mother."

Suspects, in other words.

Logan cocked his head and squinted at me. He was catching on.

Not every small-town cop is a rube. Unfortunately.

I turned away and pointed back up the street.

"How about her? The old hippie chick who runs the House of Arcana."

"Josette Berg? She and Athena weren't BFFs, I can tell you that. Josette's one of the true believers. She isn't fond of opportunists and frauds. No offense."

"None taken."

And I meant it. I'd been raised to think opportunists and frauds were the smart ones. Everyone else was a sucker—especially the true believers.

"So who else is Josette unhappy with?" I said.

"It'd be better if you never get to know them, Miss McLachlan. Staying in Berdache is something I wouldn't advise."

"Why is that? Are you saying I'm in danger? Does that mean you're not so sure my mother was killed by a burglar?"

Logan winced again.

How come she's *the one asking all the questions?* he seemed to be thinking.

"You know what?" he said. "I should probably get you back to the White Magic Five & Dime. I'd hate for you to miss the evening rush."

ON THE way back, Logan said he'd talk to my boss after all. Just so I could be sure he was being thorough.

I gave him the number and the name of the place and who to ask for.

"Innovative Sales Solutions?" he said as he typed it into his BlackBerry. "Sounds like a telemarketing firm."

"For good reason."

"You're a telemarketer?"

"Employee of the Month fifty months running."

"What do you sell?"

"What do you got?"

Logan grunted out a gruff chuckle. "You're really something, you know that?"

I did. The question was: what?

I'd been asking myself that for a long, long time.

"Oh," Logan said, "can you give me a number for you, too? In case I have follow-up questions."

"And what if *I* have follow-up questions?"

"I have a feeling that's less a *what if* than a *when*."

"You're probably right."

Logan sighed. But he gave me his card anyway.

CLARICE WAS standing in front of the White Magic Five & Dime when we walked up.

"I've been looking for you," she said to me.

"I had some things to discuss with Detective Logan here. I assume you two know each other?"

"Hello, Clarice."

"Hello," the girl replied coolly. Too coolly. It was the kind of cool you only get with effort. "Have you found out anything new?"

"A little," Logan said. "I think I'm making progress."

"Good."

"Well, thanks for the welcome to Berdache, Detective," I said. "I hope we'll be staying in touch in the days ahead."

Logan just smiled tightly and said goodbye.

I glanced back at him as Clarice and I went inside. Logan was glancing back, too. *Glowering* back. At both of us.

Was I really one of his suspects? Maybe.

But the girl beside me? Definitely.

Ignore the sex toy/Mr. Microphone in the lady's hand. It's what's tucked under her robed rump that counts. The Empress reclines on a throne of passion and pure motherly love. From it she reigns over a lush, fertile, beautiful realm—all the bounty that can flow back to you if you learn to give of yourself first. If you don't learn, you miss out on the river and the trees and the throne and end up with nothing but the sex toy, which isn't much consolation after a while.

Miss Chance, *Infinite Roads to Knowing*

I THOUGHT about turning the neon sign back on when Clarice and I walked into the Five & Dime. I decided not to bother. For the moment I had plenty to work with without any walk-ins.

"Thanks for not mentioning my freak-out in front of Logan," Clarice said.

I shrugged. "You haven't had the best week. You're owed a freak-out or two."

"Yeah, maybe. Still, I wanted to apologize. And explain."

I drifted around behind the display case and leaned on it casually. I wanted some distance between us, but I didn't want it obvious.

"The thing is," Clarice said, "Athena always told me she'd take care of me. She wasn't the most nurturing person in the world—I mean, not with me, anyway. Maybe it was different for you. But still, she was almost like a mother to me. She did her best, in her weird way. So to find out there was a will and I wasn't even in it and now I've got nothing and nowhere to go…?"

Her eyes were big and round. She even cocked her head a bit to one side. If she'd been a dog, I would've given her my lunch.

I knew what I was supposed to say to her. And I knew I wasn't quite ready to say it.

"What about your family?" I said instead.

"Not an option."

"Your friends?"

"I'm sort of an outcast at school. I've got a few friends, but their parents are sick of me already."

"I'm surprised Logan didn't arrange for you to go somewhere."

"He tried. Foster care." Clarice puckered her face as though someone had just offered her a kitty-litter sandwich. "Thank god I'm emancipated, so they couldn't force me."

"You're old enough to be emancipated?"

Clarice nodded. "Sixteen's the age you can do it in Arizona. Athena helped me. Over the summer."

"Wow. That's really...great."

And hard to believe. Mom emancipating a slave? Not her style.

I'd freed myself—or thought I had, anyway. If I'd been truly free, would I even be here now?

"Well," I sighed, "I don't know how long I'm going to be around, but you're welcome to keep staying here until you figure out something else."

"Thank you! I was hoping you'd say that!"

Yes. Yes, you were.

"I could use the help anyway," I said. "I'm going to open the shop again while I'm here, and it'll be good to have someone around who knows what they're doing."

"You're going to do readings?" Clarice looked over at *Infinite Roads to Knowing*, which was lying on top of the display case next to me. A pen was sticking out where I'd stopped reading. "Do you have any experience with that?"

"Nope. But I think I can wing it. Everything I know about customer service I learned from my mother."

Clarice looked dubious. Very dubious. I'm-staring-at-a-crazy-person dubious.

I smiled.

"Speaking of customers," I said, "Mom must have had a Rolodex or something around here...right?"

Mom was very modern, it turned out. She didn't have a Rolodex. She had spreadsheets. On her computer. Which had been stolen the night she died.

I went to the office at the back of the White Magic Five & Dime to take a look for myself. All that was left of the computer were some cables and power cords, a pair of speakers, and a lonely little webcam.

I tried to imagine a meth head going to all the trouble of unplugging everything and carrying off the PC and screen but leaving the power cords behind. Conclusion: DOES NOT COMPUTE.

"Any idea why she had this?"

I tapped the webcam.

Clarice leaned in to look over my shoulder.

I would've preferred *not* having a murder suspect looming up behind me, but life's full of little inconveniences.

"I've got an idea," she said, "but I never wanted to *know*. Know what I mean?"

I did.

Online chat rooms.

Lonely bachelors.

Cybersex.

My mom.

Ew.

Maybe it wasn't a bad thing that I couldn't nose around in her computer. Who knew what kind of pictures might be lurking in there?

I hadn't seen my mother in nearly two decades. I didn't want my first look at her as a fiftysomething-near-sixtysomething to be an outtake from hotgrannies.com.

I repeat: *ew.*

I turned to face the window at the back of the room.

"Is that where the burglar supposedly came in?"

"Yeah."

There was a latch on the window. It wasn't broken.

"It's hard to imagine my mother leaving a window open. She was pretty—"

I searched for the right word.

"Paranoid?" Clarice suggested.

"Cautious," I said.

You're not paranoid if they really are out to get you, Biddle used to say. *And if no one's out to get you, you ain't trying hard enough.*

"Yeah. You're right," Clarice said to me. "She always made sure the windows were closed and locked. Always. She was really uptight about it."

"Could a customer have come back here and unlocked the window while my mom was distracted?"

"Maybe. It'd be pretty hard to do without being seen, though. You'd have to sneak up the hall right past the reading room."

"Hmm," I said.

No burglar, no matter how skilled, could have unlocked that window from the outside. It had to be someone on the inside. Someone who was very good at sneaking around unseen.

Or someone who was right at home.

THERE WAS a filing cabinet beside the desk, and I started going through it as slowly as possible.

"Ah," I said. "Old bills."

I pretended to become absorbed in a long form letter from the electric company.

"Well, let me know if you have any more questions," Clarice eventually said. "I guess I'll go do my homework."

"Great. Thanks. See ya."

The girl went upstairs.

I relaxed. I stopped reading bills, too.

My mother wasn't the type to leave anything revealing laying around in a filing cabinet. The really juicy stuff would be buried under a rosebush in a locked strongbox or something.

I moved on to another drawer anyway, just in case Mom was getting sloppy. It was empty except for several shrink-wrapped packages of camcorder cassettes. One of the packages had been opened, but there was no sign of any used tapes.

Interesting. My mother had never been big on Kodak moments. She avoided having her picture taken and rarely bothered with snapshots of anyone else, including her adorable daughter. Home movies definitely weren't her thing.

I'd have liked to look at those tapes. Unfortunately, they were probably under that hypothetical rosebush.

I was moving on to the next drawer when the telephone on the desk rang. PAY PHONE, the caller ID said.

I picked up.

"White Magic Five & Dime."

"Who is this?" a man asked gruffly. He'd either smoked a lot of cigarettes or gargled a lot of acid.

"Miss Chance, seer and teller. How can I help you?"

"Don't worry about helping me. Help yourself. Get out of Berdache and don't come back."

Ah. So it was one of *those* calls. I'd picked up a few for my mom and Biddle back in the day, but I was a little out of practice.

I didn't reply until I was sure I could stay calm. It took me almost a full second.

"And how would that help me?" I asked.

"You'll stay alive."

"Got it. I assumed that's what you meant, but I wanted to be sure. People can be so vague when they're trying to be threatening."

"Stick around and you'll end up like your bitch mother. That clear enough for you?"

"Very. It tells me almost everything I need to know, in fact. I've only told three people that Athena Passalis was my mother, so it shouldn't be hard to figure out who you are."

The man snorted. "That doesn't mean anything. Word spreads fast around here."

"I bet it does. Practically at the speed of sound. Speaking of which…"

I'd already walked out the back door to the little gravel lot behind the building. Two cars were parked there: my mother's black Caddy and the rented Camry I'd driven up from Phoenix.

I pressed the phone hard to my ear with my left hand while pulling out the keys for the rental with my right.

I pushed the panic button.

HONK HONK HONK HONK HONK HONK HONK

52

I heard it in both ears. The sound was coming over the phone.

The caller was close. And if I was right—and lucky—I knew exactly how close.

I sprinted around the building, turned left at the street, then right at the first corner.

It took me less than thirty seconds to get to the 7-Eleven. I'd remembered it was there because I'd been planning ahead.

Arizona is hot, and I like Slurpees.

No one was using the pay phone out front, but the receiver was dangling from its cord as if it had been dropped in a big hurry.

A delivery truck was idling not far away.

"Excuse me," I said to the guy loading a dolly with big blue trays of Ho Hos and Twinkies, "was there a man here a minute ago talking on that phone?"

"Yeah."

"What did he look like?"

"I don't know. I don't stop to check out every dude I walk by."

"You must have noticed something. The color of his hair, his clothes…"

"He didn't have any hair, and he was definitely wearing clothes. That's all I remember."

"So. A bald non-nudist."

"I think he was white."

"Now we're getting somewhere. A bald non-nudist who may or may not be white. Excellent. I'll put out an APB on Vin Diesel."

The delivery guy shrugged and said, "Sorry."

He threw a puzzled glance at the white cordless phone still clutched in my hand.

"What are you? Some kind of cop?"

"I'm from AT&T," I said. I walked to the phone, stuck a finger in the coin-return slot, and pulled out a dime. "The gentleman forgot his change."

I returned to the White Magic Five & Dime ten cents richer.

Ninety-nine times out of a hundred, a threat's just bluff mixed with wishful thinking, Biddle sometimes said.

"Is this the hundredth time?" I finally asked him. He and I were frantically packing suitcases while my mother burned papers in a trashcan.

There were bullet holes in the wall behind us.

I wondered what my odds were this time.

I DID a little more searching in Mom's office, but my heart wasn't in it. I was thinking about bald men, specifically the theoretically white kind who talk like Darth Vader with strep throat and make threats and wear clothes.

I wanted to meet one. On my terms, of course.

Problem: I didn't know one. Yet.

After a while, I ordered Mexican from a joint down the street. When I asked Clarice if she wanted in, she said she'd like a vegetarian burrito.

I tried to take some comfort from that. At least the girl wouldn't kill a chicken.

I locked the front door again after getting back with the food. The back door was already locked. The windows, too, of course. For all the good it might do me.

Clarice and I ate together in the little kitchen upstairs.

"Just curious," I said between bites from a completely and utterly adequate chile relleno. (I don't kill chickens, either.) "Did you mention to anyone that Athena's daughter had showed up?"

"Why?"

"Some guy called who knows who I am."

"What was he calling about?"

"A possible appointment. He said he might pop in sometime."

"What's his name?"

"Mr. Roper."

"Never heard of him."

"Maybe I'm remembering wrong. He sounds like he's in his forties or fifties, has kind of a raspy voice, acts a little cranky. Bald."

"He mentioned that on the phone?"

"It came up. He said his nickname's Cueball."

"Well, he doesn't sound like anyone I know."

Clarice turned her attention back to her burrito.

"So," I said, "have you mentioned it? Me being here?"

"Oh. Right. Yeah, I told a couple people. Why didn't you ask the guy how he knew?"

"He was in a hurry. Who'd you tell?"

"Just some friends. How's your food?"

"It's good. Which friends?"

"People from school. I've been a vegetarian since I was nine. Athena used to make fun of me for it. She'd say, like, 'What's the use of being at the top of the food chain if you can't eat everything below you?' Or she'd take a big bite of steak and start singing 'The Circle of Life'—that kind of thing. It used to bother me until I figured out she *had* to make fun of me to keep herself from feeling bad. Because if you stop to think about where meat comes from for one second, you'll never start eating it again. And giving a shit is just *sooooo* inconvenient, you know?"

I let her keep babbling. It was obvious I wasn't going to get my questions answered tonight.

Eventually she wrapped half her burrito in foil and stuck it in the fridge and announced that she had a test to study for. I might see her in the morning if I got up early enough. Good night.

Later, after she went to her room and closed (and locked) the door, I heard her talking on her cell phone. I couldn't make out any of the words, but the conversation went on for a long, long time.

ONCE I'D finished getting ready for bed, I went through the medicine cabinet and all the drawers in the bathroom. Why wouldn't I?

My mother had always been old-fashioned about makeup. A woman just didn't look right until every visible inch of skin had been powdered, rouged, spackled, and lacquered. She practically needed a sand blaster to wash her face at night. And that's how it had been right up to the end, apparently. I found enough blush to keep every drag queen in San Francisco fabulous for years. The Avon lady must have been making her deliveries in a semi.

Mixed in with all the bronzer and foundation and foundation primer and foundation primer primer, I found three medicine bottles. The kind you only get with a prescription. Each had pills inside, but what kind I couldn't tell. The labels had been ripped off.

DON'T YOU DARE was written on one in thick black ink.

I COUNT THESE EVERY NIGHT was on another.

The third had a skull and crossbones.

I was in a little desert town I didn't know, in an apartment with a stranger who may or may not have homicidal tendencies. The floor below us was a crime scene, while outside, somewhere nearby, was a man who said I'd die if I didn't leave. And now I was lying in my dead mother's bed, thinking of her stretched out in a refrigerator a few miles up the road.

If "creepy" were a lottery, I'd just won.

So what was I reading to comfort myself? A book about interpreting the freaky imagery on a bunch of weird old playing cards, of course. Because Mom didn't have *The Power of Positive Thinking* on her shelf, and my copy of *Happiness Is a Warm Puppy* was hundreds of miles away.

Starting *Infinite Roads to Knowing* a second time, not skimming and skipping around but really digging into it, I'd come to appreciate something about the woman who'd written it. Miss Chance wasn't the touchy-feely New Age bullshit artist I'd thought her to be.

She was nuts. A certifiable multiple-personality head case. You could watch her mix and match identities practically line by line. One second she'd be blah-blah-blahing about the numerological significance of the Empress card: "As it is assigned the value III, naturally it's a combination of I (male) and II (female) and is, hence, a representation of the product of such a union: a child born of a joining both carnal and spiritual."

(Yeah, lady. And a three can also be represented by the raising of one's three middle fingers, a gesture that is often accompanied by that classic decree to seek deeper meaning, "read between the lines.")

Yet then, in the very next paragraph, she'd slip in a reference to a vibrator and the Empress's "robed rump," and her interpretation of the card would actually make a little sense. That female symbol thingie that looks like a hydrocephalic stick figure really was right beneath the Empress's booty, on the side of her La-Z-Boy/throne. A heart was there, too. So the card as a symbol of "passion and pure motherly love" worked for me (because it would be easy to remember).

Not that I believed in "pure motherly love"—that was Bigfoot to me. Plenty of people claim to have seen it, but I had good reason to be skeptical.

Around midnight I closed the book and turned off the light and stared up at nothing, thinking about the crazy, stupid thing I was doing and the odds it would get me killed. But I didn't think about leaving.

Because Clarice was right. Giving a shit is just *sooooo* inconvenient.

Smart kid. I'd learned the same lesson when I was about her age. Caring is inconvenient, a pain, dangerous. Dumb, my mother said. But if you do it, you do it. It's not a choice. It's who you are.

So I cared. And here I was.

Sorry, Mom.

Good night.

Grim, stiff, stern, humorless—the Emperor is the law, and he is not amused. Do as he says and you will be tolerated. Defy him and you will regret it...or so he'd like you to think. See that barren wasteland behind the throne? That's the old fart's kingdom. Follow all his rules and you get to live there. Yippee! Or not.

Miss Chance, *Infinite Roads to Knowing*

THE DAY got off to a good start. I was alive when I woke up.

It was almost eight, and someone—Clarice, I assumed—was clomping around in the other room. You would have thought she was building a pyramid out of concrete blocks, but that's probably just what teenagers sound like when they're getting ready for school. I wouldn't know. I hadn't heard teenagers in the morning since I'd been one.

When Clarice finally stomped off down the stairs in her combat boots or clogs or whatever, I unlocked the door to my mother's bedroom and went out to the kitchen. All I could find in the cabinets was instant coffee, so I got ready to go out for the real thing.

Usually I'm a jeans and T-shirt woman. If I'm feeling especially fancy (or cold), I might put on a pullover. My footwear runs the gamut from black Chuck Taylors to generic Payless snow boots. (It's a short gamut.) The last time I bought jewelry, it cost me two prize tickets at Chuck E. Cheese.

This wouldn't do. Not for Miss Chance.

I went to my mother's closet.

There she was. All five of her, by my count. There had been dozens over the years, but she'd whittled herself down to this handful now: the Businesswoman, the Cougar, the Frump, the Blank Slate (designed to be so boring, she was invisible), and the Gypsy.

Five different wardrobes for five different identities, all ready at a moment's notice.

They were neatly organized not just by style but by size, too. My mother, it seemed, was shrinking. From her perennial slender 6 down to a new shipwreck survivor 2. Maybe Clarice had convinced her to go vegan. You know, for the animals.

Ha.

I went for the Gypsy, size 6.

When I headed downstairs, I was wearing a white peasant blouse and a long skirt and a clunky turquoise necklace that looked like a beaded string of petrified Smurf dung. The clothes were a bit snug here and there, but at least the brown sandals on my feet fit perfectly. I'd literally stepped into my mother's shoes. I did my best not to let my thoughts get all metaphorical about that.

I picked up the phone and called Josh Logan, Berdache 5-O.

"Detective Logan speaking."

"I have another question for you."

"Miss McLachlan?"

"Yes. Where do you get good coffee around here?"

"Well…the tourists seem to like Celebrity Roast."

"We passed it yesterday, right? On Furnier?"

"That's it."

"Meet me there in two minutes."

"Is five okay?"

"Take your time. Be there in three."

I hung up.

"You're late," I said when Logan came in.

It had taken him four minutes to get to the coffee shop.

He made it up to me by getting me a cappuccino, which wasn't the same thing as buying me a cappuccino. The blond behind the cash register wouldn't *dream* of letting an officer pay.

She shot me an icy glare when he walked over and handed the cup to me.

"You're not having anything?" I asked as he took a seat across from me.

"I don't like coffee."

"A cop who doesn't like coffee? What do you drink to wash down your—?"

"Please don't go there. I don't like doughnuts either."

I looked him up and down. "It shows."

I was hoping for a blush. Flirting men don't have as many road blocks between their brains and their mouths.

I didn't get the flushed cheeks, though. Maybe too many blonds gave the guy free coffee.

He nodded down at my faux gypsywear. "You've changed *your* look."

"It's not my style, but you know how it is. Sometimes you have to wear a uniform to work."

"So you're still gonna open the White Magic Five & Dime back up?"

"For a while. What's the matter? You don't look thrilled."

Pictures of famous actors and musicians covered the walls, and Logan spent the next few seconds gazing silently into the mascara-ringed raccoon eyes of Adam Lambert.

"I don't want to offend you," he said slowly, "especially after what you've been through. But…you see…I have to think about the good of the community, and…well…"

"You're afraid I'm a con artist like my mom."

"Yes."

"I understand. Let me put your mind to rest: I'm not."

I took a sip of cappuccino. It was good.

"Golly, I'm so glad to hear that," Logan said, deadpan. "As long as I have your word on it, there's nothing to worry about, right?"

"Did you call my boss?"

"Yes."

"And?"

"It's like you said. You were in a Lombard, Illinois, boiler room pushing home refinancing all day."

"Loan modifications, actually. They're different."

"Still sounds skanky."

"It is. But it's legal. I am *not* my mother."

"Then why are you dressing like her and reopening her store?"

"Curiosity. Speaking of which, I wonder: have you told anyone who I am?"

Logan put a hand to the back of his neck. "Whoa, whiplash. You wanna put on a turn signal before you change the subject that fast?"

"I got a threatening phone call yesterday. From a man who knew Athena was my mother."

Logan's face went stony. He reached into his jacket and pulled out his BlackBerry. "Did you see who the call was from?"

I shook my head. "I'm not filing a report. I'm just telling you. And asking you: who knows I'm here?"

Logan sighed and put his BlackBerry away. "Only everybody, I assume," he said. "I discussed it with a few different people, and I didn't swear any of them to secrecy. It's a small town. Things get around fast."

"So I've been told."

"What did the guy say, exactly?"

"The usual: *get out of Dodge or you'll end up like your mother*."

"That's the usual?"

"That was a joke."

"Sorry. What did he sound like?"

"Barry White after a bender. Deep voice, super rough. Apparently he's a bald, clothes-wearing, maybe-white guy, too."

Logan looked like he wanted to bite someone.

"You know him, don't you?" I said.

"You could tell all this over the phone?"

"I'm a very good listener. Are you? I asked if you know the guy."

"I know him."

"Well, who is he?"

"I can't name names. But his family's in the same line of work as your mother."

"Is he a suspect?"

"He has an alibi, thanks to his family. I wouldn't put anything past him, though. Even if he had nothing to do with your mother's death, he's going to see you as a threat. You should take that phone call seriously."

"I do."

"Well, what are you doing about it, other than telling me?"

"I unplugged the phone for the night. They can threaten me all they want, but I'm not going to lose any sleep over it."

Logan furrowed his brow and shook his head. "You know, I don't get you," he said. "Are you nuts or do you just not give a crap?"

"What did my boss say?"

"Little bit of both."

"That might be true most of the time, but not today. I give a crap. That's why I'm sticking around."

I took another sip of my cappuccino. It was cold.

"Thanks for the coffee. And the concern." I got up to go. "If you ever have any actual *information* you'd like to share, I'd love it if you'd—"

"All right, all right. Sit down."

I sat.

"What do you know about Clarice Stewart?" Logan said.

"Almost nothing. What do *you* know?"

He took a deep breath. Then he told me.

"Clarice Stewart and Athena Passalis showed up here together three years ago," Logan said. "Athena opened the White Magic Five & Dime. Clarice started going to the junior high. Athena was the girl's legal guardian. The parents, she said, were dead.

"Eventually, we started getting reports that Athena was…less than honest. It was nothing we could follow up on, though. Almost all of the complaints came from third parties. The victims wouldn't talk. That's typical with confidence crimes. Most go unreported. People are so embarrassed by their own stupidity, they'd rather let a rip-off artist get away than admit how they were fooled.

"Still, I'd pop in on Athena from time to time, just to let her know I was watching. I thought she might back off, drop the scams, but…I don't know. I don't think it made any difference to her.

"Half the time I'd go into the Five & Dime, Clarice would be there answering the phone and taking money. This one time, she short-changed a customer right in front of me. The classic 'I love your necklace' move while she lets a twenty fall behind the counter.

I guess she thought it'd be funny to get away with something while the big dumb cop's there. I said, 'I think you dropped something,' and she just looked down and said, 'Clumsy me! Thanks!'

"Don't let her act all innocent with you. She knew what was going on around there. She didn't always go along with it, though. The last time I dropped by the shop before your mother died, I could hear them arguing from outside, and when I went in they clammed up. Athena was always a pro—she just smiled and said what a pleasant surprise it was to see me. But Clarice was still all agitated, angry. She couldn't control herself. She turned to me and she said, and I quote: 'You could accuse me of a lot of things, but you'll never be able to call me a whore.' And she stormed out the door. Your mom laughed it off, of course. 'Teenagers are such drama queens, aren't they?'—that kind of thing. I could tell she was rattled, though. For once.

"Then, just a few days later, it was Clarice who found Athena's body and called 911—at 1 AM on a school night. She claims she'd been out with a boy, and he backs her up. Funny thing, though. The second she was done talking to the dispatcher, she was calling the boyfriend, and not on his cell phone: on the landline for his house. Woke up his mother, and she had to go get him up to talk to his hysterical girlfriend. The kid had dropped Clarice off ten minutes before, supposedly, and already he was home in bed, sound asleep…?

"I should be getting the medical examiner's report later today. And when I do, who knows? Maybe I'll be dropping by the White Magic Five & Dime again. Is that enough actual information for you?"

"It's a start," I said.

"It's a *start*?"

"What's the boyfriend's name? And I'd still like to get in touch with some of my mother's former clients—the ones 'third parties' told you about. And of course I'll want to hear what the coroner has to say, so I'll be expecting a call from you this afternoon."

Logan buried his face in his hands and groaned.

"I know," I said. "I'm demanding. What can I say? She was my mother. But hey"—I reached across the table and put a comforting hand on Logan's shoulder—"just imagine what a pain in the ass I'd be if I'd *liked* her."

THE BOYFRIEND's name was Matt Gorman. I'd get an update on the medical examiner's report by the end of the day. And my mom's supersucker clients? Confidentiality privacy discretion blah blah blah.

Hey, two out of three ain't bad.

THE BLOND barista was giving me the stink-eye as Logan and I walked out. It was so blatant I decided not to come back for another of her cappuccinos anytime soon. You never know what could be hiding under all that foam.

Logan and I headed for the White Magic Five & Dime.

"If you keep squiring me around town like this, people are going to talk," I said. "In fact, I think at least one person's already jumped to the wrong conclusion."

"Who? Kathleen? In the coffee shop? You think so?"

"I was lucky to get out of there without having a café americano dumped over my head."

"Oh. Sorry. That's a sad story, actually. Kathleen's got a thing for cops, and I'm the only one in Berdache who's not married."

"So what's the problem? She's attractive in a too-old-to-be-working-at-Hooters-anymore kind of way."

Logan shivered.

"She always smells like French roast," he said. "Anyway, let her make assumptions; so much the better. She's the gossip queen of the county. By the end of the day, half the town's going to think we're engaged, and that might discourage certain people from making more threats."

"Got it."

Up ahead, I could see a middle-aged woman cupping her hands to the White Magic Five & Dime's glass door. She was trying to look inside.

"That was impressive how you spotted Clarice pulling a short-change," I said to Logan. "Most people would've been looking at the necklace."

"Well, cops aren't most people."

"Yeah."

The woman was knocking.

"Just out of curiosity," I said, "do you know what a Michigan role is?"

"Some kind of danish?"

"No. How about the Jamaican switch? Ever hear of it?"

"Sounds like a dance move."

"Right. Same with the block hustle. You know that one?"

"I don't think so."

"The badge-play comeback? The oak tree game? The precious pet?"

Logan shook his head and shook his head and shook his head.

"I think I just failed a test," he said.

"Oh, no. You passed. You are a very nice man." *Who doesn't know squat about confidence games.*

"Thanks for the coffee," I said, and I darted off after the woman who'd been trying to get into the White Magic Five & Dime. She'd started to walk off, and I couldn't let my first customer get away.

The Hierophant's got the priestly robes, the worshipful aco-
lytes, and the keys to knowledge both worldly and spiritual
just lying there at his feet. He even seems to be saying the
Boy Scout pledge. Who could be more worthy of our trust,
right? But watch out—this isn't wisdom we're seeing, it's
pomp and circumstance. Ritual. Spectacle. Dogma. And we
all remember what happened to the dogma when it got too
close to the karma.

Miss Chance, *Infinite Roads to Knowing*

"Sorry!" I called out. "Coffee break!"

The woman turned to face me, looking confused.

I waved a hand at the White Magic Five & Dime.

"We're open, if you're interested. I just ran down the street to the coffee shop. Can't get my eyes open in the morning without a cappuccino. Not even my third one."

The woman didn't stop looking confused and start looking something else.

"My third eye, I mean," I could have stammered. "You know… like psychics supposedly have? In, uh, mysticism and stuff? Sorry. I'm new at occult humor."

Instead, I smiled. Hell, I *beamed*.

A confident bastard will get a lot further than a saint with low self-esteem, Biddle used to say.

The woman peered past me at the shop. She was fortyish, heavyish, shortish, owlish—extremely *-ish* all around. As blandly American as a block of Velveeta.

Her hands looked strong and rough, though. And her arms were long enough to reach across a table.

You wouldn't see her type on wanted posters very often, but that didn't mean anything. I was looking for a victim—an angry one—not a criminal.

"Is Athena in?" the woman said.

She seemed sincere. But then again, so did I.

"I'm afraid not," I said. "There's been a change of ownership. I run the Five & Dime now. Come on in and I'll make you a cup of tea. Is Red Zinger all right? I've got friends who swear by it, but like I said, cappuccino's the only thing that gets *my* motor running."

This was hustling-the-mark-along talk. But the woman wasn't moving.

I got her unstuck the easy way.

"Did I mention? Returning customers get their first reading free."

She followed me inside.

HER NAME was Alice Fisk (she claimed), and she lived in the next county over. She didn't get into Berdache much, but the last time she had she'd come into the White Magic Five & Dime on a whim. Athena had been very persuasive. Very perceptive. Very helpful.

Very patient.

Alice hadn't cleaned out her life savings so Athena could invest in the deal she'd foreseen would make them rich. She hadn't dug out her private papers—including birth certificate and social security card—so Athena could use them to "work up a chart" that would plot the course of her entire life. All she'd brought, she told me, was forty dollars for the "special expanded reading" Athena had promised her.

"Oh," I said. "I can do those."

We didn't have any Red Zinger next to the microwave and mini-fridge in the office, so I made do. Alice got a tablespoon of Lipton Diet Lemon Iced Tea Mix stirred into boiling-hot water.

"Here you go." I put the mug on the table in the reading room.

"Thank you."

The woman picked up the tea and brought it toward her mouth, then simply blew on it and put it back down. I'd nuked it so long it wouldn't be cool enough to drink for a week.

"What happened to Athena?" Alice asked.

"Health issues. Came on very suddenly."

"Oh, no. I hope she'll be all right."

"She's stable at the moment. The doctors don't expect her to get any worse."

"Well, that's something."

"It is, it is. Now…please shuffle these." I slid a tarot deck across the table and tried to remember Josette Berg's patter at the House of Arcana the day before. "While you're doing that, meditate on your question. What is it you'd like the cards to tell you?"

"Should I say it out loud?"

"If you wish."

Alice closed her eyes as she shuffled. After about twenty seconds, she put the deck down and opened her eyes again.

She looked at me expectantly.

Silently.

Great.

You don't have to push for details, Biddle used to tell me. *Citizens never pass up an opportunity to talk about themselves.*

Sometimes Biddle was full of shit.

I put my hand over the deck and drew it toward me. I had to fight the sudden irrational impulse to palm the top card. That was how I'd been taught to play. But it was a whole new game I was trying to master now.

I started laying out the cards in the pattern I'd seen Josette use—"the Weather Vane."

"You're not going to use the whatchamacallit?" Alice asked. "The Celtics Cross?"

"No," I said. Because I didn't know what a "Celtics Cross" was. I hadn't seen anything about them in *Infinite Roads to Knowing*.

Then again, I was only on page 98.

"This is a spread of my own creation," I said. "I call it the Phoenix."

"Looks like an airplane."

"Exactly. Both move on the winds of chance."

Alice looked dubious.

I flipped over a card, fast, and found myself looking at a knight of the Round Table planting giant carrots.

"Ahhh," I said. "The Seven of Rods."

"Rods?"

"As it is called in the old texts, yes. You might have heard it referred to by its newer name"—I stole a quick squint at the little words printed faintly across the top of the card—"Wands. Now, this first card represents your current life situation. If we look at it closely, we can plainly see that you're…"

What? Sir Lancelot? A giant carrot farmer? They both seemed unlikely.

"On the defensive," I said. "The man there, he's building a wall around himself. A fortification. He feels besieged."

Alice's eyes went wide and watery.

Bingo.

I turned over another card.

"Very interesting. The Seven of Pentacles."

On the card, a guy who looked like Robin Hood was leaning against a hoe as he looked down at golden pentagrams growing on vines like a bunch of Satanic watermelons.

"Here we see what's in your conscious mind. You're contemplating past decisions and endeavors—taking stock of the fruit of your long toil. It looks like you've got a fine crop there...but is it really?"

Alice gave me an encouraging nod.

I had accurately perceived that someone who visits a fortune-teller would be thinking about the choices she's made in life.

Like, *amazing*, right? I must be psychic.

I moved on, sticking as close as I could to Josette's gibberishy script.

"And here we find what's in your subconscious mind."

"Oh-ho! The King of Swords! Now isn't *that* something?"

What kind of *something,* I didn't know. The picture didn't give me much to work with: just a dude with a sword on a throne. Maybe the illustrator ran out of ideas after the devilmelons.

"Here we see someone who's very…kingly," I said. "He's calm, cool, totally in charge. This is what you'd like to be—what you aspire to. But you're not sure if you can achieve it."

Alice nodded again, more vigorously this time.

"With the next card, we gaze into the past to see what shaped your life as you know it now—the choice that brought you to your current predicament. And we get…*ahhh.*"

"Ahhh?" Alice said. She put her hands on the table and leaned forward to stare at the card. A band of gold was wrapped around the ring finger of her left hand.

"A man," I said. "One who seemingly comes to you bearing some great gift. But see? He's upside down. Whatever's in the chalice pours out. The gift is squandered. The promise is broken."

The hogwash is blatant.

I wasn't risking anything, though. If the woman had a happy marriage, she'd think of some other man who'd let her down. There's always one, if not dozens. And if she didn't have a happy marriage...

Tears began to well up in Alice's eyes.

That answered that.

To my right, pressed up against the wall of the reading room, was a squat bookcase. Sitting on top of it were a box of Kleenex and a crystal ball so big you could take it bowling.

I passed the Kleenex to Alice. She dabbed at her eyes.

"It's so true," she said. "That's just the way things turned out. So much big talk in the beginning, but then what?"

I nodded sympathetically, although I felt bad for Mr. Alice. Here I was making him the bad guy and I didn't even know his name.

I decided to give the next card a happy spin no matter what it was.

"Now we turn to the future."

Oops.

Alice was crying again before I could even speak.

"I knew it," she sobbed. "There we are, starving in the snow!"

"That's just a possible future, Alice. How things *could* turn out. Like in…"

I was momentarily torn between *A Christmas Carol* and *Back to the Future Part II*. But I couldn't assume that Alice had read the classics or (like me) watched ungodly amounts of hotel room HBO circa 1990.

"…the writings of the great Roarke Villechaize Ricardo," I said instead. "In the words of the master, 'Yesterday *was*, now *is*, but tomorrow is only *maybe*.'"

"Huh?" Alice said.

Which was disappointing. I thought it had sounded pretty good considering how far I'd reached up my butt to get it.

"Let's move on to something positive," I said.

I smiled even as my mind screamed, *What comes next? Something about…energy?*

"Bettering energies to harness for personal engooderment," I said. "And here we get—"

A dude eating a nasty-looking grapefruit as he gazes out at the ocean from between two beanpoles.

Very helpful.

"Obviously," I lied, "what we have here is a master of his domain. He's not a king, but he's powerful and proud. He's got the whole world in his hands and he's looking to the horizon, facing the future with supreme confidence. This is who you need to be."

"Yes. Yes. You are so right."

Alice sat up a little straighter in her chair and blew her nose in a firm, resolved sort of way.

"And finally," I said, "negative energies. Energies to avoid."

I turned over the last card.

We'd be ending with an easy one. The same card had come up in my reading with Josette.

The Eight of Swords. A woman blinded and trapped by her misconceptions and limitations.

I recycled what I could remember of Josette's shtick about swords—how they were all about smarts versus heart and the need for action, etc. blah yada—then segued into the wrap-up.

"The cards are speaking to you clearly, Alice. They're saying that you've been passive for too long. Your life isn't what you'd like it to be, but you have the tools to change that. Start using them. Take control. No one's going to solve your money problems or fix your home life but you. And no one's stopping you but you. If you embrace your power today, tomorrow and all the tomorrows after that are going to look a lot brighter."

I didn't add that she should keep her feet on the ground and keep reaching for the stars, but I could have.

Alice didn't blink once through the whole spiel. Her fists were clenched. Her jaw jutted out. She had the look football coaches want to see on their players at halftime. Yes, her ribs were bruised, her kneecaps were shattered, and she had a concussion, but damn it she was there to *play*.

She bought it all. She could do anything!

There's a reason Tony Robbins is a gazillionaire.

"Thank you," Alice said to me.

"My pleasure."

"Everything you said is so true."

"It's all in the cards."

"I don't have to be a martyr anymore."

"No, you don't."

"It's time I started asserting myself."

"That's the spirit."

"I'm as smart and capable as anyone."

"Exactly."

"If Donald doesn't think llamas can turn the ranch around, well, that's too damn bad."

Pause.

"Right," I said.

"The second I get home, I'm calling up the Llama and Alpaca Association and buying a whole damn herd!"

"Wonderful."

"And when Donald gets home, I'm telling him, 'Congratulations, dipshit—you're a llama breeder!'"

"Fantastic."

"And *then* I'm going to tell him if he doesn't stop boning Julia Luchetti, he's going to end up with a steak knife where his wiener used to be."

Pause.

Pause.

Pause.

I eventually managed a feeble "you go, girl."

It seemed to make Alice happy.

"I'm sorry about Athena," Alice said as I showed her out. "But I'm glad it's you who took her place. You're every bit as good as she was."

"Thanks," I said.

Thinking: *God, I hope not.*

I locked the front door. I hadn't turned on the neon sign in the window that morning, and I didn't turn it on now.

I went back to the reading room and sat down.

The Phoenix spread was still on the table. Completely by accident, I'd picked a fitting name for it.

My mother was dead, and who comes rising out of her ashes? Me.

No thanks.

I had a debt to repay. I owed my mother justice. But I wouldn't *become* her to get it. Not for real. Not for keeps.

Not if I could help it.

I took stock of my progress.

Lesson learned #1: Unless Alice Fisk was the Meryl Streep of Arizona—and she wasn't—she didn't kill my mother. Alice hadn't spent enough time with Athena to have been *that* screwed by her, so whatever homicidal rage she had in her was safely directed at her husband. I had successfully eliminated a suspect. One down, the rest of the state to go.

Lesson learned #2: I needed to work on my tarot patter. Improving interpretations hadn't been hard. The cards looked like *The Lord of the Rings* as illustrated by Salvador Dalí. Most of them packed in enough kooky symbolism for a dozen Lady Gaga videos. It was kind of important to get the *names* right, though. And I wouldn't be able to get away with bogus spreads like the Phoenix—not with my mother's regulars. If someone wanted a Celtics Cross or a Trump Tower or a Reading Rainbow or what have you, I had to lay it out without blinking.

Lesson learned #3: Donald Fisk was shtupping Julia Luchetti. Which wasn't useful in and of itself, but generally speaking it was helpful to hear. It was a reminder that Biddle had been right all along: people love to talk about themselves. And they wouldn't come into the White Magic Five & Dime if they didn't mean to do it. Alice had held out longer than most, I guessed, but when she finally did open up, what had poured out along with the tears was pure gold.

What if this Julia Luchetti had a husband? What if she had *money*?

She'd find out she could keep one but not the other, that's what. If my mother had still been around, anyway.

I knew what to look for next.

He said/she said sometimes works out okay, Biddle used to say, *but "just listen to what you said" never fails.*

One glance around the room, and I had it.

I moved to the bookshelf I'd taken the Kleenex from a few minutes before. The crystal ball on top of it was smoky gray with a shiny black base. The thing was the size of a globe. The only other time I'd seen a crystal ball that big, the person using it had been cackling "Fly, my pretties! Fly!" to dudes in monkey suits.

I turned the ball around, but there was nothing on the back of the glass but dust. I noticed something in the base, though. A hole about half the size of a dime. Just big enough for an electrical cord to run through.

I picked the ball up—it was surprisingly light—and started messing with the bottom. After a little righty-tighty, lefty-loosey, I managed to unscrew the base.

The crystal ball was hollow. And empty.

But it hadn't always been.

GLI AMANTI   VI   THE LOVERS
LES AMANTS   LOS ENAMORADOS

DIE LIEBENDEN   DE GELIEFDEN

You've got to love a card this simple. The Lovers signifies love. Well, and sex. And marriage. Any romantic entanglement, really. Or even a non-romantic partnership that elevates those in it to some higher level. Or simply a joining of opposites—yin and yang. (Guess who's the yang.) It can indicate negative things as well, such as a crippling yearning for a lost love or a naïve faith in an over-idealized Other. So okay, it's not so simple. And if you REALLY thought a card about lovers could be, maybe you should ask yourself: what do you know about love?

Miss Chance, Infinite Roads to Knowing

I'M GOING to tell a story. A love story. A true one.

That's the kind that doesn't get told much.

Once upon a time, there was a little girl. She was seven years old, and she was standing in a casino in Atlantic City. It was 1981, so the people in the casino were dressed even more horribly than the people in casinos today. It was smokier, too. But the noise and the flashing lights and the general feeling that you were trapped in a giant pinball machine with a thousand drunks who didn't want to get out—that was all the same.

None of it bothered the little girl. She'd spent more time in casinos than in schools. Casinos, in some ways, *were* her schools.

Every now and then (but not as often as you might think), someone would walk up to the girl and say, "Are you lost? Do you need help?"

Most of the time, she said, "No, thanks."

If it was someone who worked for the casino, she smiled sweetly and said, "Mommy's in the girls' room. When she comes out, we're going to the buff-it. Does it have ice cream?"

Once it was a man with slicked-back hair and thick glasses who leaned in a little too close when he talked, and the girl said, "Back off before I start screaming, perv."

The man scurried off to the slot machines.

The girl really was waiting for her mother. When she saw her, she saw this: beauty. The tall, slender, blond, blue-eyed kind. Big smile. Stylish clothes. Long hair, feathered Farrah-style.

The big smile wasn't for the girl, though. It was for the man on the mother's arm. He looked a little like the Man from Atlantis, only with thinner hair and a thicker middle. He was smiling, too.

The girl rushed up to them and said, "Momma!"

The mother and the man stopped walking. And smiling.

"'Momma'?" the man said. He had an accent.

He turned to the woman beside him.

She wasn't *so* beside him anymore. She'd unwrapped her arm from his and slid a half-step away. She spoke to the girl, but her eyes were moving, scanning the faces around them.

"Gabrielle…my god, honey…what are you doing here?"

The girl ran up and threw her arms around the woman's waist. Her mother bent in over her, embracing her, but it looked less like a hug than a huddle. A bracing for a blow.

"I couldn't sleep," the girl said, "so I made Franco take me to the arcade here. They've got a Space Invaders *and* a Pac-Man! But then all Franco wanted to do was play blackjack and he gave me some money and left me all by myself and when I ran out of quarters I couldn't find him and I was starting to get really, *really* scared and I'm so glad I saw you!"

"Franco's here?"

"Yeah. Somewhere."

The mother straightened up and started tugging her daughter away.

"You didn't see me here," she said. "When you ran out of quarters, you found your way back to our hotel by yourself, and I was already back in our suite because I had a headache and I skipped Engelbert Humperdinck. Do you understand?"

"What?" the girl said.

The man took a few hesitant steps after them.

"Cathy, wait! What is happening?"

The woman didn't look back.

The man stopped following. Whatever country he was from, trouble looked the same there as it did in New Jersey.

He'd been taking Cathy to his room. Now he went there alone.

He could still count himself lucky, though. He'd first met the woman at a roulette table the night before. The way she'd looked at him, the way she responded when he approached—it was right out of *Diamonds Are Forever*, and he was James Bond. They'd never get to Round 2 together, he and she, but Round 1 was something he'd be telling his friends about back in Whereverbourg for the rest of his life.

A few minutes later, there was a knock on his door. When he looked out through the peephole, he saw Cathy. Just Cathy. But when he opened the door, thinking the bell was ringing for Round 2 after all, the woman stumbled in as if shoved, and a tall black man in a turtleneck and a tan leisure suit stalked in after her.

"Come on in, Gabrielle," the black guy said. "There's nothing to be scared of. This nice man is one of your mother's special friends, remember?"

The little girl peeked around the doorway.

"Listen to Franco, honey," Cathy said. Her voice trembled, and her eyes were wide and puffy and pink.

The girl came inside with small, slow steps.

"I don't wish to be rude," the man said, "but—"

"Close the door," Franco told him.

The man blinked. Twice.

He wasn't used to tall black guys in turtlenecks barking orders at him, and this had an effect.

He closed the door.

Franco was already walking across the room. It was a big room, but not a suite. Nice but not gaudy or over-furnished. The kind of room a casino gives you when you have money but you don't know how to throw it around yet. When you don't know what to *expect*.

Franco turned on the TV, then patted the queen-sized bed.

"Over here, Gabrielle," he said. "The grown-ups need to talk."

The girl walked past her mother's special friend—"Uhhh, now, hold on just a moment," he was saying—and settled herself on the edge of the bed and started watching *The Love Boat*.

She knew the show well. There were few shows she didn't know well. Half her childhood had been spent parked in front of hotel TVs or dumped for the day at public libraries or roadside tourist traps.

She'd learned a lot that way, actually. She knew who Gavin MacLeod was. She'd read *Animal Farm* (because it looked like it would be funny, but it wasn't). She knew that the Battle of Gettysburg was fought in 1863 and that the Union army had won and they must have been sweating like crazy in those blue suits of theirs because, wow, you got hot wandering around that place in July.

And she knew that if you walked up to kids at a chintzy local museum and said, "Did you see the leprechaun? They keep it in a jar in the back," about half the time you could get a buck out of them before you convinced them to go out the fire exit.

The Love Boat was a rerun. The half-whispered conversation behind her was a rerun of sorts, too, but she listened anyway.

Franco: Do you have any idea whose wife you've been messing with?

Cathy: I told you he doesn't.

The guy: I don't. I really don't.

Franco: And in front of his kid, even?

Cathy: She didn't see anything.

The guy: The lady and I were just walking together.

Franco: Just walking with the lady, he says. Just walking! To your room. *Again.*

Cathy: Oh god. You set me up, didn't you? Oh god. You bastard.

The guy: If I'd known she was—

Franco: It doesn't make any difference whether you knew or not. You did what you did, and that's going to make my employer very, very unhappy.

Cathy: Oh god.

The guy: Look, I'm just a businessman who's—

Franco: Hey, my boss is here on business, too. Atlantic City business. You understand me? He's *that* kind of businessman. Only he likes to take the wife and kid along sometimes. Because, you know, to him family is everything. *Everything.* And if he found out his wife was out bed-hopping with Eurotrash instead of catching the show at the Sands…

Cathy: Son of a bitch.

The guy: This is…I don't know…it's crazy. I don't want any trouble.

Franco: Well, you've got it. More than you can handle. Let me ask you. Do you like coming to Atlantic City?

The guy: Yes, I guess.

Franco: Do you like gambling?

The guy: Yes.

Franco: Do you like breathing?

Cathy: Oh god.

Franco: *Answer me.* Do you?

The guy: Yes.

Franco: Well, if you want to keep coming to Atlantic City and gambling and breathing, you're going to make sure our little secret doesn't leave this room. Which means you need to keep your mouth shut, and you need to convince me to keep *my* mouth shut.

Cathy: Do it. Please. Just do it. Whatever he wants.

The guy: But…but…what *do* you want?

Franco: You're a businessman. What do you think?

It was mostly technical and boring after that. There was talk about expense accounts and exchange rates and traveler's checks and casino chips. The only interesting bit came when the guy said something like "that's the best I can do" and there was the crinkly rustle of someone moving fast in polyester, and the woman cried out "Franco, *don't!*" And the guy suddenly realized he could do better after all, and not long after that they were leaving.

"What about her?" the man said, nodding at the girl as she followed her mother toward the door. "She won't say anything?"

"Say anything about what?" Franco said. He reached out a big hand and ruffled the girl's brown hair. "You like your show?"

The girl shrugged. "It was pretty funny. But the kissing parts are gross."

"I know what you mean," Franco said.

The man locked the door behind them as soon as it was shut.

The three of them walked back to their hotel—Holiday Inn, not the Sands—without saying a word. The moment they were in their room, though, the woman whirled on Franco and threw herself into his arms.

"I told you it'd work! Four thousand bucks! Ha!"

And she kissed him. He kissed her back, then broke it off.

"Yeah, you were right. We did good." He looked over his shoulder at the girl, who was standing perfectly still just inside the door. "All of us. Though I still don't think we need—"

The woman wrapped her hands around his face and jerked it toward her and kissed him again.

"Come on," she said when she let him up for air. "Let's celebrate."

She pulled him backwards toward the nearest bed.

Beside it were three suitcases, packed, closed, and ready to go.

"We've gotta get out of here," Franco said.

"We can spare twenty minutes."

"But…you know…what about…?"

"Bath time," the woman said to her daughter without looking at her.

"Now?" the girl said. "I thought we were trying to—"

"Just get in the goddamn tub, huh?"

The girl went into the bathroom and closed the door. She turned on the tap, but she didn't bother undressing. She just sat on the hard, white linoleum and listened to the water splashing and gurgling behind her.

The door opened, and Franco leaned in.

"You okay?"

The girl nodded.

"We'll take a break after this," Franco said. "Go somewhere fun. Just enjoy ourselves for a while."

"You said we were taking a break when we came here."

"Hey, you know how it is. Some dollars just belong in your pocket even when they're in someone else's. When you see 'em, you gotta take 'em."

"Bullshit," the little girl said.

Franco didn't look shocked. He looked proud.

"Yeah," he said, "but what isn't?"

"I'm waaaitiiing," the girl's mother sang out.

Franco winced.

"Here," he said before he left. "I brought you this."

He held out a copy of *Of Mice and Men* the girl had stolen from a branch of the Cleveland Public Library a few days before. She'd only read a couple pages—she'd gotten distracted by another book—but she was still wondering when the mice would show up, and when they did, would they talk? That would be fun.

The girl turned the water gushing into the tub down to a trickle, just enough to make some noise, before she took the book. Then she sat back against the john and started over from the beginning, full of hope.

"Thanks, Biddle," she said.

The Chariot is the card for people who are really going places. It signals progress, momentum, achievement. This particular charioteer is so good, he can control the strength of conflicting drives—one black, one white, each pulling in different directions—without reins or even a harness. Let's see Ben-Hur do that. Then again, Ben-Hur didn't have to worry about his horses running away. Or turning around and eating him.

Miss Chance, *Infinite Roads to Knowing*

BLACKMAIL—a classic. The video camera in the crystal ball was a nice new touch, though. Say what you will about my mother—it wouldn't be anything worse than what *I'd* say—the lady was original.

Now I knew what the camcorder cassettes in the office had been for. Of course, a digital audio recorder would've been a lot easier to hide than a Handycam, but I'm sure Mom had her reasons for going old school.

My guess: a hand-off just seems so much more *real* when there's a physical object involved. You give someone a tape and at least they can have the satisfaction of stomping on it. "Transfer the money into my PayPal account and I promise to delete the mp3 file from my hard drive" just doesn't have the right ring to it.

There'd be downsides, though. Tapes would be a pain to back up, for one thing. And knowing that—that these were most likely the original recordings, with no copies—certain someones would be tempted to steal them.

In fact, I was pretty sure a certain someone *had* stolen my mother's tapes. The camera was gone. You're going to take that and not whatever it had recorded? No. That's why all the cassettes I'd seen had been unopened. The ones that had been used were who knew where.

So who'd want them? Three kinds of certain someones came to mind.

A victim.

A rival.

An accomplice who wanted to be a rival.

I still didn't know enough about the three groups to know which it was. I needed a lot more information. And I didn't even have to leave the shop to start getting it because one of the certain someones did me a favor.

He called me.

THE CALLER ID said PAY PHONE.

It had to be him again. Mr. Phlegm. The Man with the Exfoliating Voice.

He'd be calling from somewhere farther away this time. No way he'd be waiting for me at the 7-Eleven with a cherry Slurpee.

I thought about letting him talk to voicemail.

I'm not here to murder at the moment. Just leave your death threat after the beep…

But no. He'd probably be too smart to leave a message with a distinctive voice like that. And contact with him was an opportunity.

Sometimes you've got to rattle the cage to get the monkey to play, Biddle used to say. Of course, in real life the monkey's liable to throw crap in your face or bite off your fingers, but point taken.

I cleared my throat—talking to people who want to kill me always gets me a little verklempt—and picked up the phone.

"LEX LUTHOR!" I said. "How goes it?"

Nothing.

"Hello? Mr. Luthor?"

More nothing.

"Listen, Lex, I gotta tell you: the silent intimidation thing doesn't work anymore. Everyone just assumes their cell phone dropped the call."

"You're not on a cell phone," the gruff-voiced man finally said. "You're still in the White Magic Five & Dime. Mistake."

"That's more like it! I was starting to think, 'What's this guy doing? Calling up so he can *mime* threats?'"

"Shut up and listen. If you know what's good for you—"

"Lex."

"—you won't spend another night—"

"Lex."

"—in this town."

"*Lex.* Rude! I'm trying to talk to you! That's the whole problem with this relationship. Don't get me wrong—I enjoy our chats; really, I do. All those light bulbs you've been eating have totally paid off because *man* do you have a voice for menacing phone calls. But our conversations are so one-sided. Let's have a little give and take, huh? Get to know each other. Me first. I'm a Leo, I love piano rock and reggae, I don't eat meat but I can't stand tofu, my favorite movie is *The Goonies,* and I didn't kiss a boy until I was twenty. Now—your turn. I know you're not a member of the Hair Club for Men and you were at the 7-Eleven around the corner yesterday and as a welcome wagon you leave a lot to be desired, but beyond that I'm in the dark."

"You think I'm joking with you?"

"No, Lex. I don't."

"You think I'm not serious?"

"I think you're very serious, Lex. I'd just like to know why. Come on, open up. What's your beef with me? I'm a reasonable person. Help me see things from your perspective and maybe you'll get what you want."

"Oh, I'm going to get what I want, all right. But you aren't going to like how I get it."

"Really, Lex—again with the ominous insinuations? I thought we were beyond all that."

"You're right. We are. No more insinuations. Just *action*. Starting tonight."

"I hate to break it to you, Lex, but what you just said? That was an insinuation."

Back to nothing.

"Lex? You still there?"

He wasn't. He'd hung up. And just when I was going to switch from "Lex" to "Mr. Clean," too. Damn.

I hung up the phone and took a deep breath. What had I learned? Only this: I still had it. I could push fear down so deep it was like it wasn't there at all. Biddle would have been proud.

It wasn't the kind of information I'd been angling for, but it was good to know.

As long as I was feeling fearless, I decided to get another cup of coffee.

DETECTIVE LOGAN had told me that Kathleen, the blond glaring death at me from behind the coffee shop espresso machine, was "the gossip queen of the county" with a thing for cops. As if it never occurred to him that I'd be back in the place within the hour to get all the local dish he'd been holding back. Silly man.

Kathleen didn't seem glad to see me.

I smiled. "I thought I should come back and pay for a cup," I said. "I noticed I got the last one free."

"Yeah. You did. Cappuccino again?"

"Just black this time, please. Small."

Kathleen let me bask in a couple seconds of squinted contempt before turning away to grab a cup.

"I don't want to overdo it," I said. "I'm kind of jittery already. You see, I was in here with Detective Logan to talk about…"

Beat.

Tighten throat.

Moisten eyes.

Go.

"…my mother's death."

A different Kathleen handed me my coffee. This one looked sympathetic, concerned, unthreatened. And curious.

"My god. I'm sorry," she said. "Listen—this one's on the house, too."

"No, no. Thank you, but I really want to pay."

"I'm serious. Put that money away."

She talked me into it.

There were no customers behind me in line—I'd made sure to come in when business was slow—so there was no rush for me to move.

"You're very kind," I said. "Everyone has been. It's been a pleasant surprise, actually, since…well, to be honest, my mom wasn't always Miss Popularity."

Kathleen looked confused. Apparently, word that Athena Passalis's daughter was in town had gotten around to my secret non-admirer but not to Her Royal Highness, the Queen of Gossip.

Interesting.

I told Kathleen who my mother was.

"Oh, no! I am so sorry about what happened to your mom! That was just horrible! Does Josh—Detective Logan, I mean—does he have any leads?"

"Well, I probably shouldn't say anything, but…"

I glanced over one shoulder, then the other.

Kathleen leaned toward me so far I was surprised she could stay upright.

"There is someone Detective Logan's interested in," I whispered. "He described him to me. Middle-aged, gruff voice, bald, with some kind of connection to other fortunetellers in the area."

Kathleen gasped. "Anthony Grandi's a suspect?"

I nodded. "It would seem so."

"Oh. My. God. That's—oh, hi, Tom."

One of Berdache's finest was walking up behind me.

I don't like it when cops walk up behind me. It makes me wonder how I screwed up and where the nearest exit is.

Old habits.

"Thanks again," I said to Kathleen.

She looked sad to see me go.

I took my first sip of my coffee as I headed out the door. It wasn't bad.

Good. I had a feeling I'd be back for more.

I WALKED down the street to the law offices of Wheeler & Associates. I still didn't see any associates. I didn't see any clients either.

"Change your mind about selling?" Eugene Wheeler asked. He looked like a kid about to open the biggest box under the Christmas tree.

"Tell me about Anthony Grandi," I said.

Wheeler's shoulders slumped, and his eyes lost their glow. The big box was full of wool socks.

I threw in a candy cane.

"You can bill me for your time. It'd be better if our conversations aren't gratis anyway."

Wheeler sat up straight again, nodding knowingly.

Now it was official. I wasn't just a former client's daughter, I was a client. Everything he told me or I told him would be confidential.

Wheeler didn't ask why that was important to me. He only asked about his rate.

I agreed to it—why not? I'd just inherited $45,000—so he started talking.

"Anthony Grandi," he said, "is a scumbag. He has an office just a block south of here. Star Bail Bonds. Grandi's the only bondsman in town and the worst; there is no best. He charges whatever you're dumb enough and desperate enough to agree to, then he latches on like a leech and drains you dry. In the end, you're lucky if he only ends up with all your money and not your house, too."

I nodded.

So. A crooked bondsman. Good. That was just the kind of sleaze Mom would get tangled up with. Hello, prime suspect.

I was doing okay for someone whose previous experience with police work involved running away.

"Sounds like you've had mutual clients," I said.

"We used to. If I have a client in that kind of trouble now, I tell them to call Sweet Freedom Bail Bonds in Sedona. You might not get out of jail as fast, but you won't have a bloodsucker on your back either. Sometimes people don't take my advice. Then they're not my clients anymore. Usually they listen, though."

"Grandi must love you."

Wheeler shrugged. "He wouldn't go out of his way to pull me out of a wood chipper."

"Would he go out of his way to push you in?"

"If he thought he could get away with it. But it wouldn't be out of spite. Everything with him is about money."

"Do you know if he ever did any business with my mother?"

"No idea."

"Would he have had some reason not to like her?"

"Not a clue."

"What if I told you he'd been making threatening phone calls?"

"To you?"

"Yes."

"To your cell phone?"

"To my mother's place. From pay phones."

"And you're sure it's him?"

"Does he sound like Moe the bartender with laryngitis?"

"What?"

"Does Grandi have a rough, gravelly voice?"

"Yes."

"Then it's him."

"In that case, I would advise you to go to the police immediately."

"I did that, kinda sorta."

"What does that mean?"

"It means I mentioned it, but that's as far as I want to go."

"You didn't file a report?"

"No."

"Why not?"

"Not my style."

Wheeler raised his thick, graying eyebrows.

I didn't elaborate.

"Okay," Wheeler said. "Then I think you should consider this: Arizona has some of the most liberal gun laws in the country. And by *liberal* I mean *anything goes.* You could be packing heat within the hour."

"'Packing heat' isn't my style either."

"Maybe you should think less about your style and more about your safety."

"My style *is* my safety."

"Excuse me?"

"No police reports. No guns. Any other advice?"

"Well, if you won't take steps to protect yourself, then you should probably find a new place to stay."

"Run away?"

"Remove yourself from harm's way. Don't forget, though: Grandi's a bail bondsman. He knows how to find people...and get at them. I don't know what kind of threats he's been making, but unless you go far, far away, you are going to find out whether or not he means them."

"Are you trying to scare me?"

"I'm trying to warn you."

"Hmm."

I spent a moment sizing up Wheeler again. He looked like every Kiwanis member you've ever met: a big, doughy pillar of the community.

A lot of those pillars are rotten inside, though. Believe me. I've seen "respectable" people do things that would shock Genghis Khan.

Wheeler knew I was Athena Passalis's daughter. He knew I was staying at the White Magic Five & Dime. He wanted me to sell the place and cut him in for a slice of the price. And (according to him, anyway) he'd had business dealings with a ruthless scumbag who'd started sending me RSVPs to my own murder.

Yeah. *Hmm* was right.

"Change of subject," I said. "What do you know about Clarice Stewart?"

"Absolutely nothing...including who she is."

"That's weird. She's a sixteen-year-old kid. Apparently she'd been living with my mother for years now."

"As a lodger?"

"More like a housemate."

"Athena never mentioned it to me."

"So there's nothing about Clarice in the will?"

"No. Like I've been telling you, everything went to you."

I *hmm*ed again.

"It's not that out of the ordinary," Wheeler said. "I've seen it a million times. Someone's nephew forgets to send a Christmas card, and *wham*—he's out of the will. Or your best friend keeps that jet ski he borrowed just a little too long, so he's not your best friend anymore. And then when you dive drunk into Apache Lake and never come up for air, the houseboat goes to your cousin twice removed instead of him. You hadn't seen your mother in years, right?"

"Right."

"Well, maybe that's why she suddenly decided she needed a will. She and this Clarice had some kind of falling out, and she wanted to make sure the girl didn't get anything if she died. Maybe she was even afraid Clarice would—"

Wheeler cut himself off.

"There's really no use speculating," he said.

"Let's keep going anyway. Just for one more second. Do you think my mother told anyone about the will?"

"I have no way of knowing. She never indicated one way or another."

"Okay. Thank you. *Now* there's no use speculating."

I got up to go.

"We're not done yet," Wheeler said. "We still have unfinished business."

"Can't you just bill me? All I've got on me is twenty bucks."

Wheeler pouted. I guess I'd hurt his feelings. Who knew lawyers had any?

"We never finalized plans for your mother," he said.

"Oh. That. What's the rush? She's not going anywhere."

"Actually, she is. To a crematorium picked by the county. Unless you make other arrangements."

"They can't fire up the oven till the autopsy's done, right?"

"That's right."

"Then I've still got time to think about it. You can't rush these things, you know. What to do with your mother's remains is a big decision."

I tapped my lower lip and looked thoughtful as I walked out of Wheeler's office.

"Stuffed or bronzed?" I muttered. "Stuffed or bronzed? Stuffed or bronzed...?"

I was halfway back to the White Magic Five & Dime when Fiona Apple started wailing in my handbag. My ringtone. "Criminal," of course. What can I say? A chick starts her twenties in the nineties and certain things stick.

I fished out my cell and saw that the call was from LOGAN BPD. I took the call.

"Tell me you've got those names I wanted."

"Uhhh, hello," Logan said. "Names?"

"Oh my god. You're *that* kind of guy? Disgruntled customers. From my mom's shop. You said you were going to look into it. Is that what happens when you say, 'I'll call you, babe'?"

"I'm sorry. I forgot all about that. I got busy with something else."

Logan sounded somber, subdued. The "something else" was bad news.

"What is it?"

"The autopsy report's in, and...everything's not as straightforward as we would have liked."

"What does that mean?"

"The medical examiner says cause of death was strangulation, like we thought. But the killer wasn't facing your mother, and he didn't use his hands. He was behind her, and he probably used his forearm wrapped around her neck. It's sometimes called a sleeper hold."

106

"I've heard of it."

"Then maybe I don't need to tell you it gives us less to go on. Bruises from his hands would have told us a lot, but now I don't even know if I should be calling him *him*. And it's harder to fight off someone who's behind you like that, so it's a lot less likely the killer ended up with wounds we can look for now. I'd been hoping the ME would give me enough for a warrant. We could have had this wrapped up by the end of the day, if we were lucky. Unfortunately, we weren't."

"So the autopsy's a dead end."

"Pretty much."

I wondered for a second why none of this bothered me. A second was all it took.

I hadn't been counting on the autopsy to wrap everything up nice and neat anyway. This was my mother. There wasn't going to be anything nice and neat about it.

"Thanks for letting me know, Detective," I said. "*Now* do you think you could get me those names?"

Logan sighed.

"There's one more thing—something else the ME found. It doesn't help me any, but I thought you'd want to hear it."

"She had *I HEART MY DAUGHTER* tattooed on her ass?" I almost said.

I went with "all right" instead.

"There were signs of recent weight loss and jaundice, so the ME expanded the scope of his examination. Just to be thorough."

"Yeah? And?"

"It looks like your mother had pancreatic cancer," Logan said. "If the killer had just waited a few months, it would have done the job for him."

LA FORZA
LA FORCE
VIII
STRENGTH
LA FUERZA

DIE STÄRKE
DE KRACHT

Is the woman closing the lion's mouth, opening it, or giving the lion a handful of tuna Pounce? You decide. What's important is that even the King of the Jungle is just a big pussycat if you approach him without fear. WARNING: This applies to metaphorical lions only. The author of this book is not responsible for attempts to give real live lions handfuls of tuna Pounce.

Miss Chance, *Infinite Roads to Knowing*

DETECTIVE LOGAN kept talking. Next of kin, the deceased, cremation, state law, a decision, today, sorry. I heard it and I didn't.

Mom had cancer. Which meant the killer actually did us both a favor. No long, drawn-out, agonizing death for her and—bonus!—no stack of unpaid hospital bills for me.

So why was I upset?

"Thanks," I said, and I hung up though Logan wasn't done talking.

My phone rang again almost immediately.

I didn't answer.

IT'S NOT like I'd have wanted my mother to contact me. She handled it just right, actually.

I'll call you when I'm dead.

Then I could be there for her. Not before.

So I told myself it was just my pride that was wounded. The hidden pills in the bathroom, the change in dress size, the sudden desire to make out a will. I should've seen it coming.

And now my theory was all messed up, too. I'd pictured the killer lunging across the reading table to grab my mother by the throat. A crime of passion of the how-dare-you-bitch variety. But no. She was strangled from behind, and the killer didn't even use his/her/its hands.

It seemed colder. Calmer. Less spontaneous. More businesslike.

That's what was bothering me. Yeah, sure.

I noticed a sign across the street.

STAR BAIL BONDS

Anthony Grandi's office. Perfect.

When life gives you lemons, Biddle used to say, *steal some sugar and make lemonade.*

Screw this *feelings* crap. I had work to do.

THE STAR on the sign had a tip pointed straight down, pentagram-style. You'd think that'd be a tip-off. *DEALS WITH THE DEVIL OUR SPECIALTY!* Then again, most of Anthony Grandi's potential customers wouldn't be walk-ins and they wouldn't be choosy.

It had been a long, long time since I'd been in a bondsman's office. Ahhh, good times. I felt all warm and fuzzy. Then all clammy and nauseous. The memories were hitting me like a plate of bad oysters.

I went inside anyway.

A round-faced, red-haired young woman sat slumped over the front desk, texting. She glanced up at me with heavy-lidded eyes, found me nothing worth waking up for, then turned her attention back to her phone. It looked like she was sending an urgent message to her narcolepsy support group.

"Is Mr. Grandi in?" I asked.

"No."

"Do you know when he might be back?"

"Uh-uh."

"I need to speak to him about Athena Passalis."

"Who?"

She wasn't bluffing. Contemptuous disinterest that profound is almost impossible to fake.

"Someone Mr. Grandi's done some work with," I said. "Would it be okay to leave him a note?"

"Sure. Whatever."

A moment went by.

"Do you have a piece of paper I could write the note on?"

The woman jerked her head at a tray six inches from her right elbow. It was filled with forms and ballpoint pens.

"Use one of those."

Her eyes stayed on her phone.

She was the perfect receptionist for a skeevy operation like this. When she told the cops "I never noticed anything suspicious," she'd really mean it.

I picked up one of the forms. BAIL BOND APPLICATION & CONTRACT was printed across the top. The back was blank.

I sat in a cheap plastic chair covered with cigarette burns and graffiti and wrote my message using a copy of *Rolling Stone* for backing. I didn't notice the date on the magazine, but the fact that Hootie and the Blowfish were on the cover said a lot.

This is what I wrote:

Dear Mr. Clean, (I got to use it after all!)

You can save yourself the quarters and call from here next time. Or better yet, just come on over to my place and say hi in person. I've told Detective Logan you

might be stopping by. My friends Smith
and Wesson are anxious to meet you, too.
Vice versa?
Insinuatingly yours,

The Object of Your Disaffection

I folded the form over once and slid it onto the desk beside the texting receptionist.

"You'll see that Mr. Grandi gets that?"

"I said I would, didn't I?"

No. She hadn't, actually. But I didn't bother saying so. I didn't extend a middle finger just to see how long it would take her to notice it either. (My guess: between four and five minutes.) I wanted the note in Anthony Grandi's hands, not in his garbage can.

I may not pack heat, but sometimes it's good to let people know you can burn them.

FIONA APPLE started singing again. I ignored her. There was another batch of lemonade to make.

I headed back to my mom's place and changed out of my Gypsy getup.

This was a job for Businesswoman.

IT WAS awfully nice of Principal Little to see me on such short notice. But when someone from the Lions Club drops by to talk about prize money, accommodations are made, even in the middle of a busy school day.

"Have a seat, Ms…McCoy, was it?"

"Please," I said. "Call me Julie."

Principal Little settled herself behind her desk. She was a little round dumpling of a woman you could pluck up with your chopsticks and eat in one bite.

"All right, Julie. How can I help you?"

"Well, as I said, I'm from the Sedona chapter of the Lions Club and I just happened to be in Berdache today on business so I thought I'd drop by and share the good news and see what kind of bang for the buck we can all get out of it. I assume you're familiar with our annual Up with Academics! essay contest?"

"Of course," Principal Little lied. God bless her.

"Then you'll be thrilled to know that both the grand prize winner and the runner-up come from your school. Berdache High has three hundred and fifty dollars coming its way!"

"Oh," Principal Little said. "That's great."

It was now obvious to her why she'd never heard of the Up with Academics! essay contest.

"And Matt and Clarice both have three-minute shopping sprees coming to them at the Fashion Den in Sedona," I said. "Though I suppose we should probably think about giving them a little extra time on account of their…darn it, I can never remember what I'm supposed to say instead of handicaps. Special attributes?"

"Excuse me?"

"Wait, I'll get it. Limitations? Challenges? Whatever. They'll need more time due to their uniquely demanding life situations. But I think that's what makes this such a great story. To be brutally honest with you, I'm hoping we can get a little ink for the Lions Club out of it. And for your school too, of course. I think people are going to be truly touched when they hear what Matt and Clarice have been able to achieve."

"I'm sorry, Julie. Hold on. Which students are we talking about here?"

I went with the boyfriend first. The one Logan told me Clarice was out with the night my mother died. The one the girl supposedly got out of bed with a call the second she was through with 911.

"The grand prize winner was Matt Gorman," I said. Then I watched Principal Little.

This was the whole reason for being here. Risking a pop-in instead of pulling something over the phone.

What kind of kid was Matt Gorman? It should show on his principal's face, assuming she knew him. And in a town this small, she would.

Principal Little blinked. She frowned, but not in a scornful way. She looked puzzled but not shocked.

Interpretation: Matt Gorman was an okay kid…at least as far as his principal knew.

"His essay was called 'Straight As and No Eyes,'" I said.

"I don't understand."

"It's a pun. Because of his…differently abledness."

"Julie, I have to tell you, I'm very confused. Matt Gorman is a good student, but he doesn't get straight As and he's certainly not differently abled."

"You mean he's not blind?"

"Blind? No! He does track and field! He's on the wrestling team!"

"I know that. It was in his essay."

"And you thought he was blind?"

"Are you saying blind people can't wrestle?"

114

"No no no! But Matt Gorman *isn't* blind."

"You're sure?"

"Of course I'm sure."

"Oh my. I'm almost afraid to ask if Clarice Stewart really is quadriplegic."

"She's not."

"Is she even a cheerleader?"

"What?"

"The title of her essay was 'Give Me a Q, Give Me a U, Give Me an A, Give Me a—'"

"Okay, I get it."

"First quadriplegic cheerleader in Arizona."

"*I get it.*"

"We all wondered why we'd never seen her on the news."

Principal Little buried her face in her hands.

"I am so sorry," she said into her palms.

"We got…punked, is it?"

Somehow Principal Little found the strength to face me again.

"Yes," she said. "I'm afraid so."

"Have Matt and Clarice done anything like this before?"

"Nothing like this. But there have been incidents. They're sort of…partners in crime."

"Ahhh."

"Clarice has come *this close* to expulsion more than once. But we've tried to be understanding." Principal Little gave me a significant look. "Difficult home life."

"Oh. That's a shame."

"It is. I'd be surprised if Clarice was behind this, though. She and Matt won't ever be valedictorian, but they're smart. Too smart to put their own names on fake essays for a contest."

"Do they have enemies? People who would want to get them into trouble like this?"

"Not that I know of. But I'll be looking into it, I assure you."

"I appreciate that. Though...well, I'm sorry, but you know this means your school won't be getting the three hundred and fifty dollars."

Principal Little offered me a tight smile.

"Yes. I realize that. Now why don't I show you out?"

I INSISTED that Principal Little stay put. No need to waste any more of her valuable time.

And no need for Clarice to spot us together and put me in an awkward spot. Which is exactly what would have happened.

She was sitting under a tree in front of the school when I saw her. A goth lite girl sat beside her—short, electric-blue hair and heavy eyeliner but no piercings or tats. They were huddled up talking so intensely they probably wouldn't have noticed if I'd tap-danced past them waving sparklers. All the same, I veered away, putting my back to them before they might notice me.

I didn't see any sign of Clarice's "partner in crime." But I'd be meeting him soon.

I was going to make sure of that.

I GOT another call from LOGAN BPD as I drove away. This time I picked up.

"Talk fast. I'm driving."

"Then you shouldn't be on the phone."

"Arrest me."

"Maybe I will."

I heard the beep-squawk of a police radio.

"Hey," I said. "*You're* driving."

"Guilty as charged. But I'm going to let myself off with a warning."

"Hypocrite."

"It comes with the badge."

"I know."

"This is actually good timing."

"What is?"

"Us both being in our cars."

"You want to drag race?"

"I want to show you something."

"It's not the Grand Canyon, is it? I've seen it."

"It has to do with your mother."

"Where do I go?"

I SWUNG by my mom's place before meeting Logan. I wanted to slip back into the Stevie Nicks costume he'd seen me in that morning.

Consistency should be your number-one priority. Always, Biddle used to say. *People notice something's changed, they start asking questions. And if they're asking questions, that means they're thinking, and if they're thinking, then we're screwed.*

Then about five minutes would go by, and Biddle would say something like "Why would you wear boots like that? You don't want to be noticed. Blending in should be your number-one priority. Always."

"But you said consistency was—" I'd start to say.

And he'd just smile.

It wasn't the Grand Canyon, but it was a canyon, and it was grand. Logan walked me up to a spot called Devil's Ridge where we could look out over it. From up there, the world was just three colors: red (rock), green (brush), and blue (sky). If it hadn't been for the plants, I'd have thought I was on Mars.

The town was behind us. The road, too. Nothing moved. We were alone.

Logan was standing close beside me. A gust of warm desert wind ruffled his dark curls. His hair was a little thick and longish for a cop, so it actually looked okay ruffled. In fact, I was tempted to reach up and ruffle it more myself. Or maybe I just wanted to give the guy a noogie. He seemed very noogie-able somehow.

I refocused on the view.

It was a good thing I'm not afraid of heights, because the ridge jutted out like a granite diving board to nowhere. Do a swan dive from there and you'd end up spread over the rocks below like jellied Spam.

An eagle screamed as it swooped past us into the valley.

"Beautiful," I said.

"Indeed."

"Majestic."

"Absolutely."

"Awe-inspiring."

"Totally."

"Perplexing."

"Uhhh…perplexing?"

"As in, what does a beautiful, majestic, awe-inspiring view have to do with my mother?"

"There is a connection. Do you know where we are?"

"Devil's Ridge."

"Yeah, but what *is* Devil's Ridge?"

"A ridge. What the devil has to do with it, I don't know."

"Don't you *feel* anything here? Sense something special?"

"Now that you mention it…yes…yes, I do feel something. It feels like…mild irritation. Or maybe it's just heartburn."

"It's too bad you don't pick up anything more, Alanis. Because Devil's Ridge is our claim to fame." Logan held his arms out wide. "*This* is Berdache's vortex."

"You've only got the one?"

"Yes."

"Sedona's got, like, four."

Logan let his arms drop back to his sides. "That's why Sedona gets four times as many tourists."

"So this is where all the mystical energy's supposed to be swirling around?"

"That's right."

I licked a finger and stuck it up in the air.

"Nope," I said after a moment. "Nothing."

"It's the same for me. But then again, I'm not trying to pass myself off as a psychic."

"Neither am I."

"So you're not going to reopen your mother's shop?"

"Oh, I am. But tarot readers aren't necessarily psychic. They're merely adept at using a specific set of symbols, shuffled by the random hand of chance, to assess an individual's past, present, and prospects."

Infinite Roads to Knowing, page 3.

"That's a good explanation," Logan said. "I just thought they were bullshit artists."

I shrugged. "Six to one…"

"Look, Alanis, I'm going to be blunt."

"You weren't already?"

"I like you, but Berdache doesn't need another phony. And… well…"

"Just look at what happened to the last one."

"Yeah."

"That autopsy report has you spooked."

"It threw me, anyway. If the ME's right about how your mother was killed—from behind, with something like a sleeper hold—that changes how this feels. It starts to look like it wasn't a simple B&E gone wrong after all."

I've never been a fan of the prefab snarkism "gee, ya think?" So I managed not to say it.

"I think you might be onto something," I said instead. "You know who likes sleeper holds? Bounty hunters. And from the hints you dropped about Anthony Grandi, I get the feeling he doesn't always farm out his skip tracing to freelancers."

"What do you know about Anthony Grandi?"

"Not enough. You want to tell me more?"

"No."

"Fine. You know what else a sleeper hold could mean? A pro from out of town. No murder weapon, no fingerprints—it seems pretty tidy for an amateur."

"Even amateurs get lucky."

"True. But how many of them know how to kill someone with the inside of their arm?"

"That could have been unintentional. A struggle that got out of hand."

"Maybe. It's hard to imagine someone *unintentionally* putting my mother in a headlock, though. By the way, did you know that Matt Gorman is on the Berdache High wrestling team?"

"Alanis, would you please stop…what was that?"

"Did you know that Matt Gorman is a wrestler?"

"No. No, I didn't, actually."

"Who knows what kinds of holds he's picked up, right?"

"Yeah, I get it. And I appreciate the information. Really. But you don't have to lead me around by the nose. This isn't Mayberry, and I'm not Barney Fife."

"Wow. How old are you?"

Logan gaped at me a moment before answering.

"Thirty-six."

"I didn't think thirty-six-year-olds knew who Barney Fife was anymore."

"My granddad liked that show. How old are you?"

"Thirty-six."

"So how is it *you* know who Barney Fife is?"

"I spent a lot of time in Mayberry as a kid." I spread my arms wide, just as Logan had a couple minutes before. "So here we are in a wellspring of spiritual energy, the grandeur of creation stretched out before us, a murder to solve...and we're talking about *The Andy Griffith Show.*"

"I have a murder to solve. You have a mother to bury."

"I'd rather solve a murder."

Logan put on an I'm-not-joking-around-here face. It was almost even a you-have-no-idea-how-much-you're-pissing-me-off face. It wasn't very pretty.

"Hey, I'm just messing with you," I said. "Like I'd ever interfere with a police investigation. I like to stay as far away from those as possible."

Now Logan was wearing a you're-full-of-crap-and-I-know-it face. It was only slightly more becoming.

"Don't you even care that you might be putting yourself in danger just by staying here?"

"Nah."

Logan stepped closer to me, and we were already close to begin with. If he wanted to get any closer, he'd only have about two inches to work with. I was surprised he wasn't standing on my toes.

"Alanis," he said.

I had to tilt my head back to look into his eyes. They were filled with exasperation but also tenderness and something like wistfulness. Jam-packed, those eyes. They could really multitask.

It occurred to me that I might be about to receive the most poorly timed, surprising, and inappropriate kiss of my life. Which is saying a lot, considering my life and the kisses in it. There haven't been many and they almost never felt right.

I braced myself.

Actually, "braced myself" isn't quite right. Being kissed by a big, good-looking guy like Detective Josh Logan wasn't the worst thing that could happen to me. I could take it. I'm tough.

I *prepared* myself.

"Hey, Kevin!" someone called out. "Don't forget the peace pipe!"

I turned to find a gaggle of middle-aged white guys in T-shirts and shorts trudging up the trail from the parking lot. Most of them were carrying tribal drums adorned with feathers and beads.

I felt a sudden urge to throw myself off the cliff.

"If you don't mind," I said, "I'd like to go before anyone gets in touch with his inner wild man."

"Me, too," Logan sighed. A moment before, we'd been close enough to mambo, but now he was scooting back from me. "I still have more to say, though."

"Well, you'd better get to it. In a few seconds we're going to be in the middle of a Boy Scout jamboree."

There were about thirty yards of trail left between the WASP braves and our spot at the edge of the ridge.

"It's obvious I can't tell you what to do, Alanis," Logan said. "But I can ask a favor. Steer clear of Anthony Grandi."

"What if he doesn't steer clear of me?"

"I'll take care of that. You just take care of yourself. Don't take any stupid risks."

"I promise not to go sky diving or bungee jumping. Beyond that, I do what I do."

Logan shook his head and let out a long breath. "I don't know if you're the bravest woman I've ever known or…something else I won't say."

"I'm probably the something else. What's that?"

Logan was pulling a small sheet of folded paper from his jacket pocket. He handed it to me.

"You wanted to know who'd made complaints to the police about your mother. There you go."

I unfolded the paper and looked over the list. It was shockingly short.

"Just three people in the three years she was here? Wow. Mom must have been even slicker than I remember."

"Yeah, well, good luck making amends for whatever she did. Just keep me out of it, would you? You didn't get those names from me."

I refolded the paper and stuffed it in my pocket. "What names, Officer?"

Logan smiled wryly. "You are a bad influence, you know that? You're not even in town twenty-four hours and already I feel like I'm the Bad Lieutenant."

"Welcome to the Dark Side, Detective. You might like it. It's cooler over here in the shade."

"Hey, folks!" one of the ten not-so-little non-indians said. "We're about to start a sun dance. Feel free to join in."

"Sorry," I told him. "Things to do, people to see."

Debts to pay.

Killers to find.

Dangers to ignore.

Yeah, my plate was full—and none of it was very appetizing.

So why was I feeling so good as Logan and I hiked back down the trail?

L'EREMITA / L'ERMITE — IX — THE HERMIT / EL ERMITANO
DER EREMIT — DE KLUIZENAAR

These days, hermits live in cabins in Idaho, where they write anti-government manifestos and tinker with letter bombs and develop body odors as deadly as the anthrax spores they wish they had in the fridge. That's not what the Hermit of the tarot's about at all. He uses his lantern to search for truth, not the keys to his gun rack. He's not a misanthrope, he's a wanderer in the wilderness seeking wisdom. If you come across a Hermit in the cards (or in your life), follow him (or her). You'll learn a thing or two. Just watch out for the body odor. That part might not have changed much.

Miss Chance, *Infinite Roads to Knowing*

THE THREE names on Logan's list were Victor Castellanos, Kenneth Meldon, and William Riggs. Three men. Weird.

I didn't know much about the crystal-ball crowd, but I always assumed most of their clients/prey were women. Plus, men are less likely to make a stink when they're swindled. It's pride. They hate admitting how stupid they've been—which lets the con artist move on to the next dumb mark, and the next and the next and the next. Ninety percent of confidence crimes are never reported at all. True fact—or as true as anything else Biddle ever told me.

I used my phone to look for listings, but I only came up with one address. William A. Riggs lived at 1703 O'Hara Drive. There were three Castellanoses in town, but none named Victor. And there were no Meldons at all, Ken or otherwise.

1703 O'Hara Drive, here I come.

First, though, it was back to the White Magic Five & Dime for another wardrobe change. I was about to visit someone who'd been burned by my mother. Showing up on his doorstep looking like another member of Fortunetellers Local 557 didn't seem like a good idea.

As I walked up to the Five & Dime, I was stopped by someone who could have been my union rep: Josette, the groovy gray-haired hippie dip who ran the shop across the street.

"Ms. Passalis?"

I didn't feel like explaining that my mother and I had different names. I wasn't super attached to "Alanis McLachlan" anyway. I'd made that one up when I was eighteen, and it showed.

"Yes?" I said.

"I'm so glad I saw you. There's something I need to tell you."

"Oh?"

"About an hour ago, I happened to glance this way and saw a man trying to get into your mother's store. He tried the door, banged on the glass, looked in the windows. He seemed really agitated. He was shouting something, but by the time I came outside to hear what it was, he was leaving."

"What did he look like?"

"He was an older gentleman. An *old* gentleman, really. In his seventies, maybe. Not very big. He was wearing sweatpants and a cardigan and a baseball cap."

I crossed my fingers.

"Do you know Anthony Grandi?"

Josette made a face that seemed to say she didn't know the guy, but she knew what he smelled like, and it wasn't good.

"Not really. But I'm familiar with him."

"Could it have been him?"

"No. Definitely not."

Damn. So now I had two stalkers. I was just glad one of them was an AARP member.

"I feel like I've seen him before, but I can't say where," Josette went on. "I'm sorry I can't tell you more. I thought you ought to know, though."

"Thanks. I appreciate it."

I turned to go.

"I also wanted to tell you how sorry I am about what happened to your mother," Josette said. "I had no idea who you were when I read for you yesterday."

"That's okay. How could you have known?"

"Have the police made any progress? I thought I saw you with Josh Logan this morning."

Ahhh, the joys of life in Mayberry. The neighbor-folk had taken notice of my comings and goings.

I was going to have to start using the back door.

"No. No news," I said.

"Well, I'm sure that won't be the case forever."

"Thanks. We'll see."

Again I turned to go.

"Ms. Passalis, I hope you won't mind my saying so, but…"

By the time I turned back her way, Josette seemed to have changed her mind about speaking at all. Her lips were pressed together in the kind of tight, sad smile a mother might put on before saying, "You know, honey, that dress would probably look better on someone with hips that are a little…less."

Someone else's mother, I mean. Mine would've said, "You look like a satin-wrapped ham. Put on something else." Without the sad smile.

"Yes?" I said.

Josette reached out and took my hands in hers. I didn't mind so much. At least it meant she wasn't going to hug me.

She was wearing a sleeveless, shapeless, hemp-looking smock thingie that revealed lean but muscular arms it probably would be hard to wriggle free of. Who knew yoga could give a gal such guns?

"If you need a friend," Josette said, "someone who knows this place and these people and how to run a business and build a life here, I hope you'll come talk to me."

"Thank you. That's very kind."

I gave her hands a squeeze, freed myself, and escaped into the White Magic Five & Dime.

IT WAS very kind. Too kind. The kind of kind that kind of freaks me out.

I didn't see a lot of kindness as a kid. When I did, it wasn't called kindness. It was called weakness. Or bogus.

I didn't see it as a weakness anymore.

The bogus part I was working on.

CASE IN point: I was changing clothes, going from Gypsy to Blank Slate, and I was thinking about Josette. And it occurred to me that she wasn't just being *too* kind, but her reading the day before had been *too* good. There'd been the talk about big changes and new places and death and, hovering over it all, that tricky, wicked bitch, the reversed Queen of Wands. Was I really supposed to believe Josette could be that on the nose without knowing who I was?

Maybe word had gotten around about me even sooner than I'd thought. Maybe more people than Eugene Wheeler had been expecting me.

Or maybe Josette really could see the future in a bunch of cards that looked like a Renaissance fair on acid. She'd even hinted that there was an interesting (and interested) man in my future, and then Logan comes along and…whatever was happening there. Who could have predicted that? Just because Mom was a sham didn't mean every tarot reader was.

Of course, my mother would've been ashamed of me for having such thoughts. She would've found them hopelessly, dangerously, disgustingly naïve.

So I kept having them.

1701 O'HARA Drive had an immaculately manicured lawn and blooming rose bushes and little granite cherubs frozen mid-scamper here and there around the hedges. 1705 O'Hara Drive had a tricycle on the porch and a scooter propped against the garage door and balls and dolls and plastic buckets and shovels scattered across the grass.

1703 sat between them like a suburban Sargasso Sea. The small plot was barren and sun-baked. The house was a drab brown box. The driveway was empty. No name on the mailbox. ("The Baumgartners" had the granite cherubs. "The Clarks" had the real kids.) There wasn't even a number on the house. If it hadn't been for 1701 and 1705, you'd never have known what the address was. The place looked so spartan and lifeless, it could've been a coffin waiting to be buried.

This was the home of William Riggs, disgruntled Five & Dime customer, and before I'd even stepped onto the porch I knew the man had all the warmth and vibrancy of an ice cube.

I put an unassuming smile on my face. I didn't expect it to last long.

There was a moment of silence after I rang the bell, then the sound of soft, slow footsteps. The door opened just wide enough for a woman's face to poke through. She looked wary, tentative, like a rabbit sticking her nose out of the warren to sniff for wolves.

"Yes?"

"Is this the home of William Riggs?"

"Yes."

"Is he home?"

"No. He's at work. Is he in some kind of trouble?"

"No."

"Oh," the woman said, sounding strangely disappointed. She looked a little younger than me, thirty maybe, with short blond hair and blue eyes and glasses. Her face was thin, almost gaunt, but she could've had the body of a linebacker for all I knew. The door hadn't opened any wider.

"My name is Alanis McLachlan," I said. "My mother was Athena Passalis. From the White Magic Five & Dime? On Furnier Avenue?"

"Oh!"

"I'm here because—"

"I can't talk to you!"

The rabbit jumped back into her warren. The door slammed shut.

I didn't hear it being locked, though. And I didn't hear footsteps either. The woman was still only feet away from me.

"I just wanted to talk to Mr. Riggs a moment," I said. "I've heard he was unhappy with my mother for some reason, and I wanted to see if it was anything I needed to know about. I'm in town to wrap up her affairs—you might have heard that she's dead—and I'd hate to leave with any disputes still unresolved."

The door stayed shut.

I started to back away.

"I hope you'll tell him I came by. He can find me over at the Five & Dime if he wants to talk. I'm sorry for any trouble my mother might have caused him."

I was about to turn and walk back to my car when the door opened again—wide this time.

"You *really* don't want to talk to my husband about Athena," the woman said. "But you can talk to me."

Mrs. William Riggs—Marsha—did not have the body of a linebacker, unless you were looking at the skinniest twelve-year-old in the pee wee league. She was small, even scrawny. As shapely and curvaceous as a lamppost.

She hadn't always been like that.

The inside of the house was spare and unadorned, like the outside, with bare walls and no clutter or tchotchkes and only one picture in sight: Marsha and her husband on their wedding day. He was wearing an Army uniform. She was in a bridal gown filled out with at least fifteen more pounds than she carried now. She had a rosy glow and a big smile. They were gone, too.

Something had deflated her, left her shriveled. I could guess what it was.

"Your mother was the best thing that's happened to me in this town," Marsha said.

"Really?"

"Oh, absolutely. Bill and I moved here a year ago, and at first I was so lonely. I didn't know a soul, and…well, we're not real social. But then one day I was driving home from the grocery store and I passed your mother's place and on a sudden whim I stopped and went in. And I'm so glad I did! I didn't know a thing about tarot cards, but Athena was a great listener and full of such wonderful advice."

"I'm glad to hear it."

"Do you read?"

"Yes."

She hadn't said "do you read *tarot*" so technically it wasn't a lie.

"I'm sure you must be great at it if your mom taught you. She was amazing. It was like she knew me better than I know myself."

"Yeah. Mom really understood what makes people tick."

"She sure did."

Marsha smiled. The memory of my mother seemed to make her genuinely happy.

That made one person in the world.

"So why was there a problem with your husband?" I asked.

"I begged him not to go to the police."

"Why did he?"

"The last time I spoke to Athena, I just apologized and apologized. I was bawling the whole time."

Marsha sniffed and wiped at her cheek. I wouldn't have thought she had the juice in her for tears, but there they were now. Two thin trickles, then she was dry.

"You used to talk to my mother about your husband," I said.

Marsha nodded. "I didn't have anybody else to talk to here. Sometimes I think that's why Bill moved us to Arizona—so he wouldn't have to share me with anyone. So all I'd have would be him."

"Is that what Athena used to say?"

"Pretty much. She helped me see how controlling he is. I started to stand up for myself a little bit."

"And Bill didn't like that."

"No. He said I was being brainwashed, like Athena was a cult leader or something. So he went to the police."

"Giving someone advice isn't illegal."

"It was the money he complained about."

"Oh."

Here we go.

"I admit, it got a little out of hand," Marsha said. "I just couldn't stop myself. It felt like I needed Athena's help with every conversation Bill and I had. And she was giving me a discounted rate. If I hadn't been going every day—"

"Every day?"

"Well, Tuesday through Saturday. The days Bill was at work."

"How long did that go on?"

"About two months."

"And the discounted rate was—?"

"Fifty dollars."

My eyes widened.

"She was doing special readings," Marsha said. "Not just the Celtic Cross but other spreads she created just for me and my situation. Sometimes I'd be in the White Magic Five & Dime for hours while she laid it all out and explained it to me."

"Fifty dollars a day would have added up after a couple months."

"It did. That's how Bill found out about Athena. He noticed the money I'd been taking out and he started asking questions and I didn't want to tell him everything, but…he made me. Then he went to the police."

Marsha scoffed at her own words.

The irony.

Him going to the police.

"And the cops didn't do anything," I said.

"No. They just said 'keep your wife on a tighter leash'—according to Bill, anyway."

"Seems like you were on a pretty tight leash to begin with."

"Well…now it's even tighter."

I looked at the wedding photo again. The groom had short-cropped blond hair and pale blue eyes and a big smile. I don't know much about uniforms, but I could tell Riggs had been a private when the picture was taken.

"What did your husband do in the army?" I asked.

"Not much. Sometimes people think that's why he's so…intense. But he was never in Iraq or Afghanistan. He never got out of Fort Benning. The only battles he was in were with MPs."

"I see," I said.

And I did see. I saw a lot.

"What does Bill do now?"

"He works for Eureka Resorts International. He started with them back in Orlando, where we're from, but last year he was transferred to the Sedona office. He's a sales manager there. He and his team do timeshare presentations out at the Oak Creek Golf Resort."

I nodded, smiling. Now I *knew* Bill Riggs was an asshole. He was in the same business as me.

"Berdache is actually closer to the resort than Sedona, so…" Marsha shrugged, slumped, shriveled just a little bit more. "Here we are."

"Well, I'm glad my mother could make your time here a little easier, even if it was only for a while."

"She truly was a godsend. I miss her every day."

"It must have been a shock when you heard what happened to her."

"Oh, it was. I just couldn't believe it. Poor Athena. How could anyone have done something like that to her?"

"That's what I keep wondering."

Marsha looked away for a moment, then met my gaze again.

She heard it. The question I was asking without asking.

"Of course, I hadn't seen her in weeks," she said, "so in a way I felt like I'd lost her already."

Fair enough. She was answering without answering.

Translation: *No, I don't think my husband killed her.*

Alternate translation: *No, I'm not going to admit that my husband might have killed her.*

"Oh, just listen to me!" Marsha moaned, flapping her hands like a bird that can't quite get off the ground. "What a horrible, selfish thing to say when you've lost your mother!"

I reached out and put a hand on her knee. Instantly she went still.

"It's okay. I understand."

New tears welled up in Marsha's eyes.

"You are your mother's daughter," she said. "You're every bit as sweet and kind and thoughtful as she was."

I forced myself to give her a smile as if she hadn't said something I'd prayed all my life wasn't true.

WHEN I said "I've taken up enough of your time," Marsha began talking about how she and Bill met.

When I said "I really should be going," she started asking questions I didn't want to answer about my mother.

And when I stood up and said "I'd better get back to the White Magic Five & Dime," she jumped up and hurried off down the hall.

"There's something I want to show you," she said.

I thought she might come back with manacles and clamp me to the couch. The woman needed company.

When she came back to the living room, she was carrying a deck of cards.

"I bought these from Athena. I have to keep them hidden or…" Her shoulders jerked up and down in a way that was half-shrug, half-shiver. "Hey. You said you read, right?"

She offered me the cards.

Tarot, of course.

I didn't take them.

"I'll pay you," Marsha said.

"I'm sorry. Now really isn't a good time. There's so much to take care of while I'm in town. You know. Arrangements to make."

"Of course. I'm sorry. How thoughtless of me to even ask."

"It's okay. No problem. Really. You know, you spent so much time watching Athena work, you could probably read the cards as well as I can anyway."

"You mean do a reading for myself?"

"Why not?"

"But I thought that wouldn't work. That you need somebody else—someone separate from your situation, with an unbiased point of view—or you'd miss a lot of the messages. That's what Athena always said."

"Of course she did," I said. "But really—there's nothing wrong with giving it a try on your own. You might be surprised at what you find."

Marsha looked dubious. The hand holding the cards fell to her side, the arm limp, dead.

Trying didn't seem to be her strong suit.

I started toward the door again.

"Pop into the Five & Dime sometime, if you can swing it, and I'll do that reading for you. I'd love to talk some more."

Marsha smiled sadly.

"Okay," she said. "I'll try."

I assumed I'd never see her again. But I didn't stop thinking about her.

That was one way I knew I wasn't like my mother.

"Don't you ever feel sorry for them?" I asked Biddle once.

I knew better than to ask Mom.

"Who?" Biddle said.

"You know who. The people we get money from."

"Do you feel sorry for *that*?"

We were in a Godfather's Pizza in Louisville, Kentucky. Biddle was pointing at my plate.

"Do I feel sorry for pizza?" I asked.

"For the pig that pepperoni used to be."

I thought it over.

"Yes. I guess I do."

My mother was sitting across the table from me, next to Biddle.

"Oh yeah?" she said. "Well, let me help you out then."

She swiped the pizza off my plate and took a big bite.

"The salad bar's over there," she said as she chewed.

IT HAD been a long day of pot stirring. Time to step back and let things simmer. See what boiled over. Burned. Set the place on fire.

I headed to the Five & Dime.

Clarice was there, doing homework upstairs with the gothy girl I'd seen her with at school. They looked a little disappointed that an anvil hadn't fallen on me that day.

After introductions—the friend was Ceecee or Seesee or C. C. or ¡SíSí!, I didn't ask which—I offered to spring for dinner. The girls managed to set their dislike for me aside long enough to say yes. The consensus: Mexican again. Vegetarian burritos for me and Clarice, carne asada for the friend.

I wondered if Ceecee/Seesee/etc. was on the wrestling team. It didn't seem likely.

"I just wish Matt Gorman was here," I said after phoning in the order. "I'd love to meet him."

Ceecee looked surprised.

Clarice looked completely disinterested in a way that told me she was surprised, too.

"How do you know about Matt?" she asked.

"He's your boyfriend, isn't he? It's the talk of the town. So what's he like?"

"Oh, you know. Cute. Nice. Funny. Everything I've always wanted in a man."

Ceecee snorted, then went back to looking spooked.

"And athletic, too," I said. "He's a wrestler, right?"

"And a runner. Long distance. And let me tell you, honey—that boy can *really* go the distance."

Clarice threw me a big wink.

Ceecee looked like she wanted to crawl under the table.

It was a nice move on Clarice's part. Make the conversation so unbearably awkward I'd drop it.

I nodded thoughtfully. "I guess that'd be one of the fringe benefits of dating a jock," I said. "Stamina."

"Oh yeah!" Clarice enthused.

"Him love you long time, huh?"

"Quadruple overtime."

"Hubba hubba, huh?"

"Hubba hubba *hubba*."

"Oooookay," Ceecee said, pushing back her chair and practically jumping to her feet. "Why don't *I* run over to El Zorro Azul and get the food?"

Have you ever seen a goth blush? It pretty much kills the whole bloodless/undead thing they're going for, so I'm sure they hate it.

Clarice grabbed her by the hand and pulled her back down. "Alanis was going to get it, remember?"

"You know what?" I said. "I've been running around town all day. If Ceecee wants to pick up the food while you tell me about Matt, that'd be great." I pulled out my wallet. "Make sure they don't forget the guacamole and the—"

There was a distant, muffled *thump-thump-thump*.

Someone was knocking on the front door.

"—chips," I said. I handed Ceecee a twenty-dollar bill. "This ought to cover it."

The someone thumped again. Harder and longer.

"But maybe you ought to wait till whoever that is goes away."

"Aren't you gonna go down and let 'em in?" Clarice asked me. "Someone might need an emergency palm reading."

Thump-thump-thump-thump.

Would Anthony Grandi really knock on the door before he killed me? It'd be the most polite murder I'd ever heard of.

Nah.

Thump-thump-thump-thump-thump-thump.

Whoever it was, they weren't going away.

I snatched the twenty back.

"All right, I'll see who it is. And I might as well get the food while I'm at it."

I headed for the stairs.

THE THUMP-THUMP-THUMPING was coming from the front of the building. I moved toward it slowly in the dark, careful to keep my footfalls light.

"Come on! Open up!" I heard a man shout. "I know you're in there! I see the lights on upstairs!" He pounded on the door again. "I'm not leaving until you talk to me!"

I tiptoed to the picture window and peered out around the curtains. It was dark outside and I didn't have a good angle, but I could make out the man's back half. As back halves go, it wasn't particularly scary.

He was wearing sweatpants and a cardigan and a baseball cap and walking shoes so white they practically glowed in the dark. Not what you usually picture the busy killer on the go throwing on when he heads out for an evening's homicide.

No, it looked more like Josette's geezer—the one she'd seen stomping around the White Magic Five & Dime that morning.

"I will not be ignored!" he roared. "Open that door!"

I was surprised he didn't add "dagnabbit."

I decided to show respect for my elders.

I decided to avoid more of a scene.

I decided to be stupid.

I opened the front door.

"Sir," I said, "I don't know what the problem is, but if you'll just—"

"Back back back back back!" the man barked.

I backed up. He walked in.

Between us was the gun he'd just pulled from under his sweater.

It wasn't the first time I'd had a gun pointed at me. It wasn't the second or third time either.

Practice makes perfect. I hoped.

"Welcome to the White Magic Five & Dime," I said to the man. "How can I help you?"

The wheel is spun. The ball is dropped. Will it stop on red? Black? An even number? An odd? An angel? A goose? A winged cow reading GOOD HOUSEKEEPING? There's no way to know. All you can do is be ready for anything—and then be ready for that anything to change again with the very next spin.

Miss Chance, *Infinite Roads to Knowing*

ANOTHER STORY.

Once upon a time—that time being morning in America, the mid-eighties—there was a girl who wasn't quite so little anymore. She was in either a small city or a large town in the Midwest. She didn't know the name. What did it matter?

They'd just come from another small city/large town a week before. And another a week before that and another a week before that. In a few days, they'd be someplace else.

It was a slow-motion *Cannonball Run*, Biddle had joked when it began.

The girl knew the movies he was referring to. She'd seen both of them in the theater, the second one just a week before, though pre-teen girls were hardly the target audience. Over the course of one long, dark day, she'd sneaked into *Cannonball Run II*, *Star Trek III*, *The Natural*, *Bachelor Party*, and *Friday the 13th: The Final Chapter*. She spent a lot of days like that. Abandoned in cineplexes, wandering from screen to screen, story to story, world to world.

But she didn't get the joke.

Biddle started to explain. Something about insurance policies they were taking out on cars that got stolen and wrecked and stolen and wrecked (and paid for and paid for and paid for) all across the country. But the girl's mother cut him off.

She'd been calling herself "Veronica" lately. She had brand-new jet-black hair. In a few weeks, she'd have new hair again—and a new name.

"You know the rule," she'd told Biddle.

The girl knew the rule, too.

Some quick change raising or till dipping they could use her for. The precious pet scam or the Jamaican switch, too. She was an excellent roper, a competent cap. But there were plays they didn't need her for. A lot of them. And this was one.

So, the rule: Don't talk to her. Don't tell her anything she didn't need to know. Keep her in the dark. A prop in a closet, gathering dust.

"Right, right, okay," Biddle said to the girl's mother. And he turned back to the girl and winked.

Biddle knew the rule. He just chose to ignore it from time to time.

Now, weeks later, here they were in Genericsville USA, and the girl was watching yet another game show on yet another motel television.

Morning TV sucked. *The Price Is Right*, talk shows, detergent commercials, news. There weren't any *stories*, and it was stories the girl needed. Other people, other places, other lives. Anything other. Anything.

Veronica was getting ready to go to work—though her "work" wasn't anything like what the girl saw on TV. There would be no wacky officemates, no gruff but lovable boss, no laugh track.

The girl's mother was going to spend the day visiting every insurance agent in town. She was "dressed to impress," as she liked to call it. Biddle said it was more like "dressed to undress."

"Everywhere you go, you're gonna have guys trying to give you a piece of the rock," he said.

Veronica laughed. Only Biddle could get her to do that.

Then she was gone. She didn't say goodbye. Why bother? She knew the girl would be there when she got back. Do you say goodbye to a chair, a lamp, the paper-thin towels hanging in the bathroom? Of course not. You use them when you use them and you don't when you don't.

Biddle would be leaving soon, too. He had maildrops to set up, maildrops to close down, connections to make, connections to break. But first he'd take the girl wherever she wanted to go. Almost.

One time she'd walked into a school and found a classroom of kids her age and tried to pass herself off as an exchange student from London. She did an excellent English accent, courtesy of James Bond movies and PBS, but it hadn't mattered. Questions were asked, things got complicated, and she'd ended up running out of the place and laying low at their motel the rest of the week.

The girl never told her mother, but Biddle knew. And he didn't tell on her, though he never took her anywhere near a school again. Not the kind other kids went to, anyway.

"I think I can take the day off," he announced as a contestant on TV hit BANKRUPT, lost it all, and had to keep on smiling. "Wanna have some fun?"

"Sure."

Biddle's fun and other people's fun weren't quite the same, but the girl never said no.

First they went to a Bob Evans and stuffed themselves.

"Can't skip the most important meal of the day," Biddle said. "Those chocolate chip pancakes might feel heavy in your gut now, but before long they're going to be pure energy."

"For running?" the girl asked.

Biddle smiled. But there was no need to run. Not then.

They left without paying and did it so smoothly no one noticed for ten minutes.

After leaving the restaurant, they went to a party supply store and bought a roll of pink raffle tickets. Then they drove around while Biddle scanned storefronts and signs.

"Jackpot!" he eventually announced.

He pulled over in front of the Boys & Girls Club of Who-Cares County. A few minutes later, he was walking out again with a stack of brochures and newsletters.

"People sure do love it when a man takes an interest in the youth of his community," he said.

"What's the pitch?"

"Fundraiser, of course. Raise five hundred dollars and your soccer team gets to go to Indianapolis for the state playoffs. It'd be a shame if you couldn't make it. Your coach was going to pay for the trip out of her own pocket, but after she came down with Legionnaires' disease—"

"*Biddle.*"

"Okay, you're right. Too much gravy on the steak and you get no sizzle. Just stick with the trip to Indy. Now let's see those fishhooks."

The girl pouted and opened her eyes wide.

"Beautiful," Biddle said. "You'll be reeling 'em in nonstop."

They found the right neighborhood—middle class, quiet, white—and the girl worked a few blocks while Biddle went to get cigarettes and "call a guy about a thing with some people." When he came back, she was sitting on a curb waiting for him. Half her raffle tickets were gone, and she had almost a hundred dollars in her pocket.

"Are you going to stay now?" she said. "I don't want to be out here by myself anymore."

"Hey, it's the Boys & Girls Club, not the White Girls & Big Black Guys Club. I shouldn't even be sitting here talking to you. You just *know* the police are going to get a call about that."

"Then let's go do something else. Something we can do together."

"This isn't fun?"

"No. And I don't need the money anyway. I can't buy anything. My suitcase is too full as it is."

"You liked your Atari. Don't you want another?"

"So Mom can make me leave it behind like she did last time?"

"We have to travel light. You know that. And just look—you got the money for another, like she said you would."

"Well, I don't want some dumb game I have to play back in our room. I want to do something out in the real world. With you. Can't we see if they have an amusement park or a waterslide or something around here?"

"An amusement park?"

Biddle looked thoughtful.

There are a lot of scams you can pull at an amusement park.

Movement caught his eye. A flutter of drapes in a picture window.

"Time to roll. I think someone's about to come rescue you from me."

"Let 'em try," the girl said, though she often fantasized about getting caught, arrested, even kidnapped. Just a few years before, she'd become obsessed with Sasquatch and the possibility that he'd come carry her off to his moss-covered cave. It would be scary, and she'd miss movies and TV and books and Biddle, but at least it wouldn't be another Holiday Inn. Then one day her mother walked in on her watching an *In Search of…* about Bigfoot, and the woman had laughed one of her rare laughs and said, "All this fuss over a guy in a gorilla suit? And I thought the biggest bullshitter on TV was Jim Bakker." And the girl had stopped waiting for the missing link to steal her away.

Biddle talked to a guy at a gas station. The nearest amusement park was three hours away, and it might not open till Memorial Day anyway. So Biddle bought ten scratch-off lottery tickets and gave half to the girl.

"What are these?" she said.

Official lotteries were something new. Most people weren't used to states running their own scams yet.

"Those raffle tickets gave me an idea," Biddle said. "Scratch off the gray stuff on these cards. Here, gently, like this. Just enough to see the numbers. No words. Just numbers. Then we'll have us some real fun together."

"You promise?"

"Scout's honor."

"Right. Like you were ever a Boy Scout."

Biddle pinched the girl's cheek.

"That's my girl," he said.

All the tickets were losers, but it didn't matter. They found two candidates. On one, a seven could become a nine after just a little careful work with a black Bic. On the other, a five could become a six.

Biddle did the seven, the girl the five. They agreed that hers looked better.

They had a winner.

"Now we just have to find the right neighborhood," Biddle said. "We may be in the Wonder Bread capital of the world, but they've gotta have a wrong side of the tracks around here somewhere."

It took them half an hour to find it.

Another half hour after that, the girl stepped up to a middle-aged man pushing a shopping cart out of a discount grocery store.

"Can you help me? I'm lost."

The man stopped.

"I can see that," he said.

He was black, and so was everyone in the store and the parking lot and the streets around them.

"I was on the bus and I must have gotten off at the wrong stop," the girl said. "But I didn't realize it at first and I started walking around and now I can't even find my way back to where I started from."

"All right," the man sighed, "here's what you want to do."

He started giving directions. The girl nodded as if she cared. Then another man walked up.

"Excuse me, please," he said. He had a thick accent of indeterminate pan-Caribbean origin. "I need your help."

The older man rolled his eyes. "This is my lucky day."

"Maybe it is, sir," the other man said. He held up a scratch-off lottery ticket. "I think this is a winner, but I can't turn it in."

"Why not?" the girl asked.

"I'm not from here. I'm not supposed to be here. I don't have papers. I can't collect a hundred dollars from a state lottery."

"A hundred dollars? Let me see!" The girl grabbed the ticket. "Wow. You're right. It's a winner."

The older man peeked over her shoulder. He didn't get much time to look. Just enough to see that the right numbers seemed to match.

"Where'd you buy it?" the girl asked.

"Right here. In this store."

"And it can be turned in here, too?"

"Yes. You'd get the money immediately."

"And then I'm supposed to come out and just give it to you?"

"No. I'd give you…twenty dollars."

"Hey," the older man said. He had a "What am I—chopped liver?" look on his face.

"How do I know you wouldn't take it all?" the girl said.

The man from Trinijamahaiti looked offended.

"What a thing for an innocent little girl to say! How do I know *you* wouldn't try to keep it all? Maybe you would accuse me of being a thief when I tried to collect my money!" He snatched his ticket back and turned away. "I'll find someone else to help me."

"Hey," the older man said again.

"Wait! I know how we can do this!" the girl cried out.

She jammed a hand into her Jordache jeans and pulled out a wad of crumpled bills. She counted quickly.

"I'll give you twenty-eight dollars right now. Then you just give me the ticket, and we can be done."

"Twenty-eight dollars? I don't know…"

The older man whipped out his wallet.

"I can give you thirty-nine! No! Forty! That's practically fifty percent, cash on the barrelhead."

He thrust the money at the other man.

The other man took it and handed over the ticket.

"No fair," the girl whined.

"The only fair's the one with farm animals and cotton candy," the older man said. He swung his cart around and headed back into the store. "Good luck catching that bus."

The other man and the girl stalked off in different directions.

They met again two blocks away, on the quiet side street where they'd left the car.

"Told you it'd work," Biddle said.

He unlocked the passenger door and let the girl in, then walked around and slipped behind the wheel.

"It's crude, though," Biddle went on. "There's gotta be a way to spin it into something more than a nickel-and-dime short con. The big lotto jackpots—that's the angle to play."

The girl was looking out the window. The houses lining the street were small and old. A few were boarded up. The rest looked like they should be.

"I don't like it when we take money from poor people."

"If it's good enough for McDonald's and Mogen David, it's good enough for me."

"I'm not joking."

"Neither am I. Hey, I've got family in neighborhoods like this. Believe me—plenty of these people are just as greedy and stupid as the rich people up the road. So why discriminate?"

"But it just doesn't seem…"

The girl stopped herself. She wasn't even sure if she'd been about to say "fair" or "right" or something else. But she knew the look she'd get.

She got it anyway.

Biddle cocked his head and gazed at her with eyes filled with pity.

"Sometimes I forget you're not a midget," he said.

"Oh, blow it out your ass."

"My word!" Biddle gasped. "Wherever did you learn such nasty language?"

Then he smiled.

He knew.

"Look," he said. "Are all rich people bad?"

"No."

"Are all poor people good?"

"No."

"So what makes them different?"

"Money."

Biddle shook his head. "Luck. Dumb luck. Some people are born Kennedys, and some people are born here. It has nothing to do with who deserves it. Hell, nobody *deserves* anything. We don't deserve a Russian bomb to fall on us, but it might any minute. So we may as well buy us some ice cream with the money we didn't deserve to get today."

"I don't know, Biddle."

"You don't know if you want to go to Baskin-Robbins?"

"No. I don't know if—"

There was a hard rapping sound. Metal tapped to glass three times.

The glass was the driver's-side window.

The metal was the barrel of a gun. Pointed at Biddle.

The girl made a sound that wasn't a word and wasn't quite a scream. She wasn't surprised, though. Not entirely. Some part of her had been expecting this for a long, long time.

How long could you do wrong and not be punished? Forever?

No. There had to be a *sometime*. There had to be a *finally*.

And here it was.

"Gimme your money!" someone said. He sounded young and angry. All the girl could see of him was his plain white T-shirt. It hung on him limply, like a toga. The body beneath it was lean.

Biddle pulled out his wallet, then rolled down the window and handed it over. He was moving very, very slowly.

"Men with guns either want respect or to kill you," he'd told the girl once. "If they don't kill you right off, just give them the respect and you'll be fine."

"Hers, too," the boy or man outside the car demanded. He pressed the gun against the side of Biddle's head. "Come on, come on!"

Slowly, calmly, Biddle held a hand out to the girl. Her hands were shaking so badly the bills she pulled from her pockets rustled and fluttered like wings. But she managed to give Biddle every dollar she had, and he brought it all to the window, and then it was gone.

The gun and the T-shirt disappeared, too. The girl could hear footsteps slapping on asphalt hard and fast.

"Don't look back," Biddle said.

He was staring straight ahead. After a long, silent moment, he started the car and put it in gear. He was still moving slowly, slowly, slowly. He drove away slowly, too.

The girl felt lightheaded. Her scalp and feet tingled. There was a low buzzing in her ears that sounded like the static between TV channels. Her hands were still shaking. A sob was welling up in her chest.

Biddle burst out laughing. He laughed and laughed and laughed. More than a block went by before he could even speak.

"Round and round she goes!" he said. "Where she stops, nobody knows!"

"It's not funny, Biddle! It's not funny!"

Biddle stopped laughing. But he couldn't keep the grin off his face even as he looked over at the girl and saw that she was crying.

"Oh, don't be upset, sweetie. Everything's fine. The universe just has to mess with you every once in a while, that's all. It's over now. Before you know it, you'll be eating rocky road on a sugar cone."

"What are we gonna do—steal it? That asshole took all our money!"

And the girl began crying even harder, though it wasn't the money she was crying about at all.

Biddle let her cry for a while. Then he pulled something small and stiff from his shirt pocket and put it on the girl's lap.

"Now, now," he said. "See there?"

The girl looked over at him, sniffling.

Biddle was still smiling.

"We've got another lottery ticket," he said. His smile grew wider. "People like us always do."

A blind lady swinging a sword big enough for Conan the Barbarian seems like a bad idea. But look: this Justice has the traditional sword and scales but no blindfold. (Her muumuu's a lot spiffier than the usual toga, too, but that's beside the point.) The implication: screw impartiality. If things are to work out as they should (and that's what justice is really all about), the important thing is to look at the situation—and yourself—and truly SEE.

Miss Chance, *Infinite Roads to Knowing*

"Don't try anything funny," the old man told me.

Obviously he was an amateur. Professionals never tell you not to do anything funny. They let their guns do the talking. His was either saying "geez, it's cold in here" or "earthquake!" because it was shaking like someone had slipped in a quarter for the Magic Fingers.

"Whatever the problem is, sir, I'm sure we can resolve it," I said slowly, gently. I was standing very, very still. "*Without* a gun pointed at me."

"I'll believe that when I have my jewelry back!"

"Your jewelry?"

I started wondering if someone had let grandpa go off his meds.

It was dark in the White Magic Five & Dime, with only light from a streetlamp outside to see by. Yet I could tell the old guy wasn't the jewelry type. He was dressed for a brisk shuffle around the YMCA, not a home invasion. Anything more than a plain gold wedding band would've been too froufrou for the likes of him.

"Yes, my jewelry," he said. "Don't pretend you don't know where it is. There's probably a trunk of the stuff around here someplace."

"I'm sorry, but really—I haven't run across any treasure chests. I only got here yesterday, though, so who knows? If you'd just put your gun away, we could start poking around together and maybe—"

"Don't patronize me!"

He jabbed the gun out toward me. It was too murky to make out the model, but I assumed it was the kind that goes *boom* and makes holes in things when the trigger's pulled—whether the pull was on purpose or not.

"Sir, please," I said soothingly. "If your jewelry's here, I swear I'll find it for you. But I can't even start looking if I don't know what it is or who you are."

"Just get Athena down here. She'll tell you who I am."

"Athena's…not available."

"Busy with another sucker, is she? Well, I don't give a damn. Hey! Athena! Get your buns out here this instant or your little friend's gonna have a bullet where her brains used to be!"

"Athena's dead."

The old man tilted an ear toward me. There was a hearing aid in it.

"What did you say?"

"Athena's dead."

"Ha. You must think I'm senile."

Yes.

"No," I said. "I just think you're a little behind on the news. Athena was murdered right here in the White Magic Five & Dime. They still don't know who did it. I could find a newspaper article about it if you want to see proof."

"Athena…dead?" the old man said. He lowered his gun and started swaying like a reedy little tree in the breeze. "Murdered?"

I took a hesitant step toward him.

"Can I help you sit down? There's a couch right over here."

He nodded, and I took him by the arm and guided him to the waiting area.

"I'm Alanis, by the way," I said once I had him settled. "Athena's daughter."

The old man scowled. "She never mentioned any daughter."

"We didn't get along."

He kept glaring at me a moment, then decided to believe me.

"Sorry about this," he said, putting his gun on the coffee table before him. "It's just a toy. They keep taking away my guns."

I waited for him to go on.

"They" the aliens? "They" the men in white suits?

"My name's Ken Meldon," he said. "I was your mother's fiancé."

MOM AND the old man must have had a love-hate relationship, which was really the only kind to have with my mother (love optional).

Kenneth Meldon was one of the names on Detective Logan's list. Mom's "fiancé" had complained about her to the police.

A projector whirred. Light stabbed the darkness. Images appeared. The whole thing played out like a movie in my mind— the kind where you know the ending two minutes in.

Still, I said, "Oh my goodness! How did you meet?"

ONCE A week for more than a year, Athena Passalis had donated two hours of her time to the Dry Creek Assisted Living Community. Which told me that the Dry Creek Assisted Living Community was run either by crooks or fools (but who was I to judge, being a little bit of both myself?).

Athena did free readings for residents and talked to them about tarot. Naturally, the conversations could get personal. She came to know which residents had family troubles, which had money troubles, which were lonely (which was all of them). Which, like Meldon, were widowers.

"She read my palm and she stole my heart," he said.

The jewelry had belonged to his wife. Piece by piece, it went to Athena. At first they were given out of gratitude. Then they were shows of affection. Eventually, after Athena turned up both the Lovers and the Two of Cups during a reading, Meldon offered her an engagement ring.

("The Two of Cups?" I asked.

"Yeah. That was the clincher," Meldon said. And he carried on with his story without any further explanation.)

"I'll have to think about it, Ken," Athena had said when he proposed. "Can I keep the ring in the meantime? I like how it feels on my finger."

"Of course!"

So Athena thought about it. And thought about it. And thought about it. And each time she came, she was wearing the ring… though it seemed thinner now, with a smaller setting. And hadn't the band been silver? Meldon couldn't be sure. His eyesight wasn't what it used to be, and he'd never paid much attention to jewelry anyway.

"It all looks the same to me," he said.

Then one day another resident, "an old man" (the old man called him), let Meldon in on a secret. He and the pretty lady with the blond hair and the weird cards? They were engaged—or would be soon, anyway. She was still thinking about it.

The next time Athena came to Dry Creek, Meldon demanded the jewelry back.

"What jewelry?" Athena said.

"The jewelry I gave you. My wife's brooches and pins and…oh, you know what I'm talking about. *The jewelry.*"

"I *don't* know what you're talking about."

"But you're wearing Judith's ring right there on your finger!"

"This? I've had it for years. I have to say, I'm very disappointed, Mr. Meldon. I thought we were friends, and then you go and accuse me of stealing. I don't know if I should come here anymore."

She didn't. And when Meldon started telling people about his doomed affair with the fortunetelling gold-digger, no one believed him. Not even the old-old man who'd claimed she was engaged to *him*. He could barely remember who Athena was or who Meldon was or who he was himself.

"So you went to the police," I said.

Meldon nodded. "They said they didn't believe me either. Sons of bitches. They've never liked me 'cuz I stand up for my rights."

A-ha.

The old guy's story wouldn't have any aliens after all.

"*They* keep taking away your guns," I said.

"Yes! I used to have dozens—a real collection. But take one out of its case to show some punk who's messing with your mailbox or a dumb bastard who thinks he can drive past your house playing his music so loud it rattles the windows, and *whoops*—there goes the Second Amendment! And then when my kids moved me into Dry Creek, they wanted the whole bunch. Well, I didn't give 'em up without a fight."

"I'm sure you didn't," I said. "So—the police wouldn't help you, and today you decided to get the jewelry back yourself."

"That's right. I heard some of the staff at the home whispering about her, and I thought they were laughing at me and it made so mad I walked right out and went to the sporting goods store and bought myself that pea shooter. They wouldn't sell me the real thing. Said I was too agitated. Can you believe it? In America! In *Arizona*! Anyway, I got what I could and I came here. That was a lot of walking for an old man, let me tell you. But I just had to see Athena again. For…for…"

Meldon squeezed his eyes shut and searched for the word he wanted.

"Closure?" I suggested.

The old man's eyes popped open.

"What the hell is that?" he said. "No, I just wanted your mother to do the right thing. Give me back my wife's jewelry and admit she'd done me wrong."

"Well, I'm afraid it's too late for an apology from her, but we'll see about the jewelry. If I come across it, I'll let you know."

"Oh, you will, huh? I should just crawl back into my little hole and wait for you to bring me what's mine out of the goodness of your heart?"

"Exactly," I said. "Come on. I'll give you a lift. I have to pick up some burritos anyway."

Meldon glowered at me.

"Or we could always just have the police drive you home," I said. "I'm sure they're looking for you by now."

"All right, all right."

The old man tried to push himself up off the couch. He didn't make it.

I took his hands and pulled him to his feet.

A prime suspect he was not.

He yanked his hands away and started shuffling toward the door.

"Don't you want that?" I asked.

I pointed at the air gun he'd left on the coffee table.

He didn't even look back.

"They'd just take it from me," he said.

Before I followed him out, I noticed two pairs of feet on the stairs at the back of the building. Clarice and Ceecee had been sitting on the steps, eavesdropping.

I wondered how long they'd been there.

I wondered if they'd seen the old man pointing a gun at me.

I wondered if they'd been hoping he'd pull the trigger.

It was a short drive to the Dry Creek Assisted Living Community. On the way, I thought again of Detective Logan's list. There was only one person on it left to track down.

"Does someone named Victor Castellanos live at Dry Creek?" I asked Meldon.

"No."

Damn.

A block went by.

"There was a *Mrs.* Castellanos, though," Meldon said. "She used to come to all of Athena's talks, same as me."

"'There *was* a Mrs. Castellanos'? Past tense? Meaning she's passed on?"

"You mean *died*? No. She moved out. Not long after Athena stopped coming around, too."

"Do you know her first name?"

"What do I look like? A phone book?"

Another block went by.

"Lucia," Meldon said.

I DIDN'T pull into the Dry Creek parking lot. Instead, I stopped on the street just outside the entrance.

"It'd probably be best if you didn't tell anyone I brought you back," I said. "We don't want to answer a lot of questions about what you were up to and why, right?"

"Yeah. I suppose so."

"Do you need help getting out of the car?"

"No."

Meldon tugged on the door handle a few times. The door didn't open.

"Yes," he said.

In the time it took me to walk around to his side of the car and open the door, he'd started crying.

"I'm sorry," he said. "I was just thinking about the Two of Cups, of all things. Athena used to say it was our card."

"I understand."

Or I meant to, anyway. Later.

"Mad as I was at your mother, there was a crazy part of me that actually thought we might patch things up. Me and my wife used to fight all the time. Hurt each other in a million mean little ways. There was love there, though. I guess I hoped it might be the same with Athena. That makes me an old fool, doesn't it?"

"No," I said. "Not at all."

Meldon wiped his eyes with the backs of his hands, then let me help him to his feet.

"All right, all right, I'm good now," he said, steadying himself with the door.

I let go.

He gazed off at the Dry Creek Assisted Living Community—a long white building with only one story. It looked nice enough. To me, at least. Meldon seemed in no hurry to get back.

"You say your mother was *murdered*?" he said.

"That's right. They still haven't caught the killer."

The old man gave his head a weary shake.

"Maybe she had another fiancé."

He started walking away. He was moving slowly, even by his standards. I was worried he might trip and fall in the parking lot, so I stayed and watched him until he'd gone inside.

I had to wait a long, long time.

CEECEE DIDN'T stick around for her carne asada. When I got back to Mom's place, Clarice's gothy friend had gone.

"It's a school night. She couldn't hang out here forever," Clarice said with a shrug. She took a bite of her vegetarian burrito. "So who was that banging on the door?"

"You didn't hear me talking to Mr. Meldon?"

"Who?"

"It doesn't matter."

I took a bite of my own burrito. It was cold.

"So what did Mr. What's-His-Name want?" Clarice asked.

"He was selling Girl Scout cookies. Hey, you know what? I've been wondering. I was going through my mother's clothes—"

"I noticed." Clarice looked pointedly at the turtleneck and chinos I was wearing.

"—and I see she was down to a size 2," I went on. "My mom was *never* a 2. How'd she do it?"

"Oh, she went on some crazy diet about four months ago. Yogurt and cheese and fruit and nuts. I told her she looked fine already—she always did—but of course what I said didn't matter. After a while, she got so skinny even I was saying, 'Jesus, Athena. Get yourself a Big Mac.'"

"How did it affect her mood? She put us both on the Atkins Diet when I was, like, twelve, and it turned her into a real zombie. She stumbled around glassy-eyed for months. Then one day she just said 'screw it,' drove to the nearest Pizza Hut, and that was that."

"Yeah, it was kind of like that again. She looked tired a lot. There were a few days she didn't even open the shop at all, and that never used to happen no matter how sick she was. She'd rather give twenty people the flu than miss out on one day's cash."

I nodded.

I bought it. For once, Clarice wasn't evading, dodging, or snowing me. She really had no idea Athena had been dying.

"That sounds like Mom," I said, smiling in a pseudo-wistful *oh, that wacky lady* kind of way.

No sale for me. Clarice furrowed her brow, frowning, and I knew that she knew that I knew something she didn't.

She wasn't going to ask me about it directly, though. She'd spent enough years with my mother not to do something as straightforward and sincere and boring and dumb as that.

"She was really something, wasn't she?" she said.

"That she was."

"A real original."

"Yup."

"One of a kind."

"I certainly hope so."

Clarice gave me a full-on scowl now.

"Why do you think she never talked about you?" she said. "Not one mention in all the years I knew her. It was like you didn't exist."

I shrugged. "We didn't part on good terms."

"Why not?"

"She wanted me with her. I had to change her mind."

"What does that mean?"

"It means I made things unpleasant."

"Why? You couldn't just leave? Move out or run away or whatever?"

"My mother wasn't someone you could just run away from. So I made sure she wouldn't *want* to find me."

"But then she did, supposedly. After all those years, suddenly she was thinking of you. And not long after that, she was dead and you got everything. Weird, huh?"

"Utterly frakking unbelievable," I said. "What about you?"

"What about me what?"

"Didn't you ever want to get away from her? I know what she could be like. The kinds of things she could expect of someone."

"I don't know what you're talking about."

"Really? Then you can count yourself lucky. It sounds like you never really knew my mother at all."

"I knew her better than you! That's why I can't understand why she gave you the house and the car and whatever else. You keep calling her 'mother' and 'mom,' but until a few days ago you didn't care if she was alive or dead."

"I care that somebody killed her."

"What's that supposed to mean?"

"I wish certain people wouldn't act so cagey when I ask questions."

"Oh. Yeah. Because you're so open and honest yourself. How crazy not to trust *you*."

That shut me up.

I don't mind when other people are right. I just don't like it when they're so right about *me*.

Clarice glared at me. This much she wasn't hiding: she hated me. It almost felt like she was daring me to throw her out.

I was about to give her a touché when she picked up her plate and stood.

"I've got homework to do. See you later."

She walked to her room and closed the door.

I finished my dinner with *Infinite Roads to Knowing* for company. I had homework to do, too.

It HAD been the Lovers and the Two of Cups that had convinced Ken Meldon he and my mother had a long, happy future ahead of them. The Lovers needed no explanation. The Two of Cups—aka the Two of Chalices—did.

Then I saw it.

Oh yeah. Josette Berg had turned it up when she'd read for me the day before. Her reaction (more or less): "*Ooo la la!*" It was easy to see why.

The hovering bat-lion I still didn't get, but the couple and their Big Gulps was obvious.

A man and a woman face each other, offering what they have to share.

This is a hook-up. Or "the beginning of a be-YOO-tiful friendship," as Miss Chance put it in her book. According to her, the Two of Cups was all about "partnerships commenced" and "the nurturing of fruitful symbioses." (For someone who threw in references to Bugs Bunny and Conan the Barbarian, the woman sure could be pretentious.)

I could understand the appeal of the card, especially to someone like Meldon. The poor man had lost his two true loves: his wife and his guns. He was totally alone. What did he have to cling to if not some companionship and a (carefully cultivated) dream of new romance?

Smooth one, Mom. For someone with no soul, you sure knew how to mess with other people's.

Of course, here I was thinking *I* was the soulful one—the *human* one—and I was more alone than my mother had been. After I'd made my escape, she'd picked up a replacement daughter, somehow or other. I don't know how nurturing or fruitful it had been, but at least she and Clarice did seem to have some kind of symbiosis. Yet if Anthony Grandi suddenly popped in to take me out, nobody would miss me but my boss back at the call center—and that'd be because our sales team probably wouldn't make its quota for the month. I didn't even have any pets to leave starving when I didn't come back. I was a cat lady without the cats.

If I did have a soul, I guess I hadn't figured out what to do with it yet.

I studied the Two of Cups again. The more I looked at it, the more I thought the man looked kind of cranky.

Maybe he didn't like what was in his cup. Maybe he was pissed because his gal pal was reaching out to take it. Maybe he'd had a rough childhood.

Yet there he was anyway. Commencing a partnership. Nurturing a symbiosis. Hooking up. Connecting.

If he could do it, so could I.

Maybe.

Lucky guy. Really. Usually when you get hanged it's by your neck, and that's not known for its health benefits. The Hanged Man is dangling by his ankle, though, which is an inconvenience for him, yes, but one that's paid off. He's been forced to stop and look at things from a whole new perspective, and that's given him insight into how the world really works. His frown hasn't necessarily been turned upside down, but his outlook on life sure has been.

Miss Chance, *Infinite Roads to Knowing*

I woke up. I unlocked and unbarricaded the bedroom door. I got coffee. I pulled out Detective Logan's list. Two of the names were crossed off.

I got to work on the third.

"Red Rock Elder Care Center. How can I help you?"

"Hi! I haven't been in Berdache since I was a kid, but now I'm passing through on business and I thought I'd look up an old family friend. I can't seem to find her, though, and I was wondering if maybe she lived there now."

"What's her name?"

"Lucia Castellanos."

"I'm sorry. There's no one here by that name."

"Awww, too bad. Thanks anyway."

"You're welcome. Good luck."

"Oak Creek Canyon Residential Living. How can I help you?"

"Hi! I haven't been in Sedona since I was a kid, but now I'm passing through on business and I thought I'd look up an old family friend. I can't seem to find her, though, and I was wondering if maybe she lived there now."

"What's her name?"

"Lucia Castellanos."

"I'm sorry. There's no one here by that name."

"Awww, too bad. Thanks anyway."

"You're welcome. Good luck."

"Verde River Vista Senior Residences. How can I help you?"

"Hi! I haven't been in Cottonwood since I was a kid, but now I'm passing through on business and I thought I'd look up an old family friend. I can't seem to find her, though, and I was wondering if maybe she lived there now."

"What's her name?"

"Lucia Castellanos."

"Oh yeah—she's here. Something, isn't she?"

"A real pistol. Does Victor ever come by to see her?"

"That's her son, right?"

"Right."

"He's in here pretty regularly."

"Great."

"Will you be coming by, too?"

"That's the plan."

"Wonderful! I'll tell Lucia. She'll be thrilled. What's your name?"

"Mallory Keaton."

"Mallory Keaton? Really? Wasn't that what's-her-name's character on *Family Ties*?"

"I said Valerie Keaton."

"I'm sorry. I must have misheard you."

"Big *Family Ties* fan, are you?"

"Not really."

"Me neither."

Verde River Vista Senior Residences was big and white and sterile. Lucia Castellanos was little and brown and wrinkled. A woman guided her into the Social Center (aka the Overlit Room with a Lonely-Looking Bumper Pool Table and a TV with a Screen Big Enough for a Drive-In Blasting Fox News at an Old Man Dozing in a Wheelchair) where I'd been waiting.

"Is that her?" Lucia said, stabbing a gnarled finger my way. She was somewhere between 80 and 4,000 years old.

"That's her," the woman said. "You two have a nice visit now."

She handed Lucia off to me like a football, smiled, and left.

"Well, how about a hug?" Lucia said.

I bent down (and down and down—she was *teeny*), put my arms around her hunched back, and patted. It was like trying to burp a fire hydrant.

"All right, that's good," Lucia said. "Now help me sit down."

A minute later, she was on a couch. It hadn't been easy to arrange. She seemed to have lost the ability to bend her knees, so the act of sitting was a sort of semi-controlled backwards fall. It was a good thing she was small and the couch was soft.

It was going to take ropes and pulleys to get her on her feet again.

"So," she said, "tell me what you've been up to, Valerie. Goodness, it feels like it's been forever!"

"I think there's been a mix-up, Mrs. Castellanos. My name's not Valerie."

"But they said a Valerie was here to see me. An old friend."

"Well, I guess that was good timing for me. I'm not sure they'd have let me see you otherwise."

"I don't understand."

"A nice place like this—they're not going to let just anybody waltz in and start talking to residents. Not like at Dry Creek. That's where you lived before, right?"

"That's right."

I would say the woman squinted at me, but she was always squinting at everything. Still, she seemed to squint even harder.

"So you're not Valerie?"

"No."

"Well, I hope she's still coming. I want to find out who the heck she is. I don't remember any Valerie. But they could've told me Adolf Hitler was here to see me and I'd have sprayed on some perfume and come out to say hello."

I nodded, smiling. That's what I'd been counting on.

"My name's Alanis. I think you knew my mother. Athena Passalis."

"Yes, of course! How is she?"

"I'm afraid she's passed away."

Lucia reached out toward me. After a little groping, she found a hand and patted it.

"I'm truly sorry to hear that. You never know who's going to go next, but it's never who you want it to be."

She threw a glare at the snoring man in the wheelchair. Then she looked back at me.

"But your mother—she was so young."

"It was very sudden."

"Stroke?"

"No."

"Heart attack?"

"No. It—"

"Pulmonary embolism?"

"No. It was—"

"Hit by a car?"

The old woman looked strangely hopeful.

"No. She had pancreatic cancer," I said. "Then there was an unexpected complication."

"Oooo, pancreatic cancer. That's a bad one. Mr. Garratt and Mr. Hilton and Mrs. Hettle and Mrs. Cohn all went with that. I hope she didn't suffer."

"Not for long."

"That's good. I used to hope for the car myself. Or getting struck by lightning. *Pow, sizzle* and you're done. It never happened, though. Last year I thought the carcinoma might get me, but it let me down in the end."

Lucia shook her head sadly.

"Remission."

I didn't know what to say. "Better luck next time"?

"Your mother was supposed to be helping me with all that, actually," Lucia went on, "but I guess nothing will come of that now."

A look of sudden, panicked horror came over the old woman's face.

"Please tell me you're not here to give me my jewelry back!"

"What jewelry?"

Lucia relaxed.

"You had me worried for a second there," she said.

"Worried I'd bring you jewelry?"

"Yes."

"Jewelry that belongs to you?"

"Yes."

"Which you gave to my mother?"

"Yes."

"Which you don't want back?"

"Of course not," Lucia snapped, exasperated. "Not if it's still cursed!"

HERE'S SOMETHING they never told you on *Antiques Roadshow*: jewelry can be haunted.

Lucia Castellanos's was. The rings and necklaces and chokers and lockets she'd inherited from her mother were befouled by a vengeful spirit—the ghost of a woman Lucia's father had once spurned. When Lucia brought the jewelry into her home, she brought the woman's evil with it. That was why her husband and her daughter had died not long after, while Lucia was cursed to live and live and live. It was why her son Victor couldn't find love. They were doomed to be alone. Forever.

Fortunately, Athena Passalis came along and discovered the true root of all Lucia's sorrows. And Athena knew what to do about it, too. Take the jewelry far away from Lucia and Victor. Starve the evil inside it. Cleanse it, purify it. Then and only then could it be returned, and Lucia and Victor would be free.

YES. PEOPLE actually believe this stuff.

SOME OF them, anyway. Victor Castellanos *hadn't* believed.

He'd gone to the police. He'd moved his mother into a new home—one that wasn't so welcoming to the likes of Athena Passalis. And he'd confronted Athena and demanded the jewelry back.

"What jewelry?" she'd said to him.

Because she was selfless like that. She was willing to keep cursed objects near her, putting herself at risk, rather than let them fall back into the hands of those they might destroy.

Lucia understood. That was why she'd told the police "what jewelry?" too. She was protecting Athena just as Athena was protecting her.

Her son wasn't very happy about that. In fact, he was still mad at Lucia about it. And oh—the things he said about Athena! The things he'd do to her if he could. It actually scared her sometimes.

It was a good thing Victor and Athena never met face to face.

It wouldn't have been pretty.

"WHAT DOES Victor do, by the way?"

Lucia beamed. "He's a teacher."

"Oh. How nice."

How boring. How nonviolent.

"At the high school in Berdache."

"Lovely."

And unhelpful.

"He teaches physical fitness and health enhancement. Coaches the basketball teams, too. Boys and girls."

Wait.

"He's the gym teacher?"

"I don't think they call it that anymore."

"Does he coach any of the other teams? Football? Soccer? Hopscotch?"

"No, just basketball. Oh, and field hockey. And…another one. For the boys."

"Wrestling?"

"That's it," Lucia said. "He's the wrestling coach."

I ASKED the old woman to describe the jewelry she'd given my mother to be "purified."

"I'm not sure you should mess around with it if you find it," she said when she was done. "Would you know how to cleanse it yourself?"

"Absolutely," I told her.

Windex.

As I drove away from the Verde River Vista Senior Residences, I spotted a pay phone at a gas station. That reminded me: time to give the cage another rattle.

I stopped and called Star Bail Bonds.

Press 0 to speak to a customer service representative (if she's awake).

Press 1 to speak to Anthony Grandi.

I pressed 1.

"Grandi," a man said. He had a rough, gruff voice I remembered well.

There was no doubt about it now. It was him. My fifty-cents-a-call stalker.

I exhaled. Loudly.

"Hello?" Grandi said. "I can hear you. Can you hear me?"

I exhaled again. Then again.

"Call back!" Grandi shouted. "We've got a bad connection!"

I exhaled as hard as I could.

Turns out heavy breathing isn't easy. I was starting to feel light-headed.

Fortunately, he finally got it.

"Who is this?" he growled.

But he knew. Otherwise, he would've just hung up.

I thought about hanging up myself. Or maybe huffing and puffing some more. Or asking if his refrigerator was running.

"I think you might have killed my mother," I finally said. "If you want me to think otherwise, you'll meet me at Celebrity Roast in half an hour. And you'll be ready to do some convincing."

Grandi said nothing. I said nothing.

I could hear him breathing. He could hear me breathing.

We were playing phone chicken.

He hung up first.

EXCELLENT. I had a date with a man who'd threatened to kill me. What did I have to worry about? It couldn't turn out much worse than my last "date" two years before. I keep expecting to see that one turned into a Lifetime movie: *Barf in the Lobster Tank: A Date That Will Live in Infamy*.

And I had just been thinking about trying to connect with people more. Why not Anthony Grandi? Potentially murderous scumbag-bully bail bondsmen are people too, right?

MAYBE NOT.

I SHOWED up at Celebrity Roast ready for anything…almost.

I wasn't ready for Detective Josh Logan. He was leaning against the counter chatting with Kathleen the Cop-Loving Barista. He didn't seem surprised to see me.

"I thought you didn't drink coffee," I said to him.

"I still don't. Wanna get some lunch?"

"Well, I—"

"He's not coming, so you may as well let me buy you a burger."

"I don't know what you're talking about."

"It's a little round patty of beef grilled and served on a bun. Usually with fried potatoes."

"Thanks for the explanation. I was actually thinking of the 'he's not coming' part."

"I'd rather discuss that over a little round patty of beef."

"I'm a vegetarian."

"Yours can be over a little round patty of tofu."

"Fine," I said. "Let's go."

I could tell the badinage was getting on Kathleen's nerves, and who knew when I might need to tap her for more local gossip?

"I hope this means there's been a break in the case, Detective," I said as we headed for the door.

See, Kathleen? I was really saying. *Strictly business.*

And of course it was. Though I had to wonder.

Logan had just inserted himself between me and Anthony Grandi. Between me and *answers*.

So why wasn't I pissed?

I ASSUMED Logan was going to take me to one of those old greasy spoons cops love so much. The kind that still have toadstool seats along a grimy counter and fry cooks in wife-beaters and, if the place is *really* fancy, half-frozen flies and week-old wedges of lemon meringue slowly circling on a refrigerated pie merry-go-round. In fact, we walked past just such a place, and two uniformed cops were sitting at one of the tables.

"There we go," Logan said. And he pointed across the street at a touristy French bistro called Café Vortex.

"That's where you go for a burger?"

"Best in town. But if you'd rather have authentic local flavor, we could go to Smitty's Grill here. I think the special of the day is salmonella."

I glanced back at the diner. "Doesn't look very vegetarian friendly."

Logan nodded. "Even the coffee's got grease in it."

"Café Vortex it is."

CAFÉ VORTEX didn't even have hamburgers on the menu.

"I was going to take you to Smitty's," Logan said sheepishly, "but I changed my mind at the last second."

"Because you were suddenly in the mood for *foie gras*?"

"Because I like the atmosphere here better."

"It is charming. Very Euro."

"Isn't it?"

"Yeah. More touristy, too. Less eavesdroppy. The booths are so nice and cozy and private."

Logan sighed a guilty-as-charged sigh. "I thought it was your mother who was supposed to be the psychic."

"I keep telling you: Tarot readers aren't psychic. We're just highly intuitive."

"Well, your intuition's right."

"You didn't want to talk about Anthony Grandi in front of a bunch of locals."

Logan nodded.

"Especially now that you're running errands for him," I went on. "Why couldn't Grandi make it himself? Another drug dealer jump bail?"

"I'm not running errands for him," Logan snapped.

I gave my inner bitch a whack on the nose with a rolled-up newspaper. *Down, girl! Remember—we like this guy.*

"I'm sorry," I said. "You take me out to a nice restaurant and then I won't let you explain…"

I started to say "why you're making public appearances on behalf of a murder suspect."

What can I say? My inner bitch is really poorly trained.

I tried to put a muzzle on her.

"…why you were at Celebrity Roast," I said instead.

"Grandi called me this morning," Logan said. "He and I had an agreement. He'd leave you alone and I wouldn't have to charge him with assaulting an officer for breaking my hand with his face. So what was he supposed to do when *you* started harassing *him*?"

"He admitted that he'd been threatening me?"

"Not outright, no. He's not dumb enough to do that. But we were able to talk around his non-denial denials and come to an understanding."

"Well, I really appreciate the police brutality on my behalf, Detective, but—"

"And what do we think we'll be having today?" said the waitress who came gliding up to our table, pad in hand.

Logan thought he'd be having steak frites.

I thought I'd be having the onion soup and the tarte du jour.

The waitress went gliding away.

"But," I said, "there's something pretty big I still don't understand. Why was Grandi messing with me in the first place, and why hasn't that made him your number-one suspect?"

"He's not a suspect, number one or otherwise, because he has an airtight alibi—"

I rolled my eyes. As if a crooked bail bondsman wouldn't know how to cook up a phony alibi.

"—and I know why he was messing with you, and it's not because he killed your mother."

I raised my eyebrows high.

"So," Logan said, "you need to just steer clear of Anthony Grandi and leave the police work to the pro—

"Why are you looking at me like that?"

My eyebrows were still threatening to head north of my hairline.

"I'm frozen in the moment you said 'I know why he was messing with you.' I don't think I can leave it till you explain."

"It's not a very flattering look, Alanis."

"I know. What a tragedy if I had to walk around like this for the rest of my life."

Logan sighed. "You know I've already bent all kinds of rules for you, and I don't even know why."

I reached up to my forehead and tried to tug my eyebrows down.

"Still…frozen," I grunted.

"Fine. You win. Just get that dumb expression off your face."

I smiled, and my eyebrows returned to the general vicinity of my eyes.

"Better?"

"Yes."

"So talk."

"All right, all right! Just promise me you'll keep this to yourself."

"Cross my heart and hope to die."

"Okay, here's the deal. It's not just your mother I'd been keeping tabs on. I've been investigating the Grandi family, too. Anthony's the only one in the bail bonds business. The rest are fortunetellers. They have six shops in four counties—that I know of. And the Grandis aren't like most of the psychics and aura readers and vortex guides around Berdache and Sedona. They're more like your mother."

"Con artists."

"Exactly. They convince people to give them money and valuables and bank account numbers. They make them think that they're cursed and that only a lot of mumbo jumbo—very expensive mumbo jumbo—can save them. They string them along with promises of love or better health or a better life right around the corner, and they get away with it because they know their limits. They don't take a victim for everything she's worth; instead, they take a lot of victims for a little bit at a time, and it adds up."

I was nodding.

"It makes sense," I said. "My mother used to have friends, air quote–air quote, who liked to keep a bent bondsman on the payroll for worst-case scenarios. What could be better than having one in the family? And I assume they don't like me because I spread it around that I'm reopening the White Magic Five & Dime. Not only would I be competition—or so they'd assume—if I wasn't as careful as them,

I could bring heat down on every operator in the area. Which sounds like it would be a bunch of Grandis."

"Wow," Logan marveled. "'Bring heat down on every operator in the area'? Are you sure you're not a criminal yourself?"

"Ninety-nine percent." I thought it over a moment. "Maybe ninety-eight. But wait. I still don't see why Grandi's not a suspect, alibi or not. His family had good reason to want my mother gone."

"Gone but not murdered. I've spent the last year building up a case against the Grandis, and they must know it. Now's not the best time to start bumping off rivals."

"Maybe they thought my mom was helping you somehow. You said you used to drop in on her from time to time to let her know you were watching. Grandi could have gotten the wrong idea."

"It's obvious I don't know con artists as well as you do, Alanis. But would one help a cop take down another while running the same scams in the same town?"

"Probably not. Unless the cop was crooked, too."

Logan shot me an exasperated look. "Let's assume he's not."

"Then no."

"Well, wouldn't the Grandis know that?"

"Probably. If they're smart."

"They've been operators around here for fifteen years without getting busted once."

"Okay, so they're smart. Sometimes nasty trumps that, though."

"Alanis. Forget the Grandis. Those names I gave you—focus on those. Do whatever penance you've got to do on your mom's behalf and leave the investigating to me."

"I got started on the penance yesterday. It went well."

"Good."

"I learned a lot."

Logan's shoulders slumped.

"You weren't supposed to be learning," he said. "You were supposed to be spreading sunshine and love."

"I can multitask. Don't you want to hear what I found out?"

"I—"

"First off, there's William Riggs. He went to the police after his wife, Marsha, dropped a bundle on my mom for tarot card marriage counseling. Very creepy vibe in the Riggs home. Personally, I don't think Marsha needs counseling. She needs luggage and a ticket to Anywhere Else. Her husband's got quite the temper, according to her. Got thrown out of the army for it. Used to mix it up with MPs a lot."

"So maybe—"

"Right. We don't know if he's ever used a sleeper hold on anyone, but there's a fair chance he's seen one in action—on himself. I'd say there's no better way to find out how effective they can be."

"But—"

"Then there's Victor Castellanos. My mom talked his mom out of the family jewels, and he's had some pretty ugly things to say about it, apparently. And guess what he does over at the high school?"

"Isn't—?"

"Exactly. He's a gym teacher—and he coaches the wrestling squad. Last and definitely least, but I'll mention him anyway, is Kenneth Meldon, another man with a temper. He's had more than one run-in with the police over the years, and though he acted like he didn't even know my mother was dead, his mind is so fuzzy I could almost believe it if he'd—"

"Wait. Stop. Isn't Kenneth Meldon in a *nursing home*?"

"Right, okay, you got me. I shouldn't have brought him up. But the other two are worth looking at."

"Alanis, I gave you those names because those people had complained to the police—to *me*—about your mother. Do you really think someone would do that and then decide to murder her?"

"Sure...if the police didn't do anything about her."

Logan made another pained face and turned away from me. "When is that damn steak coming?"

"One more thing."

"We should've gone to Smitty's..."

"Who would you take semi-hot jewelry to around here?"

"Oh god. Are you planning a heist now? What have I gotten myself into?"

"I said semi-hot, Logan. I'm not talking about stuff that's been outright stolen. Just stuff you don't want to answer any questions about. Stuff you wouldn't want to waste on a below-the-radar fence."

"Just tell me *you* aren't trying to sell this stuff."

"No. But I think my mom did."

"And you're going to get it back?"

"Possibly."

I also wanted to find out who else had been looking for it and what their disposition had been.

This I did not say.

"All right, fine," Logan groaned. "In Berdache, you'd go to the Fourth Street Pawn Shop. If you went a little farther afield—"

"The smart move."

188

"—you might go to the Westside Gold and Jewelry Exchange in Sedona or Jones Pawn & Loan up in Flagstaff."

"I assume you've already checked with all of them about the electronics that were stolen from the White Magic Five & Dime."

"Thank you for assuming I'm not a total idiot."

"Was a camcorder on the list of things you were looking for?"

"Yes."

"How about a bunch of missing tapes?"

Logan frowned. "No. Clarice didn't say anything about that. Should she have?"

"Well, it's not the kind of thing anyone would pawn. But yeah, she should have mentioned it. I think my mother was secretly recording some of her readings."

"Blackmail?"

"I don't think it was for *America's Funniest Home Videos*. And *someone* wanted those tapes."

Logan nodded slowly, his expression going from exasperated to pensive.

He wasn't looking for his steak anymore.

"You know," he said, "you'd actually make a pretty good cop."

I snorted. I'd never heard that one before.

"I wouldn't pass the background check," I said. "So how'd *you* get into it? You don't strike me as the usual cop material."

"Oh? What kind of material am I?"

I looked him over.

Male model?

Actor?

Singer?

"Rodeo clown," I said.

189

"*Rodeo clown?*"

"Yeah. Rodeo clown. You're just as tough as the other cowboys, but you don't feel the need to flaunt it."

"Uhhh…thanks."

"It's a compliment."

"I don't know if my dad would say so. He's the reason I'm a cop."

"Let me guess: he was a cop."

Logan nodded. "Arizona Highway Patrol."

He was suddenly beaming at the thought of his old man. Just the slightest encouragement, I knew, and he'd tell me more, everything, his whole life story. It would take a while and it would have nothing to do with what I'd come to Berdache to accomplish.

Head junk, Biddle would have called it. Useless information.

I saw the waitress finally heading our way with our food.

My stomach started growling.

My *soul* was growling, too.

Feed me, they were both saying.

I smiled at Logan.

"Tell me about him," I said.

THE CONVERSATION was good. The food was good. Life felt good.

"Oh yeah—I meant to remind you," Logan said as we left. "You *really* need to call the medical examiner's office about your mother."

Poof. Life felt like life again. Not so good.

"What's there to talk about?" I said. "All they have to do is put a stake through her heart and bury her at a crossroads and that's that."

"Look, Alanis, I know how this works. You're going to get stuck with the ashes and a bill for the cremation no matter what. You may as well have a say in how it all goes down."

"You know what I did the one and only time I had a say in any-thing to do with my mother?"

"No."

I opened my mouth.

I'd just spent the last thirty minutes hearing about Logan's saintly cop father, and now I was about to say things about my mother that would make a sailor not just blush but sick to his stom-ach?

No. Not now. Not yet.

Maybe later…when I know you're really ready, Josh Logan. When I know I'm really ready.

I forced myself to smile again.

"Thanks for lunch," I said.

I WENT to the White Magic Five & Dime and spent the next two hours looking for jewelry and camcorder cassettes. I found dust bunnies, three fat rolls of hundred-dollar bills, and the bottle of Boone's Farm Clarice had stashed in her underwear drawer.

And I found pictures. Seven of them, decades old, hidden in the pages of a Gideon Bible.

So my mother had looked back sometimes, too. She'd missed something. Longed for something. *Felt* something.

What do you know? She actually had a soul after all.

The pictures weren't of me, though. Not one.

They were of Biddle.

| LA MORTE | XIII | DEATH |
| LA MORT | | LA MUERTE |

DER TOD · DE DOOD

Don't fear the reaper, some tarot readers will tell you. The Death card doesn't mean deadly DEAD death. It's about letting go of the past and accepting—even embracing—whatever comes next. It's about change, they say. And they're not necessarily wrong. From alive to dead, though—that's a pretty big damn change. Sometimes a cigar is just a cigar. And sometimes Death is just death.

Miss Chance, *Infinite Roads to Knowing*

STORY TIME again.

It was 1986, and the girl, less little than ever, was standing in front of a mall multiplex in Cleveland, Ohio, thinking about the weird, weird film she'd just seen.

The weird, weird film wasn't *Big Trouble in Little China*, which she'd also watched that day. That movie wasn't weird. It was just goofy.

The weird, weird film wasn't *Labyrinth* or *Poltergeist 2*, which she'd also watched. Those were just dumb.

The weird, weird film—the one she couldn't wrap her adolescent mind around—was a surreal, disturbing yet oddly hypnotic science fiction fantasy called *Ferris Bueller's Day Off*.

She'd been at the mall all day. It was her babysitter.

Reading paperbacks in the B. Dalton had gotten her through a few hours. Change-raising every zombie-teen cashier in the food court had killed another while netting her enough money to buy a JC Penney necklace she didn't really want and could have easily stolen anyway. With what she had left, she'd bought a ticket for *Cobra* and a bucket of popcorn and a jumbo Mountain Dew.

She always paid for the movie she least wanted to see. She felt bad for them. She was about to spend nine hours adrift, changing seats and screens and stories and realities at a whim. Yet she didn't have ninety minutes for Sylvester Stallone as a leather-wearing criminal-killing cop? Poor guy. Here. Have $3.50. Buy yourself some shiny new bullets.

The girl had seen *Ferris Bueller's Day Off* first because it was starting when she walked in and the guy from *War Games* was in it. It was a movie about kids who weren't much older than her, who lived in the same country as her, who had the same skin color and spoke the same language, yet beyond that it was utterly alien. It may as well have been the new *Star Trek* movie. The Search for Who-Knew-What on the strange new world of Suburbia.

These people went to a nice school. They had nice friends. They had their own nice rooms in their own nice homes. They had *nice*.

And they seemed to hate it. All they wanted was to escape from it. So they ran away to the city and had an adventure. An adventure with wacky mishaps and singing and dancing.

The girl knew about adventures in the city. She'd had a lot of them.

The mishaps weren't wacky, and there was never any singing and dancing.

The first time she saw the movie, she hated it. Yet she found herself coming back to the same theater again and again, catching bits and pieces before sneaking off to see something else.

She ended the day with Ferris Bueller. And the last time he looked out into the audience after the credits and said, "You're still here? It's over. Go home!" she burst into tears, and she didn't know why.

She made sure to dry her eyes before walking outside. Then she sat on the curb and waited.

The mall was closed. The parking lot was nearly empty. Before long, she was alone.

Biddle and the girl's mother showed up after midnight. They were driving a silver Lincoln Town Car, brand-new. So brand-new it had never even been bought.

Biddle was wearing a tuxedo. The mother—she called herself Carol now—was in the kind of evening gown the lady dancers used to wear on *Lawrence Welk*. She had a big, bushy dome of over-teased '80s hair to go with it. The hair was red. Clairol 108 Natural Reddish Blonde, actually. The girl had helped dye it four days before.

"Been waiting long?" Biddle said.

Before the girl could answer, Carol told her, "Don't complain. You're the one who wanted to get dropped off at the mall."

"I'm not complaining," the girl said.

She knew better than to ask about their day. Biddle would tell her later if he was in the mood. So she just sat in the back and breathed in the Newly Stolen Car Smell and rewound and replayed and rewound and replayed *Ferris Bueller's Day Off*.

Bow bow, she thought. *Chika chikAAAAA*.

They were staying in a fancier hotel than usual. A big one, with a huge atrium lobby and glass elevators and chocolates on the pillows every day. The girl had no idea what Biddle and her mother were up to, but it had put them somewhere nice and she hadn't been involved in any way.

That was as close to nice as things ever got. She told herself to appreciate it while she could.

She was looking forward to her chocolate.

When they walked into their room, two men were waiting there. They were in their forties, heavyset, one dark-haired, one bald.

They had guns.

The bald man touched a finger to his lips. "Shhh."

The door, already closed again, was just five feet behind the girl. It could've been a mile. She knew she wouldn't reach it in time if she tried.

"Aww, geez," the other man said when he saw her. "Nobody mentioned a kid."

"Who are you?" Biddle said.

Not "What's going on?" Not "How dare you?" He didn't sound happy, but he didn't sound surprised or angry either.

It didn't matter. The man with dark hair shoved his gun into his pants—he wasn't the sort of pro to have a shoulder holster—and walked up to Biddle and punched him in the face.

Biddle stumbled sideways into the wall, his hands pressed to his nose.

"Ow," the dark-haired man said, shaking his hand. "Don't make me do that again."

"The stomach, dummy, the stomach," his friend told him. "Look—you made him bleed."

The girl started to cry. It seemed like the thing to do.

"Shut up," her mother said. She was standing very still, her eyes wide and dry.

"Clean yourself up, then we're going," the dark-haired man told Biddle. He glanced at the girl. "All of us."

"Just leave her out of it, all right?" Biddle said. "She's got nothing to do with anything."

The dark-haired man remembered. He hit Biddle in the stomach this time.

They took the Town Car. The men with the guns sat in front. The dark-haired one drove. The bald one watched Biddle and Carol in the backseat. He made sure the girl sat between them.

"You're not fast enough to jump out," he told the grown-ups. "And even if you were, just think about who you'd be leaving behind."

Still, the girl got ready to duck.

Biddle and Carol never moved, though. Twice, Biddle tried to talk, started to say "Look, guys—"

Both times the bald man brought up his hands. One held his gun. The other was putting a finger to his lips daintily, delicately. The second time, the gun was pointed at the girl.

Biddle stopped trying after that.

They drove out of the city, through the suburbs, into nowhere. The roads grew narrower and darker and more deserted.

They turned off onto a gravel driveway. Passed a farmhouse, passed a barn.

They stopped beside a field of tall green stalks. Corn in long, neat rows as straight as iron bars.

Another car was there already. It was big, boxy, ugly. Like the men standing beside it.

There were four of them. Biddle and Carol knew at least one.

"Shit," Biddle said as the headlights swept over them.

"Don't let him hurt my baby!" Carol howled. She threw her arms around her daughter. "We're sorry! We're sorry! Not my daughter! Please! Not my little girl!"

The men had to drag her out of the car. Biddle got out on his own. He started to say something to the girl before he left, but he thought better of it and just gave her hand a squeeze instead. He looked into her eyes in a way that seemed to say *let this moment last forever*. Only it didn't, and he and Carol were taken out to the field, around one corner, out of sight.

The girl they left in the backseat. The bald man was told to stay and watch her.

"What am I, Mary Poppins?" he said.

But he seemed relieved.

Half a minute went by in silence. Then the girl heard sounds coming out of the darkness.

Pleading. Weeping. And laughter, too. A man's laughter, joyless and cruel.

"Oh god oh god oh god," the girl said. "No no no no no no."

"Be quiet," the bald man said. "Everything's gonna be fine. They're just talking."

There was a scream, so brief the girl couldn't tell if it had been Biddle or her mother.

"Oh god oh god oh god."

"Be quiet," the bald man said again. His voice wasn't gentle but it wasn't harsh. He looked like he wanted to be home in bed.

Something outside caught his eye, turned his head. The girl turned to look, too.

The dark-haired man was walking back toward the car with Carol. She was crying hysterically, staggering. The dark-haired man had to hold her up with both hands, guide her. His gun was stuck in his pants again.

The bald man opened the passenger-side door. The overhead light came on.

"What's going on?" the bald man asked.

"She needs to talk to the kid."

"What? You're kidding."

It was obvious the bald man had thought he'd never see the woman again.

"Oh, baby, baby, baby!" she sobbed when she saw the girl. Her knees buckled, and the dark-haired man barely managed to keep her on her feet.

"Roll down your window," the bald man said to the girl.

She did as she was told.

"You're okay, baby?" Carol said as she lurched toward the car. "No one's touched you?"

"I'm okay."

"Oh, thank god. I just had to make sure you were all right. They say they won't hurt you, they'll let you go, if I tell them where I hid the—"

Carol's knees went again, and she started to crumple.

"Goddamn it," the dark-haired man said as he strained to keep her from falling.

And then there was a flash of light and a muffled pop and the man was falling backward.

Carol darted toward the car, no wobble to her knees now, and stuck the gun she'd just stolen from the dark-haired man into his bald friend's face.

"Scoot over and drive or you're dead," she said. All trace of panic, desperation, *emotion* was gone from her voice. Her face was blank. A mask stamped out by a machine.

"I…I don't have the keys."

"Ohhhhh no," the dark-haired man moaned as he rolled on the ground clutching his gut. "Ohhhhh no."

Carol turned just long enough to shoot him again. Then she pointed the gun back at the bald man.

"*They're still in the ignition, asshole.*"

"Hey!" someone shouted in the distance. "What the hell's going on?"

The bald man got behind the wheel and started the car. Carol swung in beside him and slammed the door shut.

"Out to the road," she said. "Not too fast and not too slow."

The car started moving.

The girl looked out the back window. She could see hazy shapes moving in the gloom. There was another flash and for a split second she could see two men running after them. Something thumped into the back of the car.

"A little faster," Carol said.

The bald man gave the car more gas. They shot onto the gravel drive, skidded, then straightened out and headed for the road.

"Wait!" the girl said. "What about Biddle?"

"Left at the end of the driveway," her mother said. "Then hit the speed limit and stay there."

"We can't just leave him! We've got to go back!"

"Take the first turn you can. Right or left, it doesn't matter."

"Mom—"

"Are they following us?"

"But—"

"*Are they following us?*"

The girl looked out the back window again. She didn't see any headlights.

"No. I don't think so," she said.

"Good."

Her mother never took her eyes off the bald man.

"We've got a gun," the girl said. "We could go back and get him."

Her mother said nothing.

"Or we could find a phone and call the police. Maybe they could get out there in time to save him."

No response.

"We can't just leave him!"

"Shut up."

"But we've got to—"

"Shut up and let me think, dammit!"

The gun wasn't pointed at the bald man anymore. It was pointed at the girl. Just for a second. But long enough.

The girl shut up and let her mother do her thinking. She assumed none of it was about Biddle.

They drove on and on, taking random turns, until the bald man said, "You know, I've got no idea where we are. It's three in the morning, there's hardly any houses around here. Just let me out anywhere and no one's gonna hear from me for hours. What do I know that they don't know already anyway? And really, you gotta believe me, I didn't want anything to do with this in the first place. They brought us in to pick you up 'cuz you wouldn't know us. Me and Phil, we're not even…"

The thought of Phil—the dark-haired man—shut him up for a moment. When he started talking again, his voice was a throaty warble, and the girl could see sweat glistening on his smooth scalp.

"Look. Really. I can't hurt you. I *won't* hurt you. You may as well let me go."

Carol nodded slowly.

"Yeah," she said. "Maybe you're right."

She looked out the window, scanning the dark countryside around them.

The girl had been weeping silently. Now she felt like throwing up. They'd be stopping soon, yes. But not just by the side of the road to let the bald man out.

The girl knew what her mother was looking for.

Another cornfield.

La Temperanza — La Tempérance — XIV — Temperance — La Templanza

Die Mässigkeit — Matiging

Talk about an angel—this one's fixing us a drink! A martini, perhaps? A cosmopolitan? Cool, refreshing pond scum with a dash of yummy mud? It doesn't matter. The important thing is the angel's a mixologist—in more ways than one. Just check out the feet. One's on land, one's in water. True balance is found by having a toehold in more than one place, more than one world, more than one outlook. Who cares if they're supposedly incompatible? What do gin and vermouth have in common? But throw them together with an olive and you've got something that'll rock your world.

Miss Chance, *Infinite Roads to Knowing*

I went to Clarice's room again. Finding my mother's pictures of Biddle had got me thinking.

Teenage girl + jock boyfriend - pictures = no way. And I hadn't seen a single picture of Matt Gorman when I'd searched Clarice's room for the missing jewelry.

Not that I knew what the kid looked like. I knew the type, though. *Homo sapiens* male. They're fairly recognizable. I didn't see any in the few pictures scattered around Clarice's room. Just her friend Ceecee and a few other girls, all of them always screaming at something hysterical that was happening just off-camera.

Maybe high-school girls don't bother with printed pictures of their boyfriends anymore. They just snap shots of them with their cell phones all day, then start over with a new phone when they run out of memory. How would I know? The last time I'd had what you could call a boyfriend, the only pictures I had of him were painted on a cave wall with mashed berries and mastodon blood. Ba-da *bing*.

Still, I found no "I ♥ M.G." doodles either. No dried-out prom corsages. No Trojans tucked in with the Strawberry Hill in the dresser. No sign of a boyfriend at all.

And no sign of a family. Clarice was half black, by the look of her, yet all the girls in her pictures were either white or Latino. Where were her parents or her favorite aunts and uncles? How about the black cousins who probably lived somewhere more racially diverse than the Arizona desert? Had Clarice's childhood really been so horrific she'd want nothing to remember her relatives by at all?

I heard a rapping sound downstairs. It was soft and timid at first, but it grew stronger, more insistent.

I went down and found Marsha Riggs knocking on the back door. It was a bit of shock to see her out of her house, in the sunlight. I'd thought of her as her husband's hamster. Something small and meek he could keep caged until he wanted to play with her.

"Oh, I'm so glad you're here," she said when I opened the door. "It took me twenty minutes to walk over from my house. It would've killed me to walk all the way back without seeing you."

"Why didn't you just call first?"

Marsha looked at her toes and shrugged.

Fear, that was the answer. Fear that someone would find out she'd made the call.

"Well, anyway, it worked out," I said. "Come on in, and I'll make you some tea. You like Red Zinger?"

"I don't have any money."

Marsha forced herself to look up again.

There was a bruise under her left eye, and her bangs were combed down over what looked like a welt on her forehead.

"Didn't I mention it?" I said. "I'm running a special for all Mom's old customers. First reading's on the house."

Marsha smiled. She did it tentatively, warily, as if smiles were something she couldn't trust. Maybe because they always ended so soon.

She followed me down the hall to the reading room.

I HAD Marsha shuffle and think about what she wanted to ask the cards. Then I took the deck and laid out a Celtic Cross: a card, another over it sideways, four cards clustered around them, then four more in a straight line along the side.

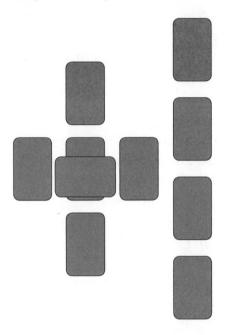

All the reading I'd done in *Infinite Roads to Knowing* was starting to pay off. I'd remembered the pattern easily, instinctively, without having to pause and think it through.

It was almost *too* easy, though. I turned over the first card and said, "Let's begin with where you're at right now," but I'd forgotten to stop and ask Marsha what her question was.

It didn't matter. I knew. And even if I hadn't, the first card would've been all the reminder I'd need.

A man on a throne, upside down.

"The Emperor reversed," I said. "Someone with strength and authority is oppressing you—using his power over you harshly."

Marsha's lips trembled, but no words came out.

Her eyes, though, said, "God, yes!"

I flipped the next card and saw a blindfolded woman holding up two swords, her arms crisscrossed over her chest. I'd seen the card before. It was the first one Josette Berg had turned over when she'd done a reading for me.

"The Two of Swords. A woman trapped, unable to take action, because she's blinded herself to her own power. She can't hold those

207

swords like that forever. She's got to either do something with them or drop them. 'Use it or lose it.' Now…on to the root of your problem."

I knew what I wanted to see. I was going to make Marsha see it no matter what card came up.

Want happiness? Run from your husband. And in the process, stop hiding anything he might want hidden. Especially if it involved more bruises on somebody else. Bruises around her neck perhaps.

Again, the cards made it easy for me. So easy, I had to stop and ask myself, *you didn't stack this deck, did you*?

"The Lovers reversed," I said. "A destructive relationship. An unhappy coupling."

"You can just say it. A lousy marriage."

I nodded. "A lousy marriage."

The next cards weren't so obvious. Yet I found I didn't have to fake my way through interpretations. What came up fit the situation with only a little imagination and intuition. And for the first time in my life, "imagination and intuition" didn't just mean BS.

The Two of Pentacles: a man awkwardly juggling two golden plates. Marsha had made an important decision—who to marry—based on worries about money.

The Seven of Wands: a man trying to fight off unseen attackers with his staff, but the card was upside down. Marsha wasn't defending herself.

The Ace of Swords: a hand clutching an Excalibur-style blade with a crown around the tip. Time to take a stand. Time to fight.

The Four of Pentacles: a man clutching gold plates to himself as if trying to keep someone from taking them. Financial troubles again. Marsha was letting anxiety about money keep her from acting on her own behalf.

Marsha looked amazed by what I was saying. I hoped I didn't, too. Because I sure *felt* amazed.

How could this be going so perfectly when I wasn't even cheating? How could I be getting at the truth without lying to do it?

There were only three cards left now. Three more chances for the tarot to send me sideways just as I tried to seal the deal and turn Marsha against her son-of-a-bitch husband.

But the cards didn't go sideways. They liked William Riggs about as much as I did.

The Devil. Strength. Justice.

"What can I say? There it is," I told Marsha. "You're shackled by your fear, just like the Devil's prisoners on his card. But you're stronger than you think. Use that strength, and the result will be justice. Balance. Karma. Things as they're supposed to be. So happiness isn't beyond you, you just have to reach for it. Does that answer your question?"

Marsha nodded. She still looked awestruck, shocked.

"Athena always read things so differently, though," she said. "She'd talk about patience and finding the willpower to persevere and helping Bill grow into his own inner peace. I see a lot of the same cards, but the way you talk about them…it's not the same at all."

"Different contexts lead to different interpretations," I said.

My mother's "context" being the need to keep another sucker on the hook.

I kept that to myself.

"The important thing is that the reading makes sense to *you*," I said. "And it sounds like it does."

"Yes. My god, *yes!*"

"Good. So do you think it's something you could act on?"

"I hope so. Eventually. When I've had more time to think about it. But I really don't have any money. Any. I never have and I never will. Bill always tells me my only skill is…well. Anyway, I can't go to my family for a million reasons and I've lost touch with whatever friends I ever had and I can't just run away with nowhere to—"

"*Hey*. Marsha. You believe in the cards, don't you?"

"Yes. I do."

"And what did they just tell you?"

"That I have the power to change my life. I just have to use it."

"There you go. Focus on that, not the things that've been holding you back."

Marsha sighed and stared off at the big crystal ball on top of the bookshelf nearby.

She mumbled something I couldn't quite hear.

"Excuse me?"

"I said it's not just the money. That's not the only reason I'm scared."

"I know."

Marsha said nothing.

"Look," I said, "I've been dealing with a lawyer here in town. Anytime you want, I'll walk you down to his office and have him talk you through your options. He can help you prepare yourself before you take the next step."

Marsha turned away from the crystal ball. "The next step?"

I moved my gaze to the gray smudge under her eye, then the flushed bump on her forehead.

Marsha moved a hand up toward her mouth.

I hadn't noticed till that moment, and I only had another second to see it, but her lower lip looked a little swollen.

"I should get back," she said through her palm. "Sometimes Bill calls during the day. If I'm not there to answer..."

Marsha stood up.

I stood, too.

"Let me give you a ride."

"No, no, that's okay. I don't want to be any trouble."

"It's no trouble. I have to go over to the high school anyway."

"The high school? Why?"

"The website says there's a wrestling match this afternoon, and I've taken an interest in the team."

Marsha looked puzzled and a little perturbed.

I guess thirtysomething women aren't supposed to take an interest in high-school wrestlers.

"It's really the coach I want to see. Victor Castellanos," I said. "His mom sort of fixed us up."

Marsha looked slightly less puzzled.

"So you're going on, like, a blind date?"

"In a way."

Victor Castellanos wouldn't see it coming, that was for sure.

"THANKS FOR the ride," Marsha said as we drove to her house. "And the free reading."

"My pleasure. It's the least I could do for one of Mom's most loyal customers."

"Still no breakthrough with the investigation?"

"No, but there are a lot of leads. I'm sure one's going to pan out sooner or later."

A block went by in silence.

"Am I a lead?" Marsha said softly.

"What do you mean?"

"I know what you've been wondering." Marsha stopped and took a deep breath before she could say it. "Did Bill kill Athena? The answer's no, Alanis…though I almost wish he had."

Marsha slapped her hands over her mouth as though trying to shut herself up a moment too late.

"I'm sorry! I know that sounds awful! But *someone* did it, and at least if we knew it was Bill you'd have some peace, and he'd be taken away, and then I'd get some, too. But I didn't lie to the police. He really was with me when Athena was murdered. He won't let me out of his sight at night, so he was always in mine. That's the simple truth. Bill didn't do it. You don't have to waste any more time on me."

I believed her, which made Marsha Riggs a dead-end. I had nothing to gain from her anymore.

"Thanks. I appreciate your honesty," I said. "You're right. You were a lead. But not now."

I looked over at Marsha. She was watching me with eyes big and sad enough for a cartoon puppy.

I put a hand on her knee and gave it a squeeze.

"Now you're just a friend," I said.

I'M OLD enough to remember the phrase "gag me with a spoon" from its heyday. And back then, it might have run through my mind at a moment like this. Yet I didn't feel spoon-gagged, even though I'd just thrown myself into treacle deep enough for the Hallmark Hall of Fame.

What was wrong with me?

I was giving empowering tarot card readings I actually kinda-sorta believed. I was declaring friendship with virtual strangers. What was next? A hug? A quick trip to Spencer's for a HANG IN THERE! poster of a kitten dangling from a branch?

Cynicism and sentimentality don't mix. People like me don't do schmaltz. I felt off, unsettled, not myself.

Then again, I'd *never* felt like myself. You've got to have a self for that. And all I had where that was supposed to be was this: "I am not my mother." Which meant I was still defining *me* based on *her*, of course.

Well, screw that.

When I dropped Marsha off, I gave her a hug.

As A general rule, you can't stroll into a school and start scoping out the students and teachers. But a game changes things. You could walk into the gym carrying a flamethrower, and as long as you look normal and have breasts and wear a smile, everyone's going to assume you're just another mother anxious to show some school spirit.

I was still on the young side compared to the genuine bona fide wrestling moms, but the people who noticed didn't seem to mind. I got more than one long look from the boys doing stretches in their wrestling tights. I hoped for their sake none of them had a MILF fetish. Given what they were wearing, it was going to show, and that's the kind of picture you definitely don't want in the yearbook.

Any of the wrestlers could have been Matt Gorman, so it would've helped if one had tipped me off by throwing kisses to Clarice. But she wasn't in the bleachers, although half a dozen other girls were.

Sad that Matt's girlfriend wasn't there to cheer him on. Or maybe sad wasn't the word for it.

It was a lot easier to figure out who Victor Castellanos was. A man about my age was talking to the Berdache team, and he was wearing the classic gym teacher uniform (as *Grease* and *Porky's* had defined it for me, anyway): gray sweats, running shoes, whistle around the neck.

He pulled the look off pretty well, to judge by the way some of the mothers were eyeing him. The guy probably needed cougar repellent at PTA meetings. He had thick black hair, chiseled features, a lean build, muscular arms and legs.

It was the arms that interested me. And what he could probably do with them.

He clapped his big hands twice, apparently wrapping up a pep talk, then turned and headed for the visiting team. A quick handshake with the opposing coach and the match would begin.

I cut him off.

"Mr. Castellanos? Excuse me. Can I have a moment?"

"Of course."

He gave me an anything-for-the-moms smile even as he stole a peek at his wristwatch.

"My name's Alanis McLachlan. I'm Athena Passalis's daughter."

The smile disappeared.

"I'm in town to wrap up my mother's affairs," I went on, "and I heard through the grapevine that you had some sort of complaint about Mom. I just wanted to let you know that, if there's any truth to it, I'll try to do the right thing."

Castellanos cocked his head and narrowed his eyes.

"*If* there's any truth to it you'll *try*?" he said.

I nodded with all the obliviousness I could muster.

"I will do my utmost to make an effort to see what I might be able to do," I said. "Assuming your little beef with Mom is valid."

"My *little beef*? Look, you—"

Castellanos managed to stop himself before he said the kind of thing that would've gotten one of his students a quick trip to the principal's office.

"Now isn't the time for this," he grated out.

Yeah. Exactly. Which made it the perfect time.

If you want someone to lose their cool, Biddle used to say, *do it when the heat's already on.*

Castellanos turned to go.

"I understand," I said to his back. "Maybe I'll catch you over at Verde River Vista sometime."

Castellanos whirled around.

"Excuse me?"

"I said maybe I'll see you at the nursing home. I stopped by yesterday to talk to your mother. I hear you're a real regular."

Castellanos looked like he wanted to start the wrestling match right then and there, Hulk Hogan–style. Pick me up, twirl me, and throw me. Or maybe smack me over the back with a folding chair.

His gaze shot past me toward his students, then ricocheted left and right into the stands on either side of the gym.

He resisted the urge to go Rowdy Roddy on me, which was a disappointment. I'd have traded some broken bones for an incriminating freak-out.

"Are you *trying* to piss me off?" Castellanos said.

"What? Oh my goodness, no! I'm trying to do the responsible thing. I've been looking for the jewelry Lucia supposedly gave my mother, but I haven't found any of it yet so I'm not sure what to think."

"Maybe it's just not around to be found anymore."

"I don't understand."

Castellanos gave me a look that was fifty percent anger, fifty percent contempt, and one thousand percent *done*.

"It's time to start the match. I have to go."

He started away again.

"One more thing," I said.

He glanced back without turning his body toward me. Beyond him, I could see someone else walking up to the other squad's coach, her hand out for a shake.

Principal Little. She hadn't noticed me. Yet.

I didn't feel like explaining why Julie McCoy of the Sedona Lions Club was now Alanis McLachlan of the Stalking Castellanoses Club.

I gave Castellanos two thumbs-ups and a grin.

"Go, BHS!" I said.

I spun on my heel and walked off.

After a dozen or so strides, I peeked over my shoulder. Little and Castellanos and the other coach were talking to each other. None of them were looking my way.

I stopped by the Berdache wrestlers. Most were still doing stretches and trying not to stare at my chest.

"Which one of you is Matt Gorman?"

The biggest kid on the squad raised his hand. He had short blond hair and pale blue eyes and a confused look on his face.

"Me," he said.

"Feeling good about today's match?"

"Yeah. I guess."

"Good. My name's Edna Garrett. I'm a scout from Arizona State. We've had our eye on you, young man. Don't let us down."

"Uhhh…okay. I won't."

"Great." I gave the rest of the team another thumbs-up. "Good luck, guys. There's hope for you, too."

I left the gym and got in my car and headed for the White Magic Five & Dime. I wasn't sure what to make of Castellanos, but there was plenty to be made from Matt Gorman.

Eight words from the kid's own mouth—that was all I needed to hear to know that Clarice was lying about the night my mother died.

You could try telling Adam and Eve there that the chains around their necks aren't THAT tight. They could probably escape and run straight to the Gap and get those privates covered. But it's no use; they won't listen. A certain trickster with horns and wings and legs that could REALLY use some Nair told them there's no such thing as spiritual energy. It's only what's right in front of them—the material world—that exists or matters. And they believe it, because they'd rather get their bare butts scorched by that torch than admit that they've been wrong. Fools.

But hey…have you checked YOUR butt for burns lately?

Miss Chance, *Infinite Roads to Knowing*

"Ping," I said when I got to the top of the stairs.

Clarice looked up at me. She was stretched out on the couch with her laptop and she looked very, very displeased with herself. Her bedroom—with its door!—was just a few feet away, yet she'd let me catch her out in the open.

"Ping?" she said.

"Yeah. *Ping.*"

"Who keeps saying *ping*?" Clarice's computer asked. It sounded a lot like Ceecee.

"I'll tell you later," Clarice said to it. "Bye."

"All right. Bye."

Clarice logged off Skype or whatever it was with a few angry pecks at the keyboard.

"So," I said. "As I was saying. *Ping.*"

I gave it jazz hands this time.

"And a big blippity-blop to you."

"You don't understand, Clarice. I just met Matt Gorman."

Clarice got that I-will-not-show-any-expression expression on her face.

"Oh? Where?"

"A wrestling match at your school. And *ping.*"

"Will you please stop saying that? What is it even supposed to mean?"

"You don't know gaydar when you hear it?"

"Gaydar? You think Matt's gay?"

"A ping is a ping."

"That is *so* offensive. You can't tell someone's gay just by talking to them at a wrestling match."

"Not always. But sometimes."

"Oh, come on! So he's a little soft-spoken. That doesn't make him gay."

"It's not just the voice. It's the whole vibe. I was taught how to look for it a long time before anyone ever talked about gaydar."

"Please. Are you saying Athena turned you into some kind of sex psychic?"

"It wasn't just her, but yeah. I learned how to pick up on subliminal cues. This guy's desperate, this guy's a liar, this guy's into girls, this guy's not. It all came in handy one way or another."

Clarice turned her attention back to her laptop.

"I'm disappointed in you, Alanis," she said as she typed. "I thought you might be a little more sophisticated than the people around here, but it turns out you're deluded *and* homophobic."

I walked over to the couch and closed her laptop.

"Hey!" Clarice protested.

"After you called 911 to report Athena's murder, you called Matt Gorman's house. You woke him up—though supposedly he'd dropped you off here just a few minutes before."

"Who told you that? That cop Logan?"

"You needed Matt to cover for you. You needed to get your stories straight. Why?"

"This is crazy."

Clarice started to get up.

I pushed her back down. "Why have you been lying?"

"Don't touch me, bitch!"

"You killed her, didn't you? *You killed my mother.*"

I didn't believe it, but I didn't disbelieve it either. I was saying it to get a reaction. And I got one.

Clarice slumped back into the cushions. Then her eyes filled with tears. Then her lips started to quiver.

"You really think that about me? That I'd...*your*...?"

Then the sobbing started.

"What am I supposed to think?" I said as gently as I could. "I'm not a psychic, but I trust my gut. And it tells me Matt Gorman is not your boyfriend."

Clarice kept crying. I let her. For a minute or so, anyway.

"Clarice. The truth. Please."

"Okay. The truth," she said, her voice shaky but the tears done. "Matt and I went out that night, but not with each other."

"I don't understand."

Clarice swiped at her face with her sleeves. "Yeah, your gaydar is *sooooo* good."

She glanced pointedly at the computer on her lap.

It took me a few seconds, but I got there.

"Oh. Well," I said. "It doesn't work as good on girls."

I PLOPPED down on the couch beside Clarice.

"You and Matt have been bearding each other."

She nodded.

I wasn't sure if she'd know what I meant.

Kids today.

"A few of the people at our school are out, but it's not easy around here," Clarice said. "Matt gets picked on sometimes even though he's a jock. He does ping a little. And if the guys on his wrestling team knew, it'd be *brutal*. So we made a deal."

"And the night my mother died, you were supposedly out late with him when you were really with Ceecee—your girlfriend."

Clarice nodded.

"You aren't going to tell Detective Logan, are you?" she asked. "If it got around about us, it'd be—"

"Don't worry. I'll play it old school: if Logan doesn't ask, I won't tell, unless he starts wasting too much of his time on you and Matt. You know he considers you a suspect, don't you?"

"Yeah. It's totally ridiculous."

"Not from his point of view. He told me he walked in on you and my mom arguing not too long ago. You were shouting something about not being a whore. Did that have anything to do with you and Ceecee?"

"No! Athena had no idea."

"So what were you fighting about?"

"Just…stuff."

"What kind of stuff?"

"Stuff she wanted me to do."

"Like what? Take out the garbage? Clean your room?"

"Yeah. Exactly."

"And doing that would've made you a whore?"

Clarice put her stone face back on.

"I hate taking out the garbage," she said.

"Clarice—"

My phone started playing "Don't Stand So Close to Me"—the ringtone I'd added that afternoon for a specific caller.

"Speak of the devil," I said when I answered.

"You were talking about me?" Logan said.

"Clarice and I were comparing notes, yeah."

"What's the verdict?"

"You're all right—for a cop."

"Thanks. You're all right—for a con artist."

"*Former* con artist."

"Right. Of course, I only have your word to go on for that."

"Would I lie to you?"

"You don't really want me to answer that, do you?"

"No. What's going on?"

"I got another call from the medical examiner's office. The last one I'm going to get about this, they say."

"Ew. Did you borrow something you weren't supposed to?"

"It's your mother, Alanis. Time's up. The cremation's first thing in the morning. If you want to see her one last time, you need to get to the county morgue before they close for the day."

Logan paused, probably waiting for the inevitable smart-ass wisecrack.

I realized I was waiting for it, too.

It wasn't inevitable, after all.

"Alanis?" Logan said.

"When do they close?"

"In forty-five minutes."

"How long would it take me to get there?"

"Forty-*four* minutes—assuming you leave this very second and drive in a way that I, as an officer of the law, cannot endorse."

I sighed.

"What is it?" Clarice said.

"Well?" said Logan.

"Tell them I'm coming, Detective," I said.

I got the address and hung up.

"Where is it you're going?" Clarice asked.

"Someplace called Prescott Valley."

"Why?"

"Because that's where my mother is, and it's time I said goodbye."

I'd just started down the stairs when Clarice called after me.

"Can I come, too?"

I WAS going soft. Fuzzy kitten soft. Fluffy pillow soft. *Twinkie* soft.
And I wasn't sure why.

I was speeding down the road to see a dead woman I hated with
a girl who seemed to hate me. Because it suddenly felt like the right
thing to do.

How my mother would've laughed at that. Yeah, sure—gotta do
the "right" thing, don't we? Because that matters *so* much. Wouldn't
want Santa to put us on his naughty list. Ho ho ho.

Maybe that was why I had to go. To see Cathy/Veronica/Carol/
Barbra/Athena dead with my own eyes. To know there was no reason I should still hear her in my head. To find—

God help me. If I caught myself thinking I was going for closure,
I'd steer for the nearest cliff and do a Thelma & Louise. I might be
going soft, but I wasn't Jell-O.

I glanced over at Clarice. She hadn't said a word other than
thanks since I'd told her she could tag along. She was angled away

from me, watching the hills fade to jagged silhouettes as the twilight sky behind them went purple-pink. Somehow I didn't sense the same old hostility from her, even if I was just looking at her back.

She surprised me by speaking.

"How we doing on time?"

"Don't worry. We'll make it."

I gave the car more gas. Not that I needed to. We'd be there soon. But it felt good.

Right.

"Sorry, next of kin only," the morgue attendant told us.

"That's fine." I wrapped an arm around Clarice. "It's just me and my daughter anyway."

"I want to say goodbye to my memaw," Clarice sniffled.

The guy gave me some forms to sign, and we were in.

"I'll give you a moment," the attendant said, and he went back to Angry Birds or updating his Facebook page or whatever it is people in his line of work do five minutes before closing time.

Clarice had stopped just a couple feet past the door. I'd only made it a step farther.

We stood there looking at the metal tray the attendant had pulled from the far wall. I could feel the frigid air that had spilled out with it swirling around my feet.

It was like they'd been storing my mother in a vegetable crisper.

"Sure you want to do this?" I asked Clarice.

"Are *you* sure?" she said.

"Of course not, but here I am."

"Well, I'm here, too."

"Okay, then. On the count of three?"

"All right."

"One. Two. Three."

We started toward the body. It was under a white sheet covering everything but the shoulders, neck, and head. When we were close enough to see the face, I stopped and gasped.

That magnificent bitch! She'd fooled everyone again!

It wasn't her.

Only it was. I just hadn't expected her to look so small and gaunt and pale. I'd been prepared to see the mother of my memories, and I got this shriveled little dead thing instead.

"You all right?" Clarice asked.

"Yeah, I'm fine. Thanks."

I made it to my mother's side. I kept my gaze on her face. Below that were bruises and incisions I didn't need to see.

"She looks so little," Clarice said.

"I was just thinking the same thing."

"I had no idea she'd gotten so thin. Without makeup and clothes…it's like it's not really her at all."

"I know."

Clarice cocked her head slightly to one side.

"You can still see how beautiful she was, though."

"Yeah. She was always pretty."

We stood in silence for a moment, unsure of what to do. We'd raced to be there, but for what? A twenty-one gun salute? A Viking funeral? A sermon?

There was only one thing I wanted to say: goodbye. But it wasn't time for that yet. Later, maybe. When I'd repaid my debt.

If I repaid my debt.

I reached out and touched my mother's shoulder. Just one finger, brushing lightly over the cold flesh for a tenth of a second.

Yup, she's dead all right, I could have said. *You up for pizza?*

But I wanted to say goodbye to that, too. Putting so much effort into joking, deflecting, pretending not to care.

Soon, I hoped. Soon.

"I'm ready whenever you are," I said.

Clarice looked a little surprised and disappointed. Like maybe she'd been waiting for the twenty-one gun salute.

She turned back to my mother, bent over her, and kissed her on the forehead. Then, without a word to me, she started toward the door.

Clarice didn't speak until we were on the road back to Berdache. It was dark by then, and I couldn't see her. But I felt her eyes on me for a while before she started to talk.

"When we were walking toward the body and you stopped and gasped…I liked that," she said. "I finally saw you have a reaction. An emotion. The rest of the time…I don't know. You're like a robot that runs on sarcasm and lies."

I flinched. "Wow. Good one. You actually managed to hurt my feelings."

"I'm sorry."

She didn't sound it.

"Well, now at least you know I *have* feelings," I said. "In fact, I could've gone into that morgue and bawled like a baby. But it wouldn't have been because my mother's dead. I would've been crying about everything she wasn't when she was alive. And I've shed those tears already."

"Then why did you come to Berdache? How come you're still here? You act like you don't give a shit, but you won't leave."

"You really want to know what I'm doing here? Why I *had* to come?"

Clarice didn't answer. She could probably tell she didn't have to. I was going to keep talking anyway.

There are so many stories I've got hoarded up inside me.

It was time I finally shared one with somebody.

Upheaval. Destruction. A sudden and violent ending. Utter rack and ruin. (Or at least ruin. What is "rack," anyway?) In other words: uh-oh. Change is on its way, whether you're ready for it or not. What comes next might turn out to be an improvement, but getting through it won't be easy. Or fun. Or even survivable.

Yippee! Don't you just love getting good news?

Miss Chance, *Infinite Roads to Knowing*

ONE DAY, the girl's mother came back to their hotel room with a scale. This was not a good sign.

The diet started the next morning.

"I don't need to lose weight," the girl said.

"I'm just trying to help you be healthier."

"No, you're trying to make me skinnier. Why?"

"Eat your Special K."

By the end of the summer, the girl was ten pounds lighter. She was a blond, too. Her mother took her to a salon to get her newly dyed hair cut just so.

"Mom, it's the nineties," the girl said as her mother told the stylist what to do. "Nobody wants to look like Farrah Fawcett anymore."

"You're going to be beautiful," her mother said. "Trust me."

"I've seen what happens to people who do *that*," the girl mumbled.

"What did you say?"

"Huh? Did I say something? I didn't hear it. I stopped listening to myself years ago because nothing I say matters anyway."

Her mother turned to the stylist and sighed. "Teenagers, right?"

She was smiling that smile of hers that always got a smile in return. But to the girl, watching her in the big salon mirror, it seemed more like she was just baring her teeth.

A few days later, her mother announced that their business in City X was done. Which meant it was time to pack up and slip out in the middle of the night.

"Where are we going?" the girl asked.

"I've been scouting something out. First we're going to need a little warm-up, though."

"That's great. *Where are we going*?"

"To an orthodontists' convention."

The girl hoped she was joking.

She wasn't.

The convention was at a big hotel in St. Louis. The mother checked them in under the name "Barbra Harper." It was a name she used sparingly, so it hadn't been permanently burned yet. Not like "Cathy Scarpelli" and "Veronica Sternwood," who were wanted in a dozen states. Not like "Olivia Lake," who'd made serious enemies on the East Coast. Not like "Mary Foster Morris," "Marlo Hollinger," "Rhoda Penmark," and twenty others, all of them banished to limbo for one reason or another.

"Barbra Harper" had outlasted them all. Sometimes the girl thought it might even be her mother's real name. Which might have made *her* real name the one she used when Mom was Barbra: Sophie Harper.

It would've been nice to have a real name. Most days, she felt like a mask with no face underneath.

"Okay," Barbra said once they were settled in their room, "let's talk."

There were two queen-sized beds. The woman was sitting on the edge of one, back straight, hands on her knees. The girl sat on the other.

Barbra was finally going to explain why they were there. The girl assumed it was a scam to get her free braces.

"You had a good summer, didn't you? Read a lot of books. Watched a lot of movies."

"Is that a good summer?"

"But the vacation's over. You know how things have been different since Stine left."

The girl grimaced. She couldn't help it. Stine always made her grimace.

She'd thought of the man as Biddle 2. As usual, the sequel hadn't been as good as the original.

When Stine disappeared, so had most of her mother's money.

"You need to start contributing," Barbra said. "I mean *really* contributing, not just as my roper or pickup. I could train a monkey to do that."

"Gee, thanks."

"There are things you can bring to the table, and it's time they were brought."

The girl went very, very still, like an animal in the forest that hears the snap of a twig and thinks *something's coming...*

The hair.

The diet.

This wasn't about braces.

"Here's the play," Barbra said. "There are three thousand orthodontists in town for this convention, and tonight they're all going to be downstairs slapping each other's backs and buying each other drinks. Orthodontists have money, and people trust them to work with their kids. Plus, they like to party. That creates an opportunity."

The girl didn't need to hear any more. She could see the "opportunity," and she knew she should either jump up and scratch her mother's bitch eyes out or run to the bathroom and barf.

Yet she stayed still.

"This is a nice place," she said, and her own words sounded distant to her, almost echoey, as if spoken by someone from the bottom of a well. "They're going to be on the lookout for anything like that. And if we're caught, that's corruption of a minor for you, on top of pandering."

Barbra shook her head. She looked almost proud of her daughter for thinking through the risks like a pro.

Almost.

"It won't be pandering, and we're not going to get caught," Barbra said. "It's not like you'll be sashaying around the lobby in hot pants and a boob tube. You're going to look like a nice, clean-cut dental hygienist from Ohio. That's the beauty of it: the mark won't even know what he's messing with till it's too late. You've always seemed older than your age. You'll pull it off."

"Even if I do, what's the take? Whatever the mark's got on him? A few hundred if we're lucky? It's not worth the risk."

"This is just a practice run. The real play's going to get us a lot more than a few hundred."

And then it all made sense.

Somewhere out there was a man—possibly a man with important responsibilities, probably a man with a high profile in his community, certainly a man with too much money. And undoubtedly a man with a weakness for skinny young blonds.

Barbra couldn't be a skinny young blond anymore, but she could create one. And now she just had to make sure the blond was ready.

The blond wasn't.

"Mom…please…no…," the girl said. And this time it didn't sound like somebody else's voice. This was her, really her, her true self. Not debating anymore. Crying.

"Oh, knock it off," Barbra said. "You've got nothing to worry about. I'll bust in before things go too far. That's the way the play works."

The girl nodded and wiped away her tears even though she knew the truth.

What gives you more leverage: something that happened or something that almost happened?

"All right, then," Barbra said. She stood and headed for the door. "You relax up here for a while. I'm going to go down and see what all the dental hygienists are wearing this year. When I come back, we'll go over the plan."

The girl started crying again the second the door was closed.

THE GIRL had run away twice since Biddle died. The first time, her mother found her within a day. The second time, it took three.

"I hope you like the pigeon drop," her mother told her. "Because we're running it till you've paid back every cent I could've earned when I was out beating the bushes for you. And don't give me that look. You think I'm bad, you just see how you like a pimp. Because that's what you'd end up with quick if I wasn't looking out for you."

And now the girl did have a pimp, more or less, and her mother was right.

She didn't like it.

THE GIRL prowled the seventh floor until she found what she wanted: a room-service tray left in the hall for the maids to clear away.

She took the salt shaker from it, stuffed it in her pocket, and hurried back to her room. Then she poured half the salt in a glass of water, stirred it with a swizzle stick, and turned on the television.

The timing would have to be just right.

An hour later, when she heard her mother at the door, she gave the water another quick stir, drank it all down, then slid the glass under the bed with the salt shaker.

It was agony waiting, but she waited.

Her mother had to see for herself. No fingers.

Barbra stepped into the room.

"Since when do you watch *Guiding Light*?" she said, glancing at the TV screen.

The girl wanted to give it a few more minutes, let the conversation play out naturally, but she couldn't.

"Mom," she croaked. "I've been thinking about tonight, and it... it makes me..."

She bolted from the bed, snatched up a trash can, and filled it with saltwater and half-digested Denny's pancakes.

"Ew," her mother said. "Don't get any of that on the carpet. I don't want the place smelling like Sunday morning in a frat house."

The girl cleaned up the mess, then crawled into bed.

Barbra came over and put her hand on her forehead.

"No fever," she said. "Just nerves."

"Can we put everything off for a while? Maybe come up with something else?"

Barbra mulled it over.

"Sure."

"Thanks, Mom."

"It's probably better that way anyway."

"Yeah?"

Barbra nodded.

"Tomorrow night everyone's going to be drunk, hung over, *and* sleep deprived," she said. "Their beer goggles'll be twice as thick."

THE NEXT morning, the girl announced that she wanted a movie day. To help her relax, she said.

"Sure, fine," Barbra told her. "Do what you've got to. Just be back by nine."

"Thanks."

The girl started toward the door.

"I mean it, though," her mother said. "Be back by nine."

What she really meant was this:

Don't make me come find you.

THE GIRL was back at eight thirty.

"So what'd you see?" Barbra asked.

Barbra almost never asked her daughter what movies she'd seen. She almost never asked her daughter anything.

"*Wild at Heart, Pump Up the Volume, Postcards from the Edge,* and then *Pump Up the Volume* again."

Barbra nodded as if the names meant something to her.

"Fun?"

"It was okay," the girl said. "One of the guys who works at the theater caught me sneaking around."

"Oh? What happened?"

"I talked him into giving me free popcorn."

"With butter?"

"And a Coke."

"That's my girl."

Barbra never said "that's my girl," either. It was a Biddle thing.

"Well," she said, "guess we'd better get you in costume."

An outfit had already been laid out on the bed. White blouse, black pumps, glasses, pinstriped pantsuit with shoulders padded enough for the NFL. Once the girl was dressed, her mother started fussing with her hair.

"If we do this right," she said, "you'll look like a thirty-year-old trying to seem twenty-four instead of a seventeen-year-old trying to seem thirty."

"What if no one...you know...takes the bait?"

"This kind of bait always gets taken. Now let's get some rouge on those cheeks."

Barbra spent fifteen minutes on her daughter's makeup. When she was done, she took a step back and looked the girl over from head to toe.

Her gaze lingered on the eyes, staring hard and deep for a long, long time.

Say it, the girl thought. *Say we don't have to do this. Say you're sorry. Say it, and everything will be okay.*

"You need more mascara," Barbra said.

She turned away to look for the applicator.

THEY WENT downstairs separately and took their positions in the lobby bar: the girl alone at a little table with her convention badge and booklet and fake ID (all supplied by her mother), and Barbra forty feet away, discouraging company with a trough-like bowl of Cobb salad and a copy of *The Watchtower*.

The last thing Barbra had said before the girl left the room—her final advice to a daughter who'd never even held hands with a boy—was this: "Just smile and let the men talk. The booze'll do the rest."

BARBRA WAS right. Orthodontists liked to party. By ten the place was packed with them. Chattering, drinking, laughing, drinking, pairing up, drinking, drinking, drinking.

The girl nursed a gin and tonic that tasted like rubbing alcohol and, for her mother's benefit, tried to look friendly.

She got stares. She got smiles. She got lascivious grins. She got a come-on-over jerk of the head she pretended not to see.

"Is anyone sitting here?"

And there he was, sliding in beside her. Just what Barbra wanted. The catch of the day throwing himself into the net.

He was mature but not too mature. Handsome but not too handsome. Married (to judge by the wedding ring on his finger) but not too married (to judge by his behavior). And, most important of all, he was acting drunk but not too drunk.

He had to be sober enough to get to her room. Sober enough to get himself in trouble. Sober enough to know he was in trouble and do whatever he could to get out of it.

The girl did what her mother told her. She let the man talk. That didn't mean she listened to him, though. She just smiled and looked into his eyes and thought, *I want this over. I want this over.*

More drinks came, and with each sip the man seemed to lean in a little closer.

He snaked an arm around her shoulders.

A few minutes later, his other hand slid under the table.

It wouldn't be long now.

I want this over. I want this over.

They went upstairs.

BARBRA HAD said she'd wait five minutes before bursting into the room. Long enough but not too long.

"What's going on here?" she would shout. "What are you doing to my daughter?"

"D-d-daughter?" the mark would sputter.

And his adrenaline would kick in and his brain would shut off (assuming it was working anyway) and he'd shed his money like a snake shedding its skin, eager to slither off under a rock and never look back. And the girl would have gained a little experience with men without losing anything in the process.

That was the plan. That was the *promise*. And the girl knew it would be broken.

How long would it be before the door finally opened? Ten minutes? Fifteen? Twenty? Every extra second that passed would be a brick the girl would carry forever. Another pound of hate weighing her down.

So when the door opened again just *three* minutes after it had closed, the girl jumped up, startled.

"Mom?" she blurted out.

Barbra stalked into the room, glaring past her.

"What's going on here? What are you doing with my daughter?" she said.

She couldn't say "what are you doing *to* my daughter" because it was obvious nothing was being done.

The girl and the man had been on the bed together, not in it. Sitting silently side by side as they waited.

"Barbra Harper," the man said now, "you're under arrest for criminal conspiracy, pandering, and the corruption of a minor. You have the right to remain silent."

Barbra whirled around and yanked open the door.

Another man stood just outside, blocking her.

Another cop.

"Anything you say or do can and will be used against you in a court of law," said the first cop—the one who'd been sitting with the girl at the bar and in the room. The one they'd eventually taken her to that afternoon when she'd walked into the police station and said "I'd like to report a crime."

Barbra turned toward him again.

"You have the right to an attorney," he said. "If you cannot afford an attorney—"

Barbra focused on the girl standing beside him.

"What have you done?" she said. "*What have you done?*"

"I'm sorry, Mom! I…I thought you were going to…that you wouldn't…"

The girl buried her face in her hands and wept.

When she looked up again, her mother and the other cop were gone.

She never saw her mother again. Not alive, anyway.

BACK AT the police station, there were forms to fill out. They'd started some that afternoon, but things had moved forward now, weren't just hypothetical, and that meant more paperwork.

Some of the forms were for the social worker who'd be placing the girl in emergency foster care.

"Name?" the social worker asked.

The girl wiped her eyes dry and thought for a long, long time.

"Good question," she said.

LE STELLE
LES ETOILES **XVII** THE STARS
LA ESTRELLA

DER STERN DE STER

It's midnight at the oasis, and after a long, hard, thirsty journey—so long, hard, and thirsty our heroine somehow lost all her clothes—there's finally water to spare. Our weary traveler even has enough left over to give the lawn a spritz now that her own thirst is quenched. Needs are met, good deeds are done, peace reigns. Enjoy it while you can, girlfriend!

Miss Chance, *Infinite Roads to Knowing*

"I was in a foster home for two days before I ran away," I said. "I don't know what happened with the charges against Mom. I assume they were dropped because I wasn't around to testify. I don't know. I never looked it up, and my mother never tracked me down. She got the message. She was better off without me. That's why I was so surprised when she left me the White Magic Five & Dime. After what I did to get away from her…well, a forgiving heart wasn't among her virtues. If she had any."

Clarice hadn't said a thing since I'd started my story, and she seemed in no hurry to say anything now, so we drove in silence for a while. All I could see ahead were a starry sky and our headlights on the road. The desert around us had disappeared into nighttime darkness. We could have been driving through a black hole.

"What did you do next?" Clarice finally asked. "After you ran off?"

It seemed to be a question she'd thought about a lot.

You run away…and then what?

"I bounced around, got into trouble, wriggled out of it. Looked for a boring life to bury myself in. Tried to stay honest, play nice. I guess I eventually got close. Kinda-sorta."

I looked over at Clarice. Her eyes were glittering moistly in the dashboard's dull glow.

"My mother wanted you to do the same thing, didn't she?" I said. "She wanted to use you as bait to trap a man. That's why you told her you're not a whore."

Clarice nodded.

"It wasn't as bad as with you, though," she said. "There was nothing in person. It was just Web stuff. Old pervs online. At first it was her stringing a few along, getting money out of them. But then she wanted me to help 'expand the operation,' 'cater to different tastes.' I tried it once, on my laptop, with her standing on the other side of the screen watching. Like, *directing*. It was awful. I couldn't believe she'd ask me to do something like that. And then she kept pushing me to do it again and again…"

Clarice turned away and put her head against the window glass. Though she'd been fighting it, she was starting to cry.

"I'm sorry she did that to you, Clarice," I said. "So, so sorry. It's obvious she was like a mother to you."

I reached out to touch her gently, cautiously on the shoulder. But then she was suddenly whipping around to face me again, her tear-streaked face full of frustration and fury, and I snatched my hand back.

"Christ, Alanis—how can you be so smart and still be so dense?" the girl raged. "Athena wasn't *like* a mother to me! She *was* my mother!"

I hit the brakes.

"Whoooooaaaaaaaaaaaahhhhhh!" Clarice cried as we skidded to a stop.

Fortunately, the road was deserted, so no one slammed into us from behind.

I eased the car onto the gravel by the side of the road, then shut it off and opened my door.

The overhead light came on.

"You don't believe me?" Clarice said.

I was staring at her. Studying her face in the dim light.

Obviously the skin and hair were different. The shape of the face and the nose, too. But there was something about her eyes and ears and neck...

"Get out of the car," I said.

"What?"

"Come on. Out."

I was already swiveling around and springing from my seat.

"Alanis, I'm not lying!"

I walked quickly around the hood to ~~Alanis's~~ Clarice's side of the car. The girl was slowly, reluctantly standing up.

I wrapped my arms around her.

She was stiff, wary at first. Maybe she thought I was trying to pick her up and throw her.

She figured out I wasn't when I started sobbing.

She hugged me back. She cried with me, too.

So there I was, in my second hug of the day. A tearful one under the stars this time. Not my style, I would've thought.

But you know what? Who needs style?

I had a sister.

"I'm an idiot," I said. "I can't believe I didn't see it."

We were on our way to Berdache again. After the initial shock wore off, I could trust myself to not drive us into a canyon.

"You just met me," Clarice said. "There are people I've known for years who never guessed."

"Why keep it a secret?"

"Athena used to say she had to 'maintain her womanly allure' and a kid would kill that. But I always assumed the black thing was a big part of it. She never thought about anything but money money money, and some of the people she was trying to cozy up to around here were pretty racist. And it's not like being a mother was a big deal to her anyway. It was more like…I don't know…"

"You were just a prop for her cons?"

"Yeah. That's it exactly. It wasn't as bad after we moved here. She didn't really need me once the store took off, so I could actually go to school and make real friends and have my own life. Then she had to start in with the online stuff…and then she was dead."

"Where's your father?"

"Beats me. You may as well ask *who's* my father 'cuz I don't know that either. I think I've seen him, though. I found old pictures of some guy stuck in Athena's Bible. I used to pull them out when she wasn't around and stare and stare and stare at him. He was always smiling. He looked happy. He looked nice."

"He was, in his own weird way," I started to say. "But that's not your dad."

I stopped myself.

She thought she'd seen her father's face, and it was a kind one. Why take that away from her? It was more than I ever had.

"Well," I said instead, "no wonder you weren't thrilled when I showed up. You don't even know I exist, then I roll into town and scoop up everything Mom had to give. Why didn't you tell me who you really were?"

"I didn't trust you. Even if you were Athena's daughter—and I wasn't sure at first if you were—that might just make you another Athena. I missed her and I was torn up about what happened to her, but I didn't need *that*. So I figured I'd be better off just waiting till you were gone."

"Makes sense. But I hope you see now that I'm not Athena. Not the evil parts, anyway. Well...not all of them."

"Sure," Clarice said.

She didn't sound entirely convinced.

"Hey, I hug people," I said. "And I use my superpowers for good."

I didn't sound entirely convinced.

I was going to have to prove it to both of us.

We traded mommy war stories for a while. Mine I'd never told anyone before. Who could've heard them without thinking *my god, what a messed-up weirdo*? While looking at *me*.

With Clarice it was different. She told me about her screwed-up childhood, I told her about mine, and instead of horror on her face I saw something like relief.

At last! she seemed to be thinking. *A freak just like me!*

I know that's what *I* was thinking.

"There's something I should show you," Clarice said when we were upstairs again at the Five & Dime.

She went to the refrigerator, dug around in the freezer, and pulled out a large plastic container. When she brought it to the counter, I saw that there was a strip of masking tape on the lid. One word was written on it: *MEATLOAF*.

I groaned.

My mother was not the meatloaf-making type, and Clarice was not the meatloaf-eating type.

Whatever really was in there, I should've found it already.

When Clarice took off the lid, I was expecting to see a bunch of frozen jewelry. Instead there was a big wad of tinfoil. Clarice peeled it back to reveal a stack of hundred-dollar bills.

"We found it five months ago," she said.

"We?"

Clarice grinned sheepishly. "Ceecee likes meatloaf."

"Lucky for us. Otherwise someone might have thrown out ten grand."

"Twenty—but it used to be forty. It dropped five thousand a month every month until a few weeks ago."

"You sure were keeping a close eye on the meatloaf."

"I used to look at it and dream…"

"You have amazing willpower. When I was your age, I would've done more than dream."

"Oh, I will, too. I've just been waiting for you to go away."

"So why are you showing it to me now?"

"It seemed like…you know." Clarice shrugged, embarrassed by what she was about to say. "A clue."

"It's more than that."

"Yeah?"

"Yeah. It's really good timing."

I helped myself to a quarter of the stack.

"Hey!"

"Sorry," I said. "I've got some shopping to do."

"What are you talking about? There's nothing open but the 7-Eleven."

"Exactly. Once I get going on those jalapeño cream cheese taquitos, I just can't stop."

Clarice glared at me, looking betrayed.

"Look," I said, "thanks for showing me the money. I do think it might be important, and I do need to take some of it right now. But I'll pay you back, I promise. As far as I'm concerned, the meatloaf's all yours. Okay?"

Clarice narrowed her eyes, then sighed and nodded.

"Okay."

"Good. Now, I'm going to be gone for a while. All night, maybe. And I don't think you should be here by yourself. Any chance you could go to Ceecee's?"

Clarice shook her head. "Her parents don't like me anymore. I think their lesbian gaydar's better than yours."

"Do you have any other friends you could stay with?"

"I could call around. Why, though? You weren't worried the last couple nights."

"Actually, I was. It's just that you were one of the things I was worried about. Now I'm gonna be worried *for* you."

"Well, thanks, but I've been doing okay on my own so far."

"That was before I showed up. If you're going to stay, do me a favor: make sure all the doors and windows are locked, and look under the mattress on Mom's bed."

A strange chill ran through me—strange because it actually felt warm.

On Mom's bed, I'd said. For the first time, I didn't mean *my* mom. I meant *our* mom.

251

"I was going to get the gun anyway," Clarice said. "It might not be real, but it's better than nothing."

"You know about that?"

"Sure. I was spying when that crazy old guy left it here last night. Sorry I didn't call the cops or try to help you, but…well, I was worried about *you*."

"And how did you know where I'd hidden the air gun?"

"Hey, if you're going to search my room, it's only fair for me to search yours."

Touché. Obviously I needed to brush up on my stealth snooping skills.

"I know you've been playing Nancy Hardy," Clarice said. "Why? Don't you think Logan can catch the murderer?"

"It's Nancy *Drew*. And I think Detective Logan is a nice man and a fine police officer."

"That doesn't answer my question."

"It's not supposed to."

"Come on, Alanis. I want to help."

I took in a deep breath.

It was tempting. It might actually be fun—in an unwholesome, totally irresponsible way.

And it would still be wrong. I kept insisting I was not Mom. Here was another chance to prove it: I wouldn't put a teenage girl in danger.

"Sorry," I said. "Why don't we bake cookies together sometime instead?"

Clarice looked like she wanted to flip me the bird.

In a sisterly way, though.

I wasn't lying about shopping, only about where I was going to do it.

I drove to Phoenix. Certain things are easier to find in a bigger town, and I didn't want to be window-shopping where I might bump into Josh Logan or anyone else who might recognize me.

My shopping list looked like this:

1. Meth

2. A stolen handgun

3. Bullets

4. 2% milk

All Clarice had in the fridge was skim. Bleah.

Once I hit Phoenix, it took me two hours to get the meth and fifteen minutes to get the gun and bullets. (Meth dealers and stolen guns go together like *rama-lama-lama-ka-dinga-da-dinga-dong*.) The milk I picked up at an all-night truck stop on the way back to Berdache. On a whim, I bought a couple bumper stickers there, too.

Then I drove to the home of William and Marsha Riggs. Thirty minutes after that, I was back in the apartment over the White Magic Five & Dime. Clarice was sound asleep. Soon I was, too.

I slept well. But not long.

William Riggs left his house and walked out to his red Camaro at 8:23 AM. I know because I was watching from half a block away with a lukewarm cup of 7-Eleven coffee to keep me awake.

His wife did not come outside with him for a kiss goodbye. I guess she was getting ready for another busy day of cowering in the house.

It was my first time seeing Riggs in person, and he didn't let me down. The man even walked like a dick. Quick, short-strided strut, feet and thighs turned out slightly, head back.

He went straight to the driver's-side door, yanked it open, and slid in behind the wheel. Like anyone would. Why would you walk around your car first thing in the morning? Why would you inspect it?

Why would you notice the busted headlight?

Why would you notice the broken taillight?

A policeman would, though. I'd made sure of that.

I'M NOT DRUNK, I JUST DRIVE LIKE THIS, one of Riggs's new bumper stickers said.

BAD COP, said the other. *NO DONUT*.

He didn't notice those, either.

He was halfway to his job peddling timeshares at the Oak Creek Golf Resort when the highway patrol pulled him over.

So much the better. Local PD might cut you slack because you're from around the corner, but not a state trooper. There would be no friendly warning. It'd be straight to license and registration.

I couldn't pull over to watch there on the highway, so I had to keep driving and miss the show. Like Riggs, I was on my way to Sedona, the difference being I was going to get there.

About two minutes after leaving Riggs behind, I heard the siren. Another highway patrol cruiser went screaming past, headed in the opposite direction.

I smiled.

Marsha Riggs was going to get a little break from her husband. Maybe a long break, though I doubted if the charges would stick. Still, when a guy opens his glove compartment and a bag of crystal meth falls out, he tends to spend a little time behind bars. More if there's a lighter, a pipe, and a gun jammed in with the owner's manual.

I hoped Marsha would use her time wisely. When I had a moment, I'd drop by and check on her. Maybe do another reading, see what the cards said. I had a feeling I knew.

There was no time for that just now, though. I had a new shopping list.

1. Jewelry

2. A camcorder

3. A killer

THANK GOD for tacky. If it had been tasteful, I never would've spotted it.

"An emerald as big as a gumdrop surrounded by the cutest little baby diamonds mounted in gold." That's how Lucia Castellanos had described her favorite ring. My mother had taken it to be cleansed of an evil spirit.

You wouldn't think it from the looks of the place, but apparently Jones Pawn & Loan in Flagstaff, Arizona, was a great place for cleansing. Because that's where I found the ring (after unproductive stops at the Westside Gold and Jewelry Exchange in Sedona and the Fourth Street Pawn Shop in Berdache).

"You Jones?" I asked the man behind the counter.

He didn't look like a Jones. He looked a Samoan Michelin Man with clothes but without the smile.

"Jones is gone. I own the place now."

"All right. I've got a question for you, Mr.—?"

"Smith."

"Right. Mr. Smith." I tapped the display case glass just above the ring. "Where'd this come from?"

"We don't release that information."

"It's hot."

"Is it yours?"

"No."

"You a cop?"

"No."

"Insurance investigator?"

"No."

Mr. Smith shrugged. "Then why do you give a shit?"

It was obvious he didn't.

I thought of the games I could play. Give me half a week and *I'd* own the place.

I was feeling magnanimous, though. And impatient.

I'd added almost two hundred miles to my rental car in the last day. Why rack up even ten feet more than I had to?

"Tell you what," I said. "I'll buy that ring and anything else that ever came in here from the same seller—as marked, no haggling—if you'll just answer one question to my satisfaction."

Mr. Smith either took some time to think about it or fell asleep with his eyes open.

"Down payment first," he said when he decided/woke up.

I pulled out my wallet and counted out three hundred dollars of Clarice's meatloaf money. It felt like normal cash now. (When I'd bought the meth the night before, the dealer had laughed and rubbed a bill against his face and said, "Damn, this is so *cold*. Who'd you blow to get it? Frosty the Snowman?")

Mr. Smith scooped up the bills and lumbered off toward the back of the store.

"I'll check our records."

He didn't have to ask what I wanted to know.

"Lady named Joan Evans brought it in," he said when he came back. "Lives in Sedona, according to her driver's license."

"Pretty, skinny lady in her late fifties?"

Mr. Smith nodded.

"So," he said, "that to your satisfaction?"

It wasn't. William Riggs of Berdache—now that would have been satisfying. Ditto Anthony Grandi of same or Billy Joe Scumbag of Up the Street. But Joan Evans of Sedona, aka Mom with a fake ID, was a dead-end as dead as they come. But at least I wasn't running into this one empty-handed.

"Pull out everything she sold you. I'll take it all," I said. "Now let's talk about computers and camcorders…"

THE COMPUTER-AND-CAMCORDER conversation was brief. He didn't have any. So I only walked out with the jewelry—half the baubles and beads in the place. I also walked out without nearly five thousand dollars I'd walked in with.

Did Mr. Smith sell me a bunch of marked-up crap that hadn't really come in via my mom? Probably. But did he throw in everything she'd brought him, too? Undoubtedly.

Stolen property on his shelves was obviously fine. Stolen property that someone could actually trace to his store, not so much. He'd be glad to be rid of it—and to have my money.

"It's not that being good is so hard," Biddle used to say. "It's just so damn *expensive*."

To my surprise, though, there was no sticker shock. In fact, I was actually looking forward to giving my new jewelry away.

EASIER SAID than done, it turned out. When I dropped by the Verde River Vista Senior Residences, I was informed that Lucia Castellanos was no longer accepting visitors.

It was my own fault. The day before, I'd tried to shake up her son, Victor, to see how he'd react. Now I knew: he'd put his mom in solitary just to keep me away from her.

The woman in the front office looked at me like I was the Angel of Death trying to sneak my way in behind an FTD bouquet. My cover was blown.

"What a shame," I said. "I'll just leave a note then. Do you have an envelope and a piece of paper I could use?"

I went out to the car to write my message.

> *Dear Lucia,*
> *The cleansing is complete! Ask your son when*
> *I can come by to drop everything off.*
> *Sincerely,*
> *Alanis*

I sealed the note in the envelope and took it inside.

In with it was an emerald the size of a gumdrop surrounded by baby diamonds mounted in gold.

I HAD no trouble getting into the Dry Creek Assisted Living Community to see Ken Meldon. Security (just like cleanliness, sunlight, and cheer) didn't seem to be a big priority there. I didn't see dingoes dragging off any of the residents, but it wouldn't have been a shock.

Meldon seemed only mildly surprised to see me. His pleasure was even milder—nonexistent even.

"Good news," I said to him. "I found some jewelry. Want to see if you recognize anything?"

I upended the bag Mr. Smith had given me. (Nothing says class like walking out of a pawn shop with five thousand dollars' worth of jewelry in a plastic bag that had probably held Fritos and a Coors tall boy the day before.) Rings, bracelets, necklaces, pearls, pendants, and brooches spilled out onto Meldon's narrow bed.

The old man stooped in over the booty and pawed through it slowly with gnarled, trembling hands.

"I don't know. I can never tell this junk apart. Why women make such a fuss over a bunch of…wait."

He lifted up a wide silver ring with a single diamond in the setting.

"I'll be damned. This is it."

"That's your wife's ring? The one you gave Athena?"

"Yeah."

Meldon shuffled to a chair in the corner. The room was the size of a luxurious linen closet, so it only took him four or five hours to get there.

He slumped into the seat with a sigh, eyes still locked on the ring.

"You said you gave my mom all kinds of jewelry." I waved a hand at the bed. "Don't you want to look for the rest?"

"Nah. I don't give a crap about any of that anymore. I just want this."

He was turning the ring this way and that, as if enchanted by the diamond's sparkles. The room was so dimly lit there weren't any, though. He may as well have been admiring a Cocoa Puff.

"We had our troubles, Judith and me. Used to go round and round. She even called the cops on me once or twice." Meldon grunted out a gruff chuckle. "But dammit…I do miss her."

I nodded knowingly.

I waited for a thank you.

I kept nodding.

I kept waiting.

Meldon just mooned over his ring.

"Well," I finally said, "I suppose my work here is done."

I waited some more. Then I gathered up the jewelry and started to leave.

"Wait," the old man said when I reached the door.

I turned back to face him.

"You still got that air gun I left at your mom's the other night?"

"Yeah."

"Good," Meldon said. "Do me a favor and go shoot some cats."

BIDDLE WOULD have laughed. Mom would have said, "What did you expect? A parade?"

But I didn't need Lucia Castellanos or Ken Meldon to thank me. I didn't care if one couldn't and the other wouldn't.

I was the ring fairy. And it felt good.

LA LUNA
LA LUNE XVIII THE MOON
LA LUNA

DER MOND DE MAAN

Tell me if you've heard this one before: Two dogs and a lob-ster walk into a bar. "Get me," the bartender says, "I'm givin' out wings!" So the lobster turns into a stack of pancakes and everyone has breakfast. BA-DA BING!

What's that? You don't get it? That's okay—you're not supposed to when the Moon card comes up. It's time to disconnect from rationality and plug into your id and your instincts. Dreams, symbols, unconscious desires, your untapped psychic self—all will be trying to assert them-selves. Try too hard to "get it" and the joke will be on you.

Miss Chance, *Infinite Roads to Knowing*

I WRAPPED the jewelry bag in tinfoil, put it in a Ziploc, labeled it *VEAL PARMESAN* with masking tape and a Sharpie and stuck it in Mom's freezer behind a wall of Hot Pockets. Then I pulled out the *MEATLOAF* and replaced the five thousand dollars I'd borrowed with fresh, unfrozen money I'd just withdrawn from the bank.

As I closed the freezer door, the phone in the White Magic Five & Dime began to ring. I hurried downstairs to get it. It had been an entire day since anyone had called to threaten me, and I was feeling neglected.

The caller ID said DONALD FISK. I didn't recognize the name. Fine. Two of the three leads Logan had given me were played out anyway, and I didn't have high hopes for Victor Castellanos as a suspect. Kids might assume their gym teacher's capable of cold-blooded murder, but I didn't think this one was. Although what I based that on I couldn't say. Maybe I just liked the way he filled out a track suit.

I picked up the phone.

"The White Magic Five & Dime, now under new management. Ask about our two-for-the-price-of-one exorcisms."

"Hi," a woman said. "Is this Alanis?"

"Yes."

"I wanted to call up and thank you. Everything you told me was right on the money. You can't believe what's happened to me the last two days!"

I couldn't imagine it, either. Because I had no idea who I was talking to.

"Oh?" I said.

"Oh yeah! I confronted Donald just like you told me to, and he admitted everything! Not just about Julia Luchetti but about how he'd been siphoning money off for their little fling. *I'd* been going broke because *they'd* been going to the Quality Suites three times a week!"

Ahhh. That hussy Julia Luchetti. Now I remembered the voice.

It was my first customer calling back. The woman I'd done a reading for a few days before—Alice. (You wouldn't get far in my old profession if you couldn't remember names—both your marks' and all the ones you've come up with for yourself.)

"That's awful, Alice," I said. "I'm so sorry to find out I was right."

"That's not the half of it. I got in touch with the Llama and Alpaca Association like I said I would, and you'll never guess what they told me."

I had a feeling she was right about that.

"Oh?" I said again.

"The biggest exotic animal breeder in central Arizona died last week. Got knocked over in one of his pens, and a camel stepped on his head. Now his family's desperate to sell off over five hundred medium-wooled curaca llamas! Isn't that great?"

"I'm thrilled."

"I know! The timing's amazing. If I'd called a week later, I'd have missed out. But as it is, I had just enough money left to scalp the poor bastards for the whole herd. Now the llamas are on their way to my ranch—and Donald's on his way out. My whole life's turning around, all because I talked to you!"

"I don't think I should get *all* the credit."

"But you should, you should! That reading was a revelation. When can I come back for another?"

"Another?"

"Of course! Now I have to decide if I'm going to tell Jack Luchetti the whole sick story or just let Donald and Julia stew in their own juices for a while."

"Hmm. That is a dilemma, isn't it?"

We made an appointment for Friday.

I STARTED to walk to the front of the White Magic Five & Dime. I was going to turn on the neon sign and lure in more customer/suspects.

I stopped halfway up the hall.

My reading for Alice Fisk hadn't accomplished anything—not for me, anyway. Alice hadn't killed my mother. Donald Fisk and Jack and Julia Luchetti hadn't either. And Mom hadn't ripped any of them off. What were the odds the next person to walk through the door would be any different?

I gave it a million to one. Maybe a gazillion. And who'd take that bet?

So why would I waste my time on another reading for Alice or anyone else? Why would I…?

I stopped and thought about it, just to be sure.

Yes. Yes, it was true.

Why would I *look forward to it*?

Easy money? A con artist's professional pride? A cheap laugh at someone else's expense?

It didn't feel like any of that. So what was it?

I was standing next to the reading room. The tarot cards were still on the table from my session with Marsha Riggs the day before.

"What are *you* looking at?" I said to them.

They didn't reply. Punks.

I gathered up the deck and started shuffling it just to show who was boss. As I worked cards in and out, out and in, a question came to mind. A good one.

"What am I really doing here?"

I put the deck down and started to turn away.

Then I turned back, whipped off the top card, and flipped it over.

Oh. Well. There you go. My question was answered.

What was I doing?

I was making Satanic plates for the Franklin Mint.

Duh. Obviously. Ask a stupid question…

It was weird, though. As much as I wanted to sneer and stomp off or go do something useful (whatever that might be), I kept standing there staring at the card.

I've never been big on arts and crafts, so pounding out pentagrams didn't strike me as a ton of fun. But the plate-making guy seemed okay with it. More than that. He seemed *content* somehow.

He was practicing a craft; using his skills to create, to build something. And maybe that made him happy.

So if this was supposed to be me, what was the craft? Meddling in police investigations? Finding long-lost relatives? Delivering rings to old folks' homes?

Reading tarot cards?

Ha. I didn't even believe in tarot cards.

Right?

"So, Josette—what do you think of the Eight of Pentacles?"

Josette Berg turned toward me and laughed. She hadn't even noticed me cross the street and come into the House of Arcana. I'd waited not particularly patiently while she finished her conversation with a tourist who didn't know the difference between a healing crystal and the kind you find in Folger's coffee. My question had been my hello.

"I hope you don't have a customer waiting over in the White Magic Five & Dime for an answer," she said.

"No. It's for me. I mean, it's just something I've been wondering about. Interpretation-wise. How do you read it?"

"Well, it depends on the context, of course. In general, though…"

Josette closed her eyes. It seemed like a strange time to start meditating, but you can never tell with New Agey types.

"You see a craftsman honing his skills," she said. She was picturing the card. "He's not in his shop, though. He's working outside—in the world—so there's a connection to something larger than himself. Beyond him, in the distance, is a doorway. A building. A town. There's a community waiting for what he makes. His skills have a purpose. They're not an end in and of themselves. There are people the craftsman can serve, and those people will, in turn, support him."

Josette opened her eyes.

"Wow. And here I was thinking it was about how to make a Frisbee," I said.

That wow kept echoing in my head, though.

Wow wow wow wow.

It must have been so loud even Josette could hear it.

She cocked her head, and her smile turned pensive, concerned.

"Is everything all right, Alanis?"

"Oh yeah. I'm fine. I've just been busy. So many arrangements to make, you know?"

"Is there going to be a service for your mother?"

"We had one yesterday, actually. Very informal, very small. Immediate family only."

"I didn't know you had more family here."

"Me neither. Well, I can see you're busy…" I flapped a hand at the throng of customers clogging the aisles. (There were two.) "So I'll toddle along. Thanks for the pearls of wisdom."

"Anytime. I hope the tapes help."

I was already halfway to the door.

I stopped and came back.

"Excuse me?"

Josette looked chagrined, as if she already regretted what she'd said.

"I said, I hope the tapes help. Detective Logan didn't mention them to you? I know you and he have been…staying in touch."

The pause before "staying in touch" was so pregnant I could have thrown it a baby shower.

Great. Let a guy buy you lunch at a French joint and everyone in town assumes something's going on. And maybe a little teeny-weeny something was or could or might, but still. The man was investigating my mother's murder. Don't get sick ideas, people! Let me mourn…for a day or two.

I pushed all that aside.

"Logan told you about the tapes?"

"No, I told him about them. They're mine, after all."

"I'm sorry…which tapes are we talking about?"

Josette turned to point at a camera mounted near the ceiling in a far corner of the store.

"The ones from my security camera. Which tapes did you think I meant?"

"The ones from my mother's crystal ball," I could've said if I'd felt like explaining, which I didn't.

"Just some of my mom's old cassettes," I said instead. "Neil Diamond, Supertramp. It doesn't matter. What do your tapes have to do with me?"

"It's what's on them. They don't just show my store. The camera's pointed at the display window."

Josette traced an invisible line from the camera to the window and the street beyond.

"You can see the White Magic Five & Dime on the tapes," I said.

"Well, the sidewalk out front and part of the door. It's pretty blurry, though."

"Still—that means you have a record of the comings and goings at my mom's place."

"Exactly. A few tapes' worth, anyway. That's why Detective Logan's going through what I've got. He's hoping the mur—uh, the person he's looking for will be on them."

"But I thought the *murderer* broke in through a back window."

Josette shrugged. "Maybe he did some sneaking around first. You know—'casing the joint.' Looking for other ways in. Speaking of which…"

Josette was peering past me, out the front window.

Across the street, a man was trying to get into my mother's store.

"Officer, I'd like to report a crime," I said as I walked up to the White Magic Five & Dime.

Detective Logan turned around to face me.

I'd recognized him right away, even from behind.

He had a highly recognizable behind.

"Yes?" he said.

"Attempted breaking and entering."

"Can you describe the suspect?"

I looked Logan up and down. "Tall. Dark hair. Conservative clothes. The kind of face that drives baristas wild."

"I'll put out an APB." Logan waggled his thumb at the door behind him. "I thought you'd be open for business. You did say you were going to try running the place for a while. I knocked, but when no one came to the door…"

"You got worried? That's sweet. I was just talking shop with Josette Berg."

"Oh yeah? Comparing notes on reading tea leaves?"

"No. Chicken entrails. I couldn't remember if gizzards represent your finances or your love life."

"I hope they never have anything to do with *my* love life."

"Don't knock it till you've tried it." I furrowed my brow and scratched my head. "I'm not even sure what I meant by that."

The banter had been flying by too fast even for me.

"So what's up, Detective?" I said. "Got some news?"

"No and yes. Care to discuss it over an early dinner?"

"All right."

"Great." Logan grinned. "I know a little place that does great chicken gizzards."

WE ENDED up at Café Vortex again.

"I don't see gizzards on the menu," I said.

"I think it's this thing called escargot."

"Got it."

I ordered onion soup and the tarte du jour. Logan ordered the escargot.

I was impressed. I'd met a few cops who were adventurous enough to eat snails, but not many. For most, French cuisine begins and ends with freedom fries.

"I can only assume you haven't cracked the case or you would've mentioned it before they brought the breadsticks," I said.

"You assume right, but I am making progress. And I still don't need help, Alanis."

I looked around the restaurant with wide eyes.

"Jinkies," I said. "I suddenly have the strongest feeling of déjà vu. As if I'd been here before having the same conversation…"

"I checked in with the Fourth Street Pawn Shop a little while ago. I had some questions related to another case. And do you know what the manager said to me?"

"He'd give you twenty dollars for that watch?"

"He wanted to know why I hadn't sent my new partner over— the one who'd come in that morning. He preferred to deal with her from now on. She was a lot cuter than me."

"It's nice to know pawn shop managers find me attractive. I never said I was a cop, though."

"Because you didn't have to. He assumed you were, so you let him."

"It's illegal to let people make an *ass* out of *u* and *me*?"

"No. But it is dumb."

"So dumb the guy answered my questions and I could move on to the next place and that's where I found a bunch of jewelry my mom was *wink wink* 'cleansing' for her clients. And I was able to buy the stuff back and start returning it this afternoon."

"Hey, that's great. I'm happy for you. You're a regular Robin Hood. Now would you please stop?"

"Don't you even want to know where I found the jewelry?"

Logan sighed. "Where did you find the jewelry?"

"Jones Pawn & Loan in Flagstaff. I assume you already checked there for the electronics that were stolen from my mother?"

"Of course I checked there. Days ago. Now may I ask a question that you haven't put in my mouth for me?"

I mulled it over.

"I shall allow it," I pronounced.

"Where were you last night?"

"Are you asking me as a policeman or the guy taking me out to dinner at a swanky French restaurant?"

"Would it make a difference?"

"No. I was at Mom's place, of course. What's up? Did someone steal the Pink Panther diamond again?"

Logan looked deeply puzzled.

Sometimes I forget that not everyone had a sociopath for a mom and a television for a dad.

"Why do you ask?" I said.

"This morning William Riggs was arrested for possession of a controlled substance, resisting arrest, and aggravated assault on a peace officer."

"Wait—what about the concealed weapon?" I wanted to ask.

But I let it go. This was Arizona. Maybe anything less than a bazooka didn't count.

I rolled my eyes up and tapped a finger against my chin.

"William Riggs...William Riggs...William Riggs. Why does that name ring a bell? Say! He was one of the guys on that list you gave me, wasn't he? Had some kind of bug up his butt about Mom?"

Logan glowered at me.

"What a coincidence," I went on. "Does he have any priors? Assault, drunk and disorderly, that kind of thing?"

"He says he was framed."

"For drunk and disorderly?"

"For the drugs."

"Why would anyone do that?"

"I don't know. They're crazy?"

"Hmm. I can't say that's very convincing, as conspiracy theories go. No, it's more likely the guy's just hopped up on goofballs. Thanks for the heads-up. I feel safer knowing he'll be off the streets for a good long time."

"We also got a call from Victor Castellanos yesterday."

I started tapping my chin again. "Victor Castellanos…"

Logan's scowl deepened.

"Oh yeah," I said. "Him."

"He said you've been harassing him and his mother."

"If a few friendly visits constitute harassment in your jurisdiction, then I'm guilty as charged. Ooo—I think that lady at the other table just smiled at me. Help, officer! I'm being harassed!"

"You don't want to mess with Castellanos, Alanis."

"What's he going to do? Make me run twenty laps around the gym?"

"A few months back, he got into a big blow-up with the owner of one of the nursing homes in town. Claimed they hadn't been taking proper care of his mother—let con artists in to swindle her and the like."

"Fascinating. Do go on."

"The nursing-home guy ended up with a broken collarbone."

Fascinating indeed.

"And Castellanos is still teaching at the high school?" I said.

"No charges were filed. The guy claimed he just tripped and fell."

"On his collarbone."

Logan nodded.

"During a big blow-up."

Logan kept nodding.

"Well, lucky for him," I said. "If Castellanos had assaulted him, it could have led to some very, very bad publicity. Maybe even an investigation of his business practices."

"Oh, that's happening anyway. But it's not the point."

"And the point *is*…what? Don't let Victor Castellanos near my collarbone?"

"Yes, Alanis. That is the goddamn point. I was stupid enough to give you three names, and two of them have turned out to be trouble one way or another."

Actually it was three for three, but I didn't feel like mentioning Ken Meldon's pop-in with a souped-up BB gun.

"You won't be getting any more help from me," Logan said. "If you bring something nasty down on yourself, you're on your own."

"You think that's anything new for me?" I snapped back.

I showed him how strong and self-reliant I am by snatching up a breadstick and snapping it in two with my bare hands.

Before I could take a big, savage bite and *really* prove how tough I am, Logan reached out and gently put a hand over one of mine.

"Look, Alanis," he said. "I don't really know you. You're so cagey I don't even know if you're knowable, if that makes any sense. But I know I like you, and I'm worried about you. Your mother just died and you're working through some pretty complicated feelings and I think that's got you so confused you can't even see how reckless you're being. You've told me you're here to make amends, but all I really see you doing is stirring up trouble—mostly for yourself. You've already had one complete stranger threaten your life. Do you really want to take that to the next level? I mean, I hate to say it, but you went to the morgue yesterday, didn't you? You saw what some-one did…"

I started to pull my hand away.

Logan clamped down hard.

"I'm not asking this as a cop," he said. "I'm asking it as the guy sitting next to you in the swanky French restaurant. Will you back off, Alanis? Please?"

And then he let go.

I thought about lifting my hand up again and taking that big bite out of my breadstick. Defiantly, Bugs Bunny-chomping-on-a-carrot style.

Instead I just dropped the two halves onto the table.

I don't even like breadsticks. Who enjoys edible pencils?

"It'd be easy to tell you yes," I said. "You're asking so nicely, and I appreciate that. Truly. But it'd be a lie. I'm closing in on something—a few somethings, it feels like—and I'm not going to give up now. For instance: five thousand dollars in cash was disappearing from my mother's place each month. That's not just a run of bad luck at the bingo hall. I'm thinking someone was shaking her down. Why don't you throw that at Grandi and see if he blinks? And another for instance: I bought back more jewelry this afternoon than Ken Meldon and Victor Castellanos's mom can account for. There are a lot more disgruntled customers out there than the three you know of, and I'm going to keep looking for them. So, no. I'm sorry. Stopping isn't an option."

When I was done, Logan didn't seem angry or disappointed. He just looked very, very tired.

Our waiter swooped in and slid a plate of escargot under his nose.

"Hey, look—your chicken entrails," I said. "What do you see in your future, O wise one?"

276

Logan picked up a fork and gave one of the glistening shells a glum tap.

"Snails," he said.

We cheered up after that. No one was trying to get anything out of anyone anymore. Not information, not cooperation, not a concession. We could just enjoy the food (or not, in Logan's case—he'd been trying to impress me with his order) and the company.

It was very date-like, and I enjoyed it, which was rare for me and date-like experiences. Most of mine had felt like con jobs.

Don't say the wrong thing. Stay in character. Convince him you're normal.

About fifteen minutes into the actual meal, just as I gave in and traded what was left of my tarte in exchange for a bunch of dead mollusks I didn't really want, Logan put a hand over his heart and said, "I'm vibrating."

"Are you declaring your love or having a heart attack?"

"Neither."

He reached inside his jacket and pulled out his BlackBerry.

"Sorry. I've gotta take this," he said after a quick glance at the screen.

He pressed the BlackBerry to his ear and hustled off.

I made use of the time alone to eat more of my tarte. When Logan returned a few minutes later, there were only two bites left.

"Hey!"

"Sorry. Couldn't resist," I said. "Tell you what: you can have what's left, and you don't even have to give me any escargot for it."

"Screw it. I'm going straight to dessert."

Logan started looking around for our waiter.

"So…?" I said. "The call…?"

"I was gonna get to that. I thought you'd find it interesting. William Riggs's bond hearing has been scheduled for next Monday morning. He'll be before Judge Crowell."

Logan waggled his eyebrows.

"And this means…?" I said, waggling mine, too.

"Judge Crowell is a hardass. One of the hardest hardasses in Arizona, and we make 'em hard here. Riggs isn't going to catch any breaks. He's going to get himself a nice little vacay in the county lockup—and maybe a long one if he can't make whatever crazy bail Crowell sets."

"Oh. Bummer for him."

Our waiter stepped out of the kitchen with a plate, and I raised a finger and caught his eye.

Suddenly I was in the mood for dessert, too.

It was dark out when we finished dinner, and Logan offered to escort me back to my mom's place.

"You don't think I'm safe on the mean streets of Berdache?" I asked.

"I just like walking with you."

I was grateful it was dark out. Turns out a girl can commit over a hundred felonies before she hits puberty and still blush when the right guy acts starry-eyed.

"Well, I wouldn't want to come between you and a good time," I said. "Escort away."

When we got to the White Magic Five & Dime, he kissed me.

He was quick about it and gentle. There was no clinch, no groping. No tongue, thank god. He just leaned in quick—but not too quick—and put his lips to mine.

I shivered, but in a good way. Like when you take that first taste of something so rich and sweet and delicious your whole body wakes up tingling and says, "Nice!"

"Whoa," I said when it was over.

"I hope it's all right that I did that."

"Yeah. Oh yeah. It's all right. It's just…whoa."

"I know what you mean."

"Aren't you worried someone's gonna see us?"

Logan shrugged. "We're the talk of the town anyway. Why fight it?"

"Good point."

I kissed *him*.

IT ENDED after the second kiss. Logan was very gentlemanly, very proper, and I understood entirely and could have kicked his ass for it.

We parted wistfully.

"Promise you won't get into any trouble?" he said.

"Promise you won't arrest me if I do?"

"I can't."

"Me neither."

There was nothing left to say after that but good night.

FROM OUTSIDE, I'd noticed that the light was on upstairs. Clarice was home. Probably doing her homework, perhaps with Ceecee.

I hoped she was alone. I was looking forward to trying this sister thing on for size.

Big Sister: *You'll never believe who just kissed me!*
Little Sister: *Oh my god! Who?*
Big Sister: *Guess!*
Little Sister: *I don't know!*
Big Sister: *Detective…Josh…Logan!*
Little Sister: *Squeeee! OMFG!*
Both jump up and down, giggling hysterically.
Cut to montage of talking, laughing, baking cookies, combing hair, putting on makeup, dancing in pajamas and singing along to "We Are Family" by Sister Sledge.

"Hey, Clarice," I said as I reached the top of the stairs. "You'll never guess—"

"Never guess what?" said the man with the gun.

He had a deep, croaky voice and a cueball-bald head.

The woman with him had a gun, too.

It was pointed at my little sister.

A new day has dawned, and today the whole world looks different. Just take a peek out your window. You never noticed all those sunflowers in your yard, did you? And check it out: a naked kid on a horse! Wow! You sure didn't see that when you peeped out through the blinds at midnight. In fact, you didn't see anything at all but the blackness of your own despair. Well, it's always darkest before the dawn, they say. And they're right. The trick is surviving the night.

Miss Chance, *Infinite Roads to Knowing*

"I'm sorry," Clarice said, her voice warbly, her face wet with tears. "I should've said something. I shouldn't have let you come up the stairs."

She was sitting on the couch, handcuffs around her wrists.

Anthony Grandi tucked his gun away, then stepped up and cuffed me, too.

The woman kept her gun trained on Clarice. She was a short, stout, fortyish woman with bright red hair and a face that was both cherubic and churlish. Her eyes were cold, her hand steady.

"It's okay," I said to Clarice. "You did the right thing."

"Move."

Grandi turned me around and shoved me toward the stairs. He wasn't as big as I'd pictured him—that rumbly-growly voice of his made him sound like Chewbacca—but he shoved hard.

"Now, just hold on a second, Grandi. Why don't we—?"

He shoved me again.

This was my we-meet-at-last moment with the man, but all I could get out was, "All right! Stop it! I'm going!"

I was scared he'd push me down the stairs, though that wouldn't have made any sense. Why risk breaking a leg when there was a cornfield somewhere I had to walk to?

282

WE WERE marched out the back door once Grandi was sure no one was around to see us. He'd confiscated the keys to my mom's black Cadillac, and soon he was driving us out of town in it. I hadn't even been in it before then. It looked too much like a hearse.

They made Clarice and me get in the back.

The woman watched us from the front passenger seat. She'd given us a little speech I remembered well, though it had been twenty-something years since I'd first heard it. You know—the one about being dead before we hit the asphalt if we tried to get out.

There weren't really any cornfields around Berdache, of course, but there was plenty of desert.

It would do.

GRANDI WAS good at making snatches, I had to give him that. All that skip tracing had paid off, apparently. He'd whisked us out of town before even I could get my mouth working. By the time I had a thought in my head other than *shit*, we were cruising past the turn-off for Devil's Ridge.

I put a hand on Clarice's knee and gave it a squeeze. She looked back at me with wide, frightened eyes.

"Don't worry," I said. "They're not dumb enough to hurt us."

Clarice nodded, but her eyes didn't look any less wide or any less frightened.

I turned toward the front seat.

"I was talking to Detective Logan not fifteen minutes ago, you know. Over dinner. If anything happens to us, the first door he's gonna kick in is yours."

Grandi didn't even glance at me in the rear-view mirror.

The woman smirked.

Obviously, the words "Detective Logan" didn't exactly strike fear into the hearts of Arizona's evildoers. I resolved not to mention it if I ever saw Logan again. Every cop secretly believes he's Batman.

I jerked my chin at Grandi.

"Tony I know," I said to the woman. "Who are you?"

"Someone who doesn't answer questions from dumbasses who don't know when to shut up."

"Wow. That's a mouthful. How do you get all that on a driver's license?"

The woman's smirk turned into a sneer. I got the feeling she was good at scowls, glowers, and glares, too.

"You're not scared, huh? Well, good for you." She brought her gun up to show me what it was pointed at: my heart. "Now show me you're not stupid."

As it turned out, I *did* know when to shut up.

Right then, that was when.

"Watch out for potholes," I said to Grandi.

That was the last thing out of my mouth until the car stopped.

GRANDI SLOWED and turned onto a gravel road. We were miles from Berdache, miles from Sedona, miles from anywhere. All I could see in the headlights were rocks and dirt and, here and gone in an instant, the glowing eyes of something watching us from the scrub by the side of the road.

Clarice whimpered. I couldn't blame her. Maybe I even joined in, I don't know.

Any second now we'd pull behind a convenient bluff and there would be the shallow pit dug earlier in the day. Or maybe just a pair of shovels. Or an abandoned well or mine shaft.

284

We reached the end of the road.

THERE WAS the bluff, just as I'd expected. And on the other side of it, not a hole. A house.

It was one story, ranch style. Not much bigger than a mobile home. There was no mailbox, no yard, no car in the driveway. No driveway, for that matter, unless you counted the road that simply stopped thirty yards away.

"Inside," Grandi said.

He didn't bother pulling out his gun again. Where were we going to run to?

We followed him into the house, the woman a few steps behind us. *She* wasn't taking any chances. Her gun was pointed at my back.

The house was a mess. It looked like a run-down spring break rental after two dozen college kids were through with it. There were crumpled soda cans and junk food wrappers everywhere, and the air smelled of cigarettes and garbage someone should have taken out weeks ago.

"Don't tell me you kidnapped us because you're too cheap to hire Merry Maids," I said.

Grandi finally came alive.

He smiled.

"Hey, that's not a bad idea."

He went into the kitchen and came back with some plastic bags. He handed one to me, one to Clarice. One he kept for himself.

"Start cleaning," he said.

WHEN WE were done picking up trash, Grandi brought me a broom and told me to sweep.

I held up my hands. Handcuffs still dangled from the wrists.

"That'd be a lot easier without these."

"Yeah, probably," Grandi said. And he shoved the broom into my hands and walked off.

Clarice was sent into the bathroom with a roll of paper towels.

"Ew," I heard her say.

"Shut up and scrub," the woman snapped.

"Geez, Grandi—we're in Arizona and you need *us* for slave labor?" I said. "I thought that's what illegal immigrants were for."

He didn't bother answering.

He was trying to find the 409.

I STARTED sweeping down the hall, moving closer to the red-headed woman.

Closer.

Closer...

Almost close enough to bring the broom handle down on her hand, then up again into her face.

"Back off or you'll be sweeping up your own guts," she said.

I started sweeping up the hall, moving farther away from the red-headed woman.

Farther.

Farther...

"ALL RIGHT. That's enough," Grandi announced.

I leaned my broom against the wall. "Can we wait till tomorrow to start on the lawn? I'm exhausted."

Grandi pulled out his gun again. "End of the hall, room on the right. Go."

I didn't move.

Would they have plastic sheeting ready back there? A tarp? Something to keep the splatter off the walls?

No. They had miles of darkened desert all around. Why make a mess in the house? The one you just cleaned?

None of this made any sense.

Grandi hadn't been pointing his gun anywhere in particular, but he corrected that now by aiming at my face.

"*Go.*"

I went.

THE ROOM was small and bare. A single light bulb overhead, nothing on the walls, no furniture other than a ratty mattress in one corner and, across from it, a bucket.

I stayed as far away from the bucket as possible.

The room's one window was barred, and there was a padlock on the outside of the door.

Grandi took off our handcuffs—while his sister covered us from the doorway, of course—then stepped outside and locked us in.

"Oh my god, Alanis," Clarice said the second the door was closed. "What the hell is going on?"

"I don't know. This isn't how I expected things to play out."

"What *did* you expect?"

"Not spring cleaning, that's for sure." I waved a hand at the room around us. "Obviously this is Grandi's private Guantánamo. I assume he sweats people here from time to time. Maybe when he's looking for leads on someone who's jumped bail. Maybe when he wants to give someone a choice: back to jail or…I don't know. Whatever they've got to give."

"But why bring *us* here?"

"To show he's serious about me leaving town?" I said with a shrug.

"It doesn't sound like you really think that."

"I don't know what to think, Clarice. Grandi suddenly starts threatening me, then he suddenly stops, then he suddenly hauls us off at gunpoint. I don't get it."

"Maybe he's nuts."

"That's a comforting thought."

I walked to the door and brought an ear in close. I could hear Grandi and the woman talking in the living room, but they kept their voices low and I could only catch the occasional word. One kept coming up again and again, though. From both of them.

Mom.

If it had been *mother*, I might have assumed they were talking about mine. But not *mom*. That was too informal, too personal.

"I think that woman might be Grandi's sister," I said.

"Jesus. What a family."

"Judge not. What are we, the Huxtables?"

"Who the hell are the Huxtables?"

"They're…never mind."

Clarice started to sit on the mattress, then changed her mind when she got a good look at it. She kicked it instead.

"Maybe this is why Athena left the Five & Dime to you," she said. "She knew it'd suck you into all this shit."

I barked out a bitter little laugh. "That'd be so perfect, wouldn't it? Her last will and testament is really her last scam, and I'm the... Jesus."

"You're the Jesus?"

"No. I think you might be right. I'm the *mark*."

"Oh, come on, Alanis. I was only joking."

I wasn't.

I'd thought maybe my mother had forgiven me.

Ha. Now there's a joke.

She was getting her revenge.

MOM HAD known she was dying, so she had started squaring things away.

She'd made sure Clarice was legally emancipated. There'd be no social workers or foster homes for her to run away from.

Fly free, little bird...and maybe starve. That's up to you.

So that was one daughter taken care of, as Mom would see it. What to do about the other? The one who'd freed herself?

To me she left everything—except an explanation. Which pretty much guaranteed that Clarice would hate my guts. And when I came to collect my inheritance, I'd find all Mom's schemes brewing and the Grandis seething about it and a police detective sniffing around the whole rotten mess. If I was still up to my old ways—*her* ways—I'd slide right into her place and right into her troubles. And if I'd gone straight, maybe this was just the setup that would bend me crooked again.

She'd prove I was no better than her by helping me *become* her. And if I didn't go along with it—well, maybe I'd just get myself killed.

You had to give it to her: The woman was good. Even dead, she could still out-con me.

Time passed. We brooded.

"Alanis," Clarice eventually said, "I want you to be honest with me."

"All right."

"Are the Grandis going to kill us?"

"I don't know."

"But if you had to guess—?"

"What do you think?"

"I'm asking you."

"Because you're hoping I'll say something different."

"Yeah. Probably."

"Then don't tell me to be honest."

I listened to the voices down the hall rise and fall, rise and fall, rise and fall. After a while, I thought I heard more than just the two I recognized. Perhaps another man. Perhaps another woman.

Maybe that's what Grandi had been making us wait for.

The burial detail.

There were footsteps in the hall.

"They're coming," I said.

Clarice cringed against the far wall.

I positioned myself in the middle of the room, between her and the door. As if that would help. But it seemed like the thing to do.

The door opened, and Grandi's sister came in. Still with her gun, of course.

Grandi was behind her. With a folding table.

He walked up to me, set up the table, then left the room. He returned almost immediately with two folding chairs.

"Hell of a time for poker," I said.

He unfolded the chairs. One he pushed over to me. The other he left on the opposite side of the table.

"All right," Grandi said loudly. Not to me—to someone out in the hall.

There was a long, ominous silence. Then she came into the room. Slowly, almost shuffling.

The most adorable little grandma you ever saw.

She was short but plump, a little dumpling in a powder-blue pantsuit. She had a hunched back and wrinkly wattles that swayed with each step and hair permed up into a wavy-gray mushroom cloud erupting from her head.

She set her white handbag on the table, eased herself into the chair across from me, then looked up at Grandi.

"Now get out," she said.

"But Mom—"

"Get. *Out*. Anthony. Thomas."

I think it was the *Anthony Thomas* that did the trick. My mother never pulled the First Name-Middle Name thing with me—which of my names would she even use?—but I've seen it work wonders in "normal" families.

Grandi's blocky face reddened, and he stalked out of the room.

"You, too, Rosalee," the old woman said.

Grandi's sister knew better than to argue. Instead, she spoke to me.

"Touch one hair on her head, and I'll feed you to the coyotes in pieces."

Then out she went, too.

"And close the goddamn door!" her mother barked after her.

Now I knew why they'd made us clean.

Mrs. Grandi looked me up and down. The up part seemed to displease her. The down part filled her with disgust.

"So," she said. "You're the nosy bitch who's been causing all the trouble."

A CUSSING granny's kind of funny in a bad movie.

Isn't that cute? Baba Phoebe called the stuck-up father-in-law "ass-munch"...and now she's rapping about his tiny penis!

It's not funny in real life. Not when you look into the little old lady's little old eyes and see that the blankness there isn't just cataracts. Whatever soul the crone ever had is as withered and warped as the rest of her.

The Grandis wouldn't spare Clarice and me because Mom was in the house. They'd just try a little harder not to make a mess.

"YES," I said. "I am the nosy bitch."

Mrs. Grandi held a trembling claw out toward the chair beside me.

"You hoping I'll break my neck staring up at you like this? *Sit.*"

I sat.

Behind me I could hear Clarice moving around to the right to get a better view of the two of us.

The old lady ignored her.

"There were times," she said, "when I thought I was going to have this conversation with your mother. But I never did. Live and let live—that worked for us."

"Until it didn't."

Mrs. Grandi shrugged. "It didn't work for *someone*. But I'm here to talk about you. You know what we do, right? My family?"

"I know your son's a bail bondsman and some of your other relatives read tarot cards and as a sideline there's a little extortion and blackmail."

"'Some of my other relatives read tarot cards,'" Mrs. Grandi sneered. "I have two sisters, four daughters, three nieces, and one granddaughter in the business. You get your fortune told in Arizona or New Mexico, even money it's one of us who's doing it. And it all started from one shop—the one I opened thirty-two years ago."

I held my applause.

"What about the blackmail?" I said. "Did you start that, too?"

"I don't see you in a habit, Mother Teresa. What is it you do wherever you come from?"

"I'm in telemarketing."

Mrs. Grandi grimaced to let me know what she thought of *that*.

"And do you want to *stay* in telemarketing?" she asked.

"I'd certainly prefer it to what I'm doing right now."

The old woman snorted.

"Jokes," she said with another grimace to show what she thought of *those*. "My son thinks you're—"

She touched her forehead, then raised her hand high, the fingers fluttering.

"A bird?" I said.

"Crazy."

"Oh."

"I don't like dealing with crazy people. They're unpredictable."

"Well, then you'd better—"

"And I don't like smartasses, either."

I didn't finish my thought.

"I hear you've reopened the White Magic Five & Dime," Mrs. Grandi said. "Do you even read tarot?"

"I'm learning."

"What do you think so far?"

"It's not what I expected."

"What did you expect?"

"Bullshit."

"And you don't think it's bullshit now?"

"I don't think it has to be."

"Do you believe the cards foretell the future?"

"I believe they can be used to identify and explore possible outcomes."

"Don't double-talk me. *Do you believe the cards foretell the future*?"

"Well…I wouldn't say *foretell* so much as *foreshadow*."

The old woman swiped a hand at me. "Bah!"

"Look," I said. "If you want me to say it, I'll say it: The cards aren't just a scam. There's something there if you really look."

A small, sly smile tightened the sagging corners of Mrs. Grandi's mouth.

"There we go. Was that so hard to admit? Wait. Never mind. I know the answer." The woman cocked her head, and her smile went a little wider. "Now you're starting to wonder if the old dingbat's senile, am I right?"

"I just don't know why you would care what I think about tarot."

"I'll tell you."

Mrs. Grandi reached into her handbag and pulled out a small silver case engraved with swirling stars and crescent moons. She popped open the lid and took out a deck of tarot cards.

"You're going to do a reading for me. How do you like to start?"

I glanced to my right, at Clarice.

If this is a dream, please wake me up, the look on my face was supposed to say.

Clarice just stared back at me.

"Well," I said, "first you should shuffle while thinking about what you want to ask. When you feel like you have the right words for your question, say them out loud. Then give me the deck."

Mrs. Grandi nodded, still smiling. Her fingers may have looked like a bunch of knobby white twigs, but they shuffled the cards smoothly and quickly.

"Oh, I know my question already. It's very simple," the old woman said. "Yes or no: should I have you killed?"

She handed me the deck.

"No," I said.

Mrs. Grandi squinted at me.

"What do you mean, *no*?"

"That's what the cards are going to say: no. I can feel it already. I've gotten really good at reading their vibe before I even deal them."

Mrs. Grandi reached for her handbag again.

"Maybe I'll just flip a coin."

"No!"

The old woman froze, glaring at me.

"I mean…let's see how the cards play out, shall we?" I said. "The answer's going to be no, like I said, but we ought to at least see the reasons why. Now I'm thinking we don't need a full Celtic Cross for something this straightforward. A five-card Dilemma spread will do the trick."

It also had the advantage of being in *Infinite Roads to Knowing*. I'd read about it the day before. I'd just have to leave out one little detail.

"Five cards. Good choice," Mrs. Grandi said. "If most are reversed, the answer's no. If most are right-side up, the answer's yes."

"Uhhh…exactly."

That was the little detail.

I started to wonder if I should have gone with the coin toss.

I laid out five cards in a line between us, then pointed at the first two.

"Reasons for a yes."

I pointed at the next two.

"Reasons for a no."

I tapped the last card.

"The most important thing to keep in mind when making your decision."

"All right. Get on with it."

"Fine. Reasons for a yes."

I flipped over the first card. It was right-side up for Mrs. Grandi—which meant it was reversed for the person reading the cards, and that's what counted.

It was a no.

Chalk one up for mercy.

I let out a breath I didn't even know I'd been holding.

"The Five of Wands reversed. A card of conflict."

"Five always means conflict," Mrs. Grandi said.

I nodded as if I knew this already and it made perfect sense.

"So there's turmoil ahead," I said, "but you'll only make it worse if you…follow through on the proposed action."

I turned over the next card. It was reversed for Mrs. Grandi, right-side up for me.

A yes.

Score one for "kill!"

"The Five of Swords," I tried to say.

It came out "the Fi uv Swuh."

I swallowed and tried again.

"The Five of Swords. Another five. More conflict, but we don't see it this time. They're cleaning up after the battle. The fight's over."

That was all the interpretation I was going to give. Best not to dwell on a yes.

I reached for the next card.

Mrs. Grandi stretched out a hand and stabbed the triumphant knight on the Five of Swords with a long, blood-red fingernail.

"That's the winner," she said, "and it's not us. That's why the card says yes."

"Yeah, but look at who he just beat. They're alive. He's letting them get away. They lost, but at least they weren't utterly destroyed."

Mrs. Grandi looked unconvinced.

I was surprised she needed convincing. Did she really believe all this stuff?

I didn't know. I couldn't even tell if *I* did or didn't anymore.

I turned over the next card. It was reversed.

Another no.

"We're on to reasons you shouldn't kill me," I said, "and we see the King of Swords turned on his head. A malevolent patriarchal figure upended. Someone with power over you will be undone."

Mrs. Grandi rolled her eyes. "'A malevolent patriarchal figure.' That's one way to put it."

"How would you put it?"

Mrs. Grandi just shook her head and pointed at the next card.

One more no and the spread will have spoken: let them go.

I flipped the card. It was reversed…to Mrs. Grandi. Right-side up to me.

A yes to death.

"Well," I said. "That's clear enough."

"That's an end to conflict—a really, really definitive one. You'll be rid of an enemy." I tried to smile. "Not that *I'm* your enemy. Have I mentioned yet that I don't even know what your family has against me?"

"We don't have anything against *you*. This is a business decision." Clarice started moving toward the table.

"That's close enough," Mrs. Grandi said without looking at her. Her voice was loud, firm. Just a little louder and it would be heard down the hall.

Clarice stopped. "So two say yes and two say no?" she asked me.

"That's right."

It was down to the last card.

"But we're all smart, educated people here, right?" I said. "No matter what the spread might say, I'm sure we'd talk through all the possible repercussions of—"

"Show me the card," Mrs. Grandi said.

"—whatever decision might be made here tonight. Because the last thing anyone should do is act rashly when there's so much at—"

"*Show me the goddamn card.*"

I showed her.

IL GIUDIZIO LE JUGEMENT XX JUDGEMENT EL JUICIO

GERICHT HET OORDEEL

Do you see a fiery pit? Do you see a guy with a pitchfork and a tail who looks like he's spent WAY too much time in a tanning booth? No, you don't. Because in the tarot, Judgement isn't about deciding who's good and who's bad and who's punished and who's not. It's about dying and rising again; hearing the call to start a new life. Sure, Armageddon will be stressful. The screaming and the sulfur and the Beast and the blood are no fun. But without all that, no one gets to begin again.

Miss Chance, *Infinite Roads to Knowing*

"No, Mrs. Grandi," I said. I took in a deep breath, held it a moment, savoring it, then let it out. "That's your answer: no."

I'd turned up the Ten of Pentacles. Reversed.

The cards were saying to let us go. Or not to kill us, anyway, and I didn't expect the Grandis to ask us to move in.

I looked over at Clarice and smiled.

"Why?" Mrs. Grandi said.

"Hmm?"

I turned toward her again.

"I want to hear your interpretation," she said. "Why shouldn't I end this while I have the chance?"

"Oh. Well. All right."

I looked down at the card again. It was one I'd never really noticed before, probably because it was so cluttered. Instead of the usual clean, simple design with one or two or, at most, three main figures, it was hard to tell who or what the card was focused on.

An old man in a Technicolor Dreamcoat sits near an arch—perhaps the entrance to a city—while a dog watches him attentively. Just beyond them are what seem to be three lost extras from *Clash of the Titans*: a man, a woman, and a child, all dressed in robes. Hovering in the air, meanwhile, are ten of the golden pentagram-plate-Frisbee-balloons that pop up on all the Pentacle cards.

It was a mess. And Mrs. Grandi was waiting for me to make sense of it.

The cards had said no, but in her eyes I still saw a maybe.

"Obviously," I said with all the certainty I could muster, "we're looking at a family and its financial well-being. Grandfather, parents, child, even pets—they're all here, while around them we see something they don't seem to notice: The Pentacles. Giant coins. The family's wealth. Times are good, but they don't even realize how good they have it because the card's reversed, meaning all this is at risk. The other cards told us there's conflict ahead; that's inevitable. But only a bad decision here—doing the wrong thing at the wrong time—could *destroy* the family and everything it's built up. And it's not Swords or even Wands we've been given to represent the family. These people aren't warriors—aren't killers. Their business is business, and that's what they should stick to. That's what the card's telling you. And it's right."

And I believed it. By god, I really, truly believed it.

As for Mrs. Grandi…

The old woman looked at me, looked at the cards, looked at Clarice, looked at me, looked at the cards. Then she leaned back in her seat until it squeaked and looked at me some more.

It was Judgment Day, only instead of having my fate decided by God or Satan or St. Peter, I was facing one of the Golden Girls. The little, crabby one.

Her eyes narrowed, her lips puckered. Then she nodded brusquely—one quick dip of the chin. She'd made up her mind.

She reached into her handbag and pulled out a gun.

"Whoa! Hold on!"

"No!" Clarice cried.

Mrs. Grandi shushed us. Then she put the gun on the table and pushed it toward me.

"You're going to need a hostage to get out of here," she said.

She gathered up the tarot cards and put them back in their box.

"You *want* me to take the gun?" I said.

"Would I give it to you if I didn't?"

"But…I don't understand."

Mrs. Grandi waggled her perm toward the door—and her son and daughter waiting down the hall.

"Neither do they." She held up the card case. "This is just mumbo jumbo to them. They've never respected it. And if *I* want to keep their respect, I have to act like I don't either. If I walk out of here and tell them to let you go because I got a reversed Ten of Pentacles—? They'd stick me in an old folks' home the second they were done burying you."

She stuffed the case into her purse, then folded her hands together on the table, eyeing me coldly, expectantly.

"Well?" her look seemed to say. "You gonna save yourself or not, dipshit?"

I put a hand over the gun without picking it up. It was a little silver automatic—a pretty, petite, ladylike thing. A piece of jewelry that could blow a person's brains out.

Call me old-fashioned. I hated it.

"You can't just tell them to let us go?" I said. "They act like they're scared of you."

"That's habit. I'm an old woman now. They still listen to me most of the time, but tonight, about this—?" Mrs. Grandi shrugged. "You really want them to put it to a vote?"

I picked up the gun and pointed it at a spot just above the old woman's nose.

"You know, there's another way we could play this: a straight-up shootout. I'd have the element of surprise on my side, and if I pulled it off I'd have three less Grandis to worry about down the line."

Mrs. Grandi rolled her eyes. "Oh *please*."

"I'm serious, lady. I'll do it—unless you tell me what I want to know. Who killed my mother?"

Mrs. Grandi tapped the cards on the table. "Why don't you ask them?"

"I'm asking you. And I think you know the answer."

"Maybe yes, maybe no."

"No maybes. Tell me or I'll blow a big hole in all that talcum powder you've got plastered to your wrinkled old—"

"It's not loaded, Einstein."

"What?"

"No bullets. You think I'm nuts?"

I slumped and lowered the gun. "Shit."

"You do know, though, don't you?" Clarice said. "Who killed my—killed Athena."

Mrs. Grandi gave her a long, scowling stare.

Clarice didn't look away, didn't blink.

If it was a test, she passed.

"I don't *know*, but I've seen enough to guess," Mrs. Grandi said. She turned to me. "And so have you."

The old woman planted her palms on the table and started pushing herself slowly to her feet.

"Now let's get this over with," she said. "I want to be home in time for *The Tonight Show*."

"ANTHONY! ROSALEE! Come here!" Mrs. Grandi called out.

When they reached the end of the hall, they found their mother with a gun to her head. I was holding the gun.

"Which one of you morons searched this bitch?" Mrs. Grandi snapped at her children.

Grandi looked like he'd just been slapped across the face with a herring, yet he didn't miss a beat.

"Rosalee did," he said, pointing at his sister.

"Ooo, you bastard!" She pointed right back. "It was *him*, Mom!"

"Shut up! All of you!" I pushed the little bulletless automatic harder into Mrs. Grandi's crunchy-stiff Aqua Net–shellacked hair. "Guns on the floor! Now!"

Rosalee started to slide a hand under her windbreaker.

"Slowly," I said. "With just the tips of your fingers."

You don't subject yourself to every episode of *T. J. Hooker* as a kid and not pick up a thing or two.

Moving in slow motion, Rosalee pulled out her gun and, pinching it by one end like a pair of diapers bound for the trash bin, gingerly placed it on the floor.

Grandi didn't move.

I tried to fix him with a steely glare.

"Put down your gun or the old bat gets it!"

Grandi seemed to be thinking it over.

"Anthony Thomas!" his mother barked.

He put his gun down beside his sister's. Clarice scuttled up and collected them.

"Cell phones and car keys, too," I said. "On the floor."

Grandi slowly snaked a hand into his pants pocket.

"We just brought you out here to talk, you know," he said. "Why don't you lower that gun, and we can—?"

"She's not an idiot—unlike some others around here," Mrs. Grandi cut in. "Just do what she says, and let's get this over with."

A few seconds later, Clarice and I were locking the Grandis into their own homemade prison.

"Wow," Clarice said. "I can't believe that actually worked."

"Anthony, put that down!" I heard Mrs. Grandi say.

I pushed Clarice up the hallway. "Run run run!"

There was a sharp, high *pop*, like the tinny blast of a firecracker, then another and another. Anthony Grandi was shooting at us. The gun was small—tiny enough to fit in an ankle holster, say—but the door was so cheap and thin you probably could shoot through it with a water pistol. Bullets whizzed past us up the hall.

Lesson learned.

Searching prisoners. Important.

"I dropped the guns!" Clarice said when we reached the end of the hall and hooked around the corner. "Should I go back for them?"

"What do *you* think?"

I never stopped running.

We flew out the front door and threw ourselves into my mother's Caddy, and I was very, very happy when it didn't do the classic horror movie dead-battery sputter. It roared to life when I jammed in the key and gave it gas, and soon we were zooming up the road toward the highway.

"Oh my god oh my god," Clarice panted. "I've never been so scared in my life."

"The night is young," I said.

I CALLED Detective Josh Logan.

"Hello?" he said.

"Josh."

"Alanis. Is everything all right?"

"Not really. How soon can you meet me at the Five & Dime?"

"I can be there in twenty minutes. What's wrong?"

"That remains to be seen. How good are you with traps?"

"Traps? I don't know. Are you in one?"

"Not anymore. But I need you to help me spring a new one."

"Christ, are you going to be this cryptic all night?"

"Perhaps."

"Dammit, Alanis—"

"All right, all right. How's this? I know who killed my mother."

Someone opened the back door of the White Magic Five & Dime.

"I'm down here!" I called out from the reading room.

There were footsteps in the hall.

"I came as fast as I could."

Logan appeared in the doorway.

"What are you doing?" he asked me.

The table was covered with tarot cards.

"What else do you do with cards when you're alone?" I said. "I'm playing solitaire. It almost works if you ignore the Major Arcana. Have a seat."

"Enough with the games, Alanis," Logan said. He sat down, though. "If you really think you know who killed your mother, you need to tell me."

I reached out and separated a card from several others of the same suit. On it, a man wearing a crown and flowing robes sat on a throne, a sword in one hand.

I slid the card toward Logan.

"The murderer is…King Arthur?" he said.

"The King of Swords," I corrected. "Reversed."

Logan groaned and rolled his eyes. "Oh god. The cards told you?"

"Yeah, kind of. I did a reading tonight, and there he was, right in the middle of everything."

"No offense, Alanis, but I thought you were too cynical and manipulative to believe in crap like this."

"No offense taken. I used to think that, too. I wouldn't have called you if it was just the reading, though." I patted the King of Swords. "It fits."

"So does that represent someone specific or am I supposed to haul a playing card off to jail?"

"It represents someone—someone who was blackmailing my mother. The five thousand dollars a month, remember? And I think the Grandi family's being blackmailed, too. That's why Anthony Grandi started threatening me before I even had any idea who he was. He was told to. And he was told to stop when I tracked him down—because that took me a step too close to the person giving the orders. And tonight he was told to get rid of me."

"Get rid of you? Did Grandi attack you?"

"Let's set the Grandis aside." I slid my hands under the table and sat up a little straighter. "I'd like to talk about *you*."

Logan cocked his head to the side and half smiled, looking like a man who'd laugh at a joke if he could only figure out what the punch line meant.

If only I'd been joking. For once, I was all wisecracked out.

"What about me?" Logan said.

"You send a lot of mixed signals, you know that? Since the day I got here, you've been telling me to back off, back off—yet you've kept yourself so very close at the same time."

"I was concerned."

"Right. So concerned you steered me toward William Riggs, who had a history of assaults and probably wife beating. Ken Meldon, who'd had run-ins with the police over guns. And Victor Castellanos, who recently broke a man's collarbone during an argument about the treatment of his mother."

"Jesus, Alanis—I was sticking my neck out to do you a favor. *You're* the one who wanted to meet people who'd complained about your mom."

"And those were the only three you could find? Really? After she's been here three years? I don't think so. I think you hoped dealing with them would be so unpleasant or even dangerous that I'd stop snooping around."

Logan started shaking his head. "Oh, Alanis…"

"That's why you kept pushing me to go see my mom's body, too. You weren't trying to help me find closure. You wanted me to look at a murdered woman and freak out and get out of town."

Logan put his face in his hands and sighed.

"I knew you didn't respect me as a cop. But this? Ouch." He peeked up at me with eyes filled with pain. "That you could actually think that I'd—"

"Why did you come in through the back door just now?"

"What?"

"I left both doors open—front *and* back. You came in through the back. Why?"

"Because I parked in the back."

"*Why?*"

"Because there are rumors flying around town about us already. People see me popping in for a late-night visit, they're going to take that as proof."

"Good answer," I said. "But I've got a better one: the security camera in the House of Arcana. You don't want your car on tape— like it was the night my mother died, I'm assuming. That's why you got the tape from Josette, right? So you could destroy it?"

Logan gave his head another sad shake. "This is crazy…"

"At least the tape thing makes me think you didn't come here to kill her," I went on. "You probably thought you were just dropping by for your monthly cut—your *investigation* into phony fortunetelling had really paid off. But then Mom tried to turn the tables on you. Too bad for her you figured out where she had her camera hidden."

Logan had gone on shaking his head, pouting, looking hurt. But now his eyes suddenly widened and he jumped to his feet and practically threw himself on the big crystal ball on the bookshelf by the table. He fumbled with it a few seconds, then simply threw it hard into the hallway.

It shattered against the wall, sending shards of glass and plastic—*just* glass and plastic—flying everywhere.

Damn. Up till that moment, the romantic part of me still had been hoping I was wrong.

Your romantic parts can be really dumb.

"Give me some points for originality, please," I said. "I'm not going to pull the same gag as my mother. Thanks for confirming that you knew where the camera was, though. It's obvious why you took it and the tapes. I assume taking the PC was just playing it safe. It's not like you'd have to work that hard to make it look like a robbery, given that you'd be investigating a murder that you actually—"

"That's enough."

Logan reached under his jacket and pulled out his gun.

"Whoa whoa whoa!" I cried. "We're still having a conversation here!"

"Where's Clarice?"

The gun was aimed at me.

That had been happening a lot lately, but I still wasn't used to it.

"Just take it easy, huh?" I squeaked. I swallowed, and my voice dropped an octave. "Why don't you point that thing at something else so we can keep this nice and relaxed? We've got more talking to do if everyone's going to come out of this with what they want."

Logan did as I asked and found something new to aim at.

Instead of pointing his gun at my chest, he pointed it at my forehead.

"What are you talking about?" he said.

"What goes around comes around, Josh. My mom was blackmailing clients, so you started blackmailing her, so she tried to blackmail you, so you killed her. And now I'm going to blackmail you for it, only I've learned from my mother's mistake. She was running her game solo, and that made her vulnerable. Once you took her out of the picture, it was Game Over. Almost."

"Where's Clarice?" Logan asked again.

I nodded. "Now you're getting it. Clarice. I'll tell you where she is: 721 Fulton Drive."

Logan blinked. His aim wavered.

721 Fulton Drive was his address.

"She won't find anything," he said, his voice sounding strained, weak.

"Really? You didn't keep any of it? My mom's tapes? Her computer? I mean, for a guy who's partial to blackmail, those would be a treasure trove."

"She won't find anything," Logan said again. Firmly this time.

"Okay. You destroyed the evidence. Good for you. That was smart. That means you only kept one thing. But that'll be enough."

"I didn't keep anything."

"Of course you did."

"I didn't."

"Josh, you did. We wouldn't be having this conversation if you didn't."

Logan stared at me blankly.

"Geez, dude—the money!" I said. "I don't know if you stuffed it under your mattress or just put it in the bank, but either way it's out there somewhere and it can be found. I'm guessing you made it a lot easier than you should've."

Logan's jaw clenched. His face twitched.

I'd guessed right.

I shrugged sadly. "Crime's a job for criminals, Josh. Now would you *please*—?"

I looked pointedly at his gun and fluttered my hands downward.

He finally lowered the gun.

"What is it you want?" he said.

"Not much. Just fifty thousand dollars."

"Fifty thousand dollars and you'd let me get away with killing your mother?"

"Hey, I hated the bitch, remember? If I hadn't run away when I did, I might've offed her myself. And if either of us is entitled to trust issues, it's me. At dinner tonight I tell you my mom was paying someone off, then you give me a kiss and *wheeeee*—I get a little ride out to the country. That's what your 'work call' at dinner was really about, wasn't it? Bringing the hammer down?"

"So I'm supposed to trust you to stick to a deal because you and your mommy didn't get along?"

"You're supposed to trust me because you're going to give me fifty grand, and money and I get along great."

Logan looked dubious, unconvinced. But I saw something new in his eyes. *Behind* his eyes. He was busy back there.

He was running the numbers.

*If I kill her now, I can be home in fifteen minutes to find
and kill the girl, after which I should have seven more
hours of darkness to clean up the mess, and if I do it right
it'll be at least twenty-four hours before anyone reports
them missing, which will buy me time to get the money
somewhere safer and really cover my ass...*

vs.

*I'm out fifty thousand dollars to someone who might never
let me off the hook and who might just be angling for proof
of my guilt anyway.*

Logan was no criminal mastermind, but this math was easy
enough for a first grader.

He hadn't brought up his gun again yet, but he would.

"Meatloaf," I said.

"Meatloaf?" said Logan.

"Yeah. Meatloaf. Meatloaf meatloaf meatloaf."

Clarice appeared in the doorway with a gun in her hand.

"It's our safe word," she explained.

At this point, Logan was supposed to freeze, Clarice was supposed to tell him to put down his gun, and I was supposed to
explain our trap. Gloat, in other words. I'd really been looking forward to that part in particular.

Logan didn't stick to the plan.

He started to swing his gun toward Clarice. There was no time to
reach out and grab it; my hands were in my lap. So I just pushed up
as hard as I could.

My side of the table flipped up and hit Logan's hand. There was a deafening blast; suddenly plaster and tarot cards were flying everywhere. Through the ringing in my ears I could hear Clarice scream.

Logan started to turn the gun on me.

We were less than three feet from each other in a glorified closet. There was nowhere to turn, nowhere to run.

Sometimes the best defense is a good offense, Biddle used to say. *And make it as offensive as possible.*

There was no way to go for a knee to the crotch with an over-turned table between us. So I threw myself forward and punched Logan in the throat with all my might.

My mother had taught me that one, actually.

Logan staggered back, his hands instinctively going to his throat. I twisted his gun from his grip as he slid toward the floor, back against the wall, gasping.

I turned toward Clarice. There was a new hole in the wall just to the left of her chest.

"You okay?" I asked her.

It was hard to tell if she nodded yes or was just trembling so hard her chin dipped. Whichever—she was alive and unharmed.

Logan's ass had hit the floor by now, and I could see he'd finally noticed what I'd been fiddling with in my lap, under the table. It had landed a few inches from his splayed-out feet, and I checked to make sure it was still working before turning it around and adjusting the screen so that he could see it.

Clarice's laptop. With two programs running.

Oh boy! I'd get to gloat after all!

"Can you believe anyone would still use a camcorder to bug a room?" I said. "Mom was *so* twentieth century."

I hit *stop* and *save* on the audio-recording program.

"Show's over. Good night," I said to the computer. And I logged off the video chat room at foxyladydating.com. My mother's old account there had come in handy. Pervs around the world had heard Logan's confession. It wasn't much of a backup in case things went horribly wrong, but it was better than nothing. At least I'd have died knowing my murder was about to go viral.

Logan wheezed at me, trying to say something. His hands were still around his throat and his face had turned an unflattering shade of blue, but it looked like enough air was getting through to keep him alive.

"In...ad...missible," he was saying.

"Sure it is. But it'll get the ball rolling. And it'll justify this."

I turned toward the doorway. Clarice was half in, half out of the room, swaying slightly, hands shaking. Gunfire will do that to some people.

"Go ahead," I said to her. "For Mom."

Clarice took in a deep breath and managed a wobbly smile.

Then she steadied her aim and shot Logan in the face.

I don't know about your world, but mine doesn't include
any floating heads or baton-twirling majorettes dressed in
nothing but dirty scarves. So ignore all that for the moment
and just focus on what the World, the last and highest card
of the Major Arcana, really represents: the finish line. The
Fool's journey is complete. You've done what you set out to
do, and all is in balance, all is well. Congratulations! If you
want to strip down, break out the batons, and dance your
happy dance for the cloud-heads, go for it. You've earned it.

Miss Chance, *Infinite Roads to Knowing*

"Ow," LOGAN said.

A BB might not look like much, but it can really hurt if it hits you on the cheek.

Clarice and I wouldn't be shooting any cats with Ken Meldon's air gun, but we'd managed to shoot a cop. I got the feeling the old man would like that even better.

LOGAN TRIED to spin Mom's death as self-defense. An argument turned violent, he put her in a sleeper hold—as Berdache police are trained to do—but she kept struggling and asphyxiated. Oops!

Judge Crowell didn't buy it. The man was one of the hardest hardasses in Arizona, after all.

He denied Logan bail. I'm sure Anthony Grandi didn't mind losing out on the business. He had other things to worry about, like what Logan would say about the Grandis once the bargaining with the DA began in earnest.

They found the money in that American classic, the duffel bag in the attic. More than seventy thousand dollars in cash. I guess Logan hadn't figured out how to launder it yet. He was amateur through and through, but maybe prison would change that— assuming he survived it. A cop wouldn't exactly be Mr. Popularity on cell block H.

The Sedona newspaper dug up Logan's dad, the retired highway patrolman. My favorite quote: "My son is 100 percent innocent, and we're going to prove it in court."

Now there's a parent for you. Standing behind his kid to the bitter end. It made me feel a little better about my mother.

"How about that?" I said to her. "Maybe I would've turned out this screwed up even if you hadn't been awful."

AT THE time, my mother was in her TCC—her temporary cremains container. A white plastic box about the size of a loaf of bread stood on end. Tupperware for people.

Clarice and I hadn't decided what to do with her yet, so she was just sitting on the kitchen counter beside the flour and sugar. I kept suggesting that we bake her, but Clarice stood firm.

"Alanis, that's gross," she'd say. "We're vegetarians, remember?"

AFTER EVERYTHING hit the papers, people stopped by to check on us and make sure we were okay. That was new for me. And nice.

Marsha Riggs I walked down the street to meet Eugene Wheeler.

"He's a little weaselly, but what good lawyer isn't? I think you two could find a lot to talk about, Marsha. Current events, the weather, divorce proceedings, restraining orders. Whatever. If it ends up being billable, have him send me an invoice."

Josette Berg I teased about her poor showing as a prophet.

"The first day I'm in town, you do a reading for me, and what do you see?"

"Death," Josette said.

"Yeah, that was in there. But I was thinking of the lovey-dovey card. The lovers at Oktoberfest. You know—with the giant mugs?"

"You mean the Two of Cups?"

"That's it! When you saw that, you practically promised me a boyfriend—and then the first guy who takes me out tries to kill me."

Josette shrugged. "Maybe I was seeing a different kind of love. Or maybe the man with the cup wasn't Josh Logan."

"Or maybe you were just plain wrong."

"We'll see," Josette said with a smile.

Victor Castellanos I showed my veal parmesan. Which is to say, I pulled the jewelry from its hiding place in the freezer and gave it to him to take to his mother. Whatever she thought was hers, she could keep. The rest Victor could bring back.

"I'm sorry I was so hostile when we met," he said. "It's just that after what happened with my mom—"

"Don't worry. I'm not offended. You were right to be suspicious."

"Thanks, but still…I feel horrible. I wish I could make it up to you somehow."

I patted him on the shoulder. It was like patting a ham. The guy obviously didn't just hang out in a gym all day. He hit one at night, too.

"You'll think of something," I said.

ANTHONY GRANDI never dropped by with cookies and balloons, but I did see him around town from time to time.

I waved. He glowered.

You'd think he'd be more grateful. I hadn't started recording Logan till I was done talking about the Grandis, and I'd been coy about them with the cops, too. I owed his mother one.

I got the feeling Anthony thought he owed *me* one. But not a good one. The payback kind.

You escape from your would-be-murderer, and *he's* mad at *you*. Go figure.

It made a certain sense, though. I was still a threat to the family because of what I knew and who I was. The longer I stayed in Berdache, the greater the odds that the Grandis and I were going to have another run-in. And the second time around, the cards might not come up in my favor.

The smart play was obvious.

Leave. And don't come back.

ARRANGEMENTS WERE made.

Eugene Wheeler would find a renter for the White Magic Five & Dime (for a small percentage).

Clarice would stay upstairs (because she didn't want to trade Berdache—and Ceecee—for the Chicago suburbs).

And I would fly back to Chicagoland, nothing parenthetical about it. Just:

THE END

THE THREE of us drove into the desert: Clarice, me, Mom. Taking our first and last family trip.

A group of tourists was already at Devil's Ridge when we arrived, up at the edge of the canyon communing with the Great Whatever. Clarice and I waited at the foot of the hill, sipping Snapples under the afternoon sun until the pilgrims finished holding hands and chanting and started streaming back down to the black bus that had brought them. The words THE MAGICAL MYSTERY TOUR were splashed on the side in huge, groovy-shimmery letters so aswirl with color it looked like a rainbow had barfed them.

That was a nice angle for a business, I thought. Help true believers become one with the universe while infringing copyrights at the same time.

There's crime everywhere, even the astral plane.

Clarice and I threw away our bottles and started up the trail. I was carrying our Mom-in-a-Box. Clarice had our Bible: *Infinite Roads to Knowing* by Miss Chance.

I'd been surprised when she said she wanted to read something from it. I was even more surprised when I heard it.

It was from the last chapter of the book. I'd only skimmed that part, as what I was interested in—the nuts-and-bolts how-to stuff— had ended the chapter before.

This was what I'd missed:

Cards can't tell you what to do. Nothing and no one can tell you what to do. Every decision is yours to make. The trick is knowing who you are. Are you the kind of person who'd do this, the kind of person who'd do that, or the kind of person who'd do the thing the first two people would think was nuts? The tarot isn't a window you look through for an answer. It's a mirror. It offers seventy-eight paths to self-discovery in thousands of possible combinations. Existence offers an infinite number more if we open our hearts and minds to them, which isn't always easy. Life can be a bitch, they say, but she's beautiful, too. Love the beauty without limit, and the bitchy you might learn to love…even if you never understand it.

Clarice closed the book.

"Wow," I said.

Clarice nodded. "Deep, huh?"

"It really says 'Life's a bitch, but she's beautiful, too'?"

"Yeah."

"Biddle used to say that."

"Who's Biddle?"

"An old friend. Mom's partner back in the day."

"Oh. Well, that makes sense. She stole half the book from other tarot guides. Why not steal from people she knew, too?"

I felt my forehead. It was warm there on the edge of the gorge, but not broiling hot. Plus, I'd just had a Snapple. It didn't seem like the time for heat stroke.

So why couldn't I understand anything Clarice had just said?

"Huh?" I ventured.

"Didn't you know? I assumed you'd figured it out by now." Clarice gave *Infinite Roads to Knowing* a little shake. "Athena wrote this."

I switched up my approach.

"*Chuh?*" I said.

"She wanted to sell tarot books in the shop, but she didn't like the idea of paying anyone for them. So she copied stuff from other books and websites and linked it together with her own BS. She had me go through it before it was printed up, to make sure everything fit together, and I ended up adding a bunch, too. It was fun, actually."

"So Miss Chance is Mom?"

"Mostly. With a little bit of me and whoever she ripped off. That's why I wanted to read that part of the book. That 'Life's a bitch, but isn't she beautiful' line—I thought that was her talking about herself."

"God knows it fits. That's probably why Biddle used to say it. Still…" I put my hands to my head again just in case it was about to spin off my neck and fly into the canyon. "This is too weird. My mother wrote *Infinite Roads to Knowing*? Unbelievable. I mean, it gets all snarky sometimes, but it seems sincere, too. And Mom didn't do sincere. Not sincerely, anyway."

"I know what you mean. But by the end I think she did kind of believe in the tarot. She used to say that anyone who knew the things she did about people could do amazing things with the cards. At first I thought she just meant a con artist could make a lot of money. But when I read what she wrote…?"

Clarice gave her bony shoulders a shrug.

I looked down at the box of person powder in my hands.

Okay, Mom: Which was it? Did you believe or not? Was the White Magic Five & Dime a gift or a trap? Were you trying to destroy me or show me a new road?

Of course, it's a little late for a heart to heart when one of the hearts is half a cup of ash.

I'd never get an answer. And that was okay.

Life's a bitch, but she's beautiful, too.

Clarice turned to look back down at the parking lot.

"Tour van's pulling in," she said. "Five minutes and there's gonna be another fanny pack powwow up here. We'd better get this over with."

"Right."

I loosened the lid of the TCC.

I hadn't decided on what I was going to say. "All we are is dust in the wind" maybe, and I'd chuck Mom into the gorge, takeout box and all. Blatantly illegal, yeah, but wouldn't that be apropos for my mother? The last act she had any part in: desecration of hallowed ground and a violation of public health codes. If only there were some way to scam money out of it, we'd hit the trifecta.

"They're coming, Alanis. Do it. Fast."

"Let's keep her," I said, blurting it out like a kid talking about a stray dog.

"What?"

"Let's keep her. Let's take her back to the White Magic Five & Dime and put her on the mantle."

"The Five & Dime doesn't have a mantle."

"We'll buy one. Or build one. Or we'll just keep her on top of the john, next to the Kleenex. That way, if we ever change our minds about having her around, we can give her a quick goldfish funeral and start using the cremains container as a napkin holder."

A small, guarded smile puckered up one side of Clarice's mouth.

"You make it sound like you're staying."

"I am." I gave the plastic box a hug. "Mom talked me into it."

Clarice's smile widened.

"All right," she said. "But I think she should go downstairs in the display case. You know—so she can be close to the cash register."

"Perfect! That'll keep her restful."

"Yeah. The last thing I want is her haunting me."

"Oh, don't worry about that." I turned away from the chasm and started toward the trail. "It doesn't last."

We walked down the hill and drove home.

THE END

STEVE HOCKENSMITH (CALIFORNIA) IS the author
of the Pride and Prejudice and Zombies novels *Dawn
of the Dreadfuls* (Quirk Classics, 2010) and *Dreadfully
Ever After* (Quirk Classics, 2011). His book *Holmes on
the Range* (Minotaur Books, 2006) was a finalist for
the Edgar, Shamus, and Anthony Awards for Best First
Novel. He also writes a series of middle-grade mysteries
with "Science Bob" Pflugfelder. For more information,
visit his website at stevehockensmith.com.

LISA FALCO (LOS ANGELES) received her first tarot deck at the age of eight years old. She holds degrees from both Northwestern University and Cal State University Northridge, and is the author of *A Mother's Promise* (Illumination Arts, 2004).

www.MidnightInkBooks.com

From the gritty streets of New York City to sacred tombs in the Middle East, it's always midnight somewhere. Join us online at any hour for fresh new voices in mystery fiction.

At midnightinkbooks.com you'll also find our author blog, new and upcoming books, events, book club questions, excerpts, mystery resources, and more.

Midnight Ink Ordering Information

 ### Order Online:
• Visit our website www.midnightinkbooks.com, select your books, and order them on our secure server.

 ### Order by Phone:
• Call toll-free within the U.S. and Canada at
  1-888-NITE-INK (1-888-648-3465)
• We accept VISA, MasterCard, and American Express

 ### Order by Mail:
Send the full price of your order (MN residents add 6.5% sales tax) in U.S. funds, plus postage & handling to:

Midnight Ink
2143 Wooddale Drive
Woodbury, MN 55125-2989

Postage & Handling:

Standard (U.S. & Canada). If your order is:
$24.99 and under, add $3.00
$25.00 and over, FREE STANDARD SHIPPING

AK, HI, PR: $15.00 for one book plus $1.00 for each additional book.

International Orders (airmail only):
$16.00 for one book plus $3.00 for each additional book.

Orders are processed within 12 business days.
Please allow for normal shipping time.
Postage and handling rates subject to change.